MARY CRAWFORD

Love Naturally

HIDDEN BEAUTY BOOK 4

COPYRIGHT

Published on October 23, 2015, by Diversity Ink Press and Mary Crawford.

ISBN: 978-1-945637-42-1

Cover by Covers Unbound.

HIDDEN BEAUTY SERIES

Until the Stars Fall from the Sky

So the Heart Can Dance

Joy and Tiers

Love Naturally

Love Seasoned

Love Claimed

If You Knew Me (and other silent musings) (novella)

Jude's Song

The Price of Freedom (novella)

Paths Not Taken

Dreams Change (novella)

Heart Wish

Tempting Fate

The Letter

The Power of Will

HIDDEN HEARTS SERIES

Identity of the Heart

Sheltered Hearts

Hearts of Jade

Port in the Storm (novella)

Love is More Than Skin Deep

Tough

Rectify

Pieces (a crossover novel)

Hearts Set Free

Freedom (a crossover novel)

The Long Road to Love (novella)

Love and Injustice (Protection Unit)

Out of Thin Air (Protection Unit)

Soul Scars (Protection Unit)

OTHER WORKS:

The Power of Dictation

Use Your Voice

Vision of the Heart

#AmWriting: A Collection of Letters to Benefit The
Wayne Foundation

DEDICATION

To all the people who have
overcome seemingly insurmountable
fear and accomplished the impossible.
To all those standing in the wings who help
make those dreams possible.

CHAPTER ONE

MADISON

I leave the stifling environment of the rental car and stretch my back. Give me a crowded subway any day — at least I don't have to drive. Still, as I look around at the tall pine trees surrounding me, I spot a field of wilting sunflowers. I can't believe it's fall and everything isn't buried in snow and concrete. As I take a deep breath of crisp, clean autumn air, I decide Oregon isn't completely without charm. I'm not sure I'd want to live here, but it's a nice place to visit.

I peek into the darkness of the big red barn and yell to my sister, "Heather, I don't understand why you had to move to the middle of nowhere. I mean, Oregon is nice and all, but you can get perfectly good greenery at a florist which doesn't have bugs. Do I even want to know what all this dirt is doing to your shoes?"

I'm immediately accosted by a spider-web. I love Charlotte's Web as much as the next girl, but come on ...

farm life is not really the utopia I was led to believe as a child. I still can't wrap my brain around the fact my somewhat over-the-top stylish big sister has chosen this quiet, rural life. Last I knew, she pretty much hated the whole animal kingdom. Okay to be fair, she didn't really hate them; she was just so scared of them she wanted them to live on another planet.

I take one more step and slip on some hay. Pardon the pun, but that's just about the very last straw I can take. I steady myself and yell deeper into the barn, "This was all Tyler's idea, wasn't it? Of course it was. He's a guy. That explains it all right there. All men are imbecilic, moronic, and downright evil creatures. I don't know why you had to go and marry yourself one. For God's sake the man isn't even here. He had to go play G.I. Joe over in the desert."

"Are you finished?" a deep, gravelly male voice asks, causing me to jump about a mile in the air.

"Who the heck are you?" I pull the pepper-spray out of my purse and I almost drop the stupid thing. My hands are sweaty and shaking with shock. No one ever gets the drop on me. I've got multiple obscure MMA certifications to prove it. I take a defensive stand, aiming the pepper spray at the guy's eyes.

"I advise you to stand down," he says with an icy calmness that sends a chill up my spine.

Well, heck. This isn't how the script is supposed to go. He's supposed to be cowering in the corner, crying for his mommy.

"Suppose I don't?" I dare as I display an insane amount of bravado. My sensei would have me scrubbing down mats for a month if he could watch this bizarre little exchange.

"Look, lady. Please don't ask me to answer that because you really don't want to hear my honest answer anymore than I want to tell you. It's not even eleven o'clock in the morning and it's already been a epically bad day. I've had one horse go down with an infected hoof and the other with colic. With all due respect, I don't think you really want me to touch you. Trust me, if I were to touch you right now, you would be offended in every sense of the word."

"Oh, so you're the stable hand?" I search around for my sister, taking a good long look at him. He's very handsome in a rugged-surviving-the-wilderness-oops-did-I-misplace-my-razor kind of way. I generally prefer my guys a bit neater. Still, my eyes are drawn to his impeccably defined shoulders and forearms.

He just smiles mysteriously and shrugs. "Sometimes." He's watching me openly ogle him. Yet, unlike most guys, he doesn't flex or preen. His quiet confidence ticks me off.

I narrow my eyes suspiciously. "Wait, does my sister even know you're here?"

This time, he doesn't even bother to hide his smirk. "I imagine so, since I manage to cook breakfast for her three or four times a week."

"You're kidding me. Heather's always been on the flighty side, but I never figured her for a cheater."

"Lady, you seem to have a universally lousy opinion of everybody. If that's the way you treat somebody you love, I'd hate to see how you treat your enemies." He shakes his head.

I draw in a deep breath as he hits a little too close to home.

"It just so happens your sister is the adorable wife of my commanding officer. I am his tenant at his request because I got sprung early. Do you have issues with me stepping up to take care of Heather while he's gone? If so, that's too darn bad. You can take your faulty assumptions and go climb back on a tin whirly bird and go back home for all I care. It's no skin off my nose."

"Pardon me if I don't believe your macho jerky-ishness. My sister hasn't said one word about you. It's not like Heather to miss an opportunity to wax poetically about a cute guy." I gasp and cover my mouth when I realize what I've just clumsily admitted out loud.

The stranger just wipes his hands on the back of his jeans and gives me an indulgent look of pity. "Well, considering your sister is one of the happiest newlyweds I've ever seen — especially given the fact she never sees her husband — I doubt she much cares about my level of handsomeness. Frankly, if she knew she would face these accusations by innuendo from you; that in itself, would explain why she hasn't been forthcoming."

"Oh, look at all those big words coming from somebody who shovels horse crap for a living." I roll my eyes.

A strangled gasp erupts behind me. "Madison Paige LaBianca! Did you leave your manners in the baggage carousel or something? Why on God's green earth would you talk to Trevor that way?" my sister scolds.

"I don't know the man from Adam," I argue

defensively.

"Exactly. You have absolutely no reason to treat him like pond scum. You've been hanging around Mom and Dad too long. Obviously, I need to help you reintegrate into polite society." Heather shakes her head in disbelief.

"You can't be too careful these days. He might've been here to hurt you," I trail off, not quite willing to give up the point.

"For the record, I was doing the functional equivalent of cleaning fungus out of Velvet's toenails when you came bursting in here like there was a shoe sale at Neiman Marcus. How many evil guys with nefarious intentions do you know who would take the time to give a horse a pedicure?"

Crap. The man makes a good point. "It's hard to know what to think. You're out here mucking out barns like a high school dropout, but you speak like a college professor. Talk about your mixed messages," I sputter defensively as I find another bit of spider web on my face. "I don't even know your name."

"All you had to do was ask. I'm Lieutenant Trevor Black. It's been an interesting experience meeting you, to say the least." He turns to Heather. "I'm still not used to calling myself Lieutenant. Has Colton gotten used to his new rank?"

Heather smiles at Trevor. "I don't know — it's still so odd for me to hear Tyler called Colton. He doesn't talk about his rank very much. So, I'm not sure how he's adjusting," she admits with a sigh. "I just got off the phone with him. He sounded weird and secretive again like he always does before something big is going to go down. This cloak-and-dagger stuff is killing me. I don't suppose you're in the loop on this one?"

A pained expression crosses Trevor's face. "No, they won't let me talk mission stuff with anyone from the unit since I appealed the decision about the separation. But, I would take it as a great sign he has the time to call you. It shows they're not in bug-out mode, ma'am."

"That's kind of the way I read it too. Tyler sounded excited, but not in a doomsday way. You know how he gets. He wasn't asking me to double check if the life insurance premiums are paid this time. Maybe it's good news for a change," Heather replies with a slightly watery grin.

Trevor gently smiles at her. "I hope so, ma'am. I really do."

When I see the compassionate expression on Trevor's face, I'm even more embarrassed by my snap judgments earlier. When exactly did I turn into such a witch?

"Trevor, I'm sorry for the belated introduction, but this lovely creature is my pesky little sister, Madison LaBianca. You'll have to excuse her. She's from the East Coast. They do things at a different pace there. It'll take her a while to get acclimated to farm life in Oregon."

I smirk at the accuracy of Heather's explanation. There is more truth to it than she could ever know. There are about a million and one reasons I can't be in Boston and I can't tell my sister about any of them. Fortunately, her upcoming wedding gives me the perfect excuse to hide in the middle of nowhere, all the way across the country.

Trevor is examining me carefully. I don't blame him. The difference between my older sister and me is astounding. It's hard to believe we're sisters at all. She's cute and fashionable in her vintage-looking retro clothes, and I'm just not. I easily fade into the background. I look like a nondescript vanilla bean. Nothing really stands out about me. I'm tall and skinny and basically brown. I've got brown eyes, brown hair, and olive-toned skin. When I stand next to my sister, people are always asking if I'm adopted because my skin tone isn't peaches and cream tone like Heather's. I look like I could work in the wine vineyards in Italy like my ancestors.

I stick my hand out. "It's nice to meet you, Trevor. Look, I'm sorry for being a putz. I'm not usually such a jerk. Can we chalk it up to jet lag or something?"

Trevor nods at me, but doesn't take my hand. "I don't think you want to touch these hands. They've been in some pretty nasty places today, and I haven't had a chance to properly wash up."

"Oh, I'm familiar with the dirty side of horses. Didn't Heather tell you I own four Arabian horses?"

CHAPTER TWO

TREVOR

I GUESS I'M NOT the only one with a few surprises up my sleeve. Although, Madison can't be hiding much of anything under her outfit. It's not as if she's trying to be deliberately provocative, but it's downright sexy nonetheless. She's wearing a burnt orange turtleneck sweater and a pair of dark skinny jeans. She has a scarf with fall colors casually draped over her shoulder that highlights her stunning copper brown eyes. Her hair is a rich, deep brown. It flows softly around her shoulders. She looks like she has far more in common with the model who might walk on fashion row in New York City than someone who would own Arabian horses.

I'm actually confused. I thought Tyler told me she was an investigative journalist and her specialty is looking into bogus charities. Raising and breeding Arabian horses isn't a cheap hobby. My confusion must show on my face because Madison snaps at me, "Please don't tell me you're one of 'those guys' who thinks only men should own and raise Arabian horses."

My jaw drops open for several seconds before I think to close it. "Excuse me? I didn't say anything like that."

"You don't have to. Your face said it all."

"I don't think so. My face said, 'Wow, impressive. She must be doing really well as a journalist. Arabian horses are hellishly expensive.' If you read anything else into that, I'm sorry."

Madison flushes and hides her face. "I'm really batting a thousand with the bad judgment calls today. I think I need to go inside and take a nap."

"Maddie, if you're hungry, I made you some tomato bisque soup with some homemade sourdough bread," Heather offers. "It sounds like you could use something to eat. You always get obnoxiously cranky when you're hungry."

For a second, it looks like Madison will take offense at Heather's words. But, then her stomach lets out an audible growl. Madison blushes slightly and shrugs as she concedes, "I just hate it when you're right. I'll admit, I could eat an entire buffet at the Golden Corral. I couldn't believe it. The cut-rate airline I flew, didn't even offer peanuts or pretzels. It's such a rip off to fly these days. That is one long flight. Why didn't you remind me?"

As she has to stop and take a breath, I take a moment to admire the color in her cheeks and the fire in her eyes. Tyler was right on a certain level. The sisters are quite different. You have to look close to find any family resemblance. Madison has rich mahogany straight, brown hair whereas Heather's hair is a mass of curly blonde corkscrew curls. Madison is tall and thin, and Heather is well endowed. But, as different as they are on the surface, I have a hunch deep down, they're probably a lot alike.

When the living conditions in Iraq caused maintenance issues with my prosthetic and contributed to pressure sores on my stump, the National Guard ordered me to bail on my team early. I'm part of a pilot program to see if injured vets who have lost a limb have what it takes to re-enter the military. To say I'm less than pleased with some bureaucrat's random decision when they've never even met me is the frickin' understatement of the century. I had it handled. They just needed to give me a couple more days of healing time. Heck, they showed more leniency to people who are sleeping off hangovers than they did for one small decubitus sore.

Heather and Tyler allowed me to patch my skills together and build a semblance of a career. I'm extremely grateful they gave me a chance to salvage my pride here on their farm. But, one of the things I've learned is although Heather looks like she might be about as ferocious as a Maltese puppy, she's every bit as tough and tenacious as my soon-to-be-former commanding officer. Tyler did the right thing when he married Heather before he shipped out—even if it was only a simple civil ceremony. He can get all fancy about it when he gets back.

As I watch the sparks fly from Madison's eyes, I wonder if she's always this prickly or if it's simply the fatigue from the trip. Yet, as I observe her when she thinks no one is watching, she seems to be surreptitiously looking over her shoulder and checking her text messages.

"Got a husband or boyfriend back home?" I ask before I can stop the question from popping out of my mouth.

She is so startled by the inappropriateness of my inquiry she reflexively answers, "Good God no!"

"Oh, I'm sorry. I guess I should've said, 'significant other'."

"That's just sad that you think just because I'm plain I must be playing for the other team," Madison replies with a menacing glare.

"Hey now! Don't put words in my mouth. I never said that. I don't think you're plain at all, nor do I think you're gay. I didn't know what you call your boyfriend. I was trying to be sensitive and all that. In case you haven't noticed, figuring out relationship statuses is like navigating minefields these days. Have you looked at options on Facebook? It's more complicated than a voter's ballot in November."

"Not that this is even remotely your business, but I have enough stuff going on in my life right now without having to worry about adding a guy to the mix. With all due respect, you're not worth the trouble."

"Yes, ma'am, you've made your opinions clear on the subject," I try to keep the sarcasm out of my voice.

Madison cringes. "I suppose I did. Knock it off with the ma'am stuff; it's likely I'm younger than you and it makes me feel weird — like I'm some strange dominatrix."

I choke as my coffee goes down my windpipe. "Pardon?" I wheeze.

"You know, 'Red Room of Pain?' Ma'am, Sir and all that jazz? Where have you been lately — living under a rock?"

Her casual question is like a right uppercut out of nowhere. I'm not even sure how to form a socially acceptable answer to her tossed away punch line.

"You could say that," I respond dryly.

"Turnabout is fair play. What about you, Mister Nosy-Pants — where is your 'significant other'?"

I know Madison intends her question to be taken as yet another example of her snarkiness. But, there is just enough of a hint of pain in her eyes that it prompts me to be brutally honest for once. I'll probably regret this later. There is no probably about it. I will regret this. I can pretty much count on it.

"I lost her," I reply, my gruff voice betraying my emotion. Shoot, it never gets any easier to say that out loud.

"What? Who did you lose?" Madison's face is full of confusion. "How do you lose a person?"

I carry my dishes over to the kitchen sink and rinse them off. Topping off my mug of coffee, I head to my favorite leather chair in Heather and Ty's den. I motion for Madison to proceed in front of me.

She takes one glance at the recliner and whispers softly, "Oh, look! She rescued Grandpa's favorite chair." When Madison spots Ethel laying on the couch, she gasps with delight. She practically skips over and cuddles up beside her, kicking off her boots and tucking her feet underneath her. Ethel responds by plopping her big blood-hound head on Madison's lap and thumping her tail wildly. "I missed you too, Sweetie," she murmurs as she strokes Ethel's long velvet-soft ears.

Well, I guess there is more to her than prickles after all. Madison glances up and notices my bemused curiosity. "What can I say? Ethel used to be my grandma's dog. I've known her since she was barely bigger than my hand. I miss her that's all," she explains defensively.

"Did I say anything negative? I think it's cute. It makes you seem almost human."

"Almost human? What the heck do you mean by that? I'm certainly not a robot or zombie! Although after my flight, I might not argue with the zombie part," she adds with a quick grin.

I'm a little stunned by the difference one small facial expression can make. If I thought she was pretty before, Madison with a sincere, unaffected smile is simply breathtaking.

"Well, even you can admit you've been giving a pretty good impression of a ticked off porcupine today."

Madison takes such a deep long shuddering breath that I think she might start to cry. Instead, she acquiesces. "Part of me wants to take issue with your characterization of my behavior, but the more honest part of me knows you pretty much nailed it. I don't suppose it would do me any good to argue that I rarely act this way."

"This is America, you're free to tell me anything you want to."

"I can read between the lines. What you're saying is you may not necessarily believe me, right?"

"I don't really have enough information to make that decision right now, but I'll keep you posted."

"Speaking of information, you never did share the rest of your story. How exactly does someone lose a girlfriend?"

Immediately, my expression sobers and my stomach crunches painfully as it does every time. I turn to look in Madison's general direction. I choose to look at a spot on the wall right above her left ear. Experience has taught me that I can't stare directly at people while I share my story because it gets too intense. However, if I look away to avoid the onslaught of pity, people draw all sorts of negative conclusions, so this has become my coping mechanism.

Even though I'm trying not to specifically focus on the expression on Madison's face, it's impossible to miss the avid curiosity displayed there. I have a hunch that she's sliding comfortably into investigative reporter mode as she looks at me with an expectant gaze.

Finally, I take a deep breath and swallow hard as I admit, "I lost my wife, Melinda Jo."

"You're married?" Madison asks incredulously.

"No ma'am — not anymore. Melinda Jo is most likely dead," I answer, fighting the words. I still wince as the words leave my mouth.

Madison pales and sways slightly. "Oh no! What happened?" she asks, her tone hushed.

"The only girl I ever loved finally decided to listen to me when I told her to get the heck out of my life. She disappeared and is presumed dead. She vanished while I was overseas, leaving only her car and her purse behind."

"I don't know if you can shoulder all the blame. There might be other factors involved you don't even know about." Madison tries to comfort me. I have to give her credit for trying. Most people don't know what to say and can't stand to even look at me after I tell them my story.

"We didn't really have any secrets from each other," I explain.

Madison shrugs. "Everyone's got secrets."

"So, Madison, care to share a few of yours? You might be here for Heather's wedding-for-show, but I've got a very real hunch there is much more going on."

"How can you tell?" she asks quietly, her voice barely above a whisper as she draws her hands and legs together. She curls up into a little ball on the couch. Ethel tries to lick her hands to comfort her.

"Madison, you play the game well. I just play it better because secrets and lies are my job."

Chapter Three

Madison

It's a little intimidating to have someone study me as intensely as Trevor is doing at the moment. I'm frantically waiting for my skills as a reporter to kick in. I'm used to putting on a false, pleasant face even when I am feeling entirely shattered on the inside. Yet, under his scrutiny, I can't seem to hide behind my professional mask.

As the minutes tick by, it becomes apparent I won't be able to simply out-wait him. I thought I could literally escape him by coming out to the barn and hanging out with the horses. But this strategy is totally ineffective with Trevor. He is just silently waiting for me to provide an explanation. The silence becomes unbearable as I pick up a curry brush and start aimlessly brushing one of Heather's horses. Even though I usually find the mundane, monotonous activity soothing, I can't escape the feeling Trevor can discern my every thought as he carefully observes me.

Finally, the pressure is too much and I turn to face him "Okay fine. I've got something serious going on in

Boston. I don't want to talk about it because if I do, it becomes real. I am so not ready for anything to become more real in my life."

"Believe me, I understand the sentiment well. Unfortunately, the downside to that approach is no one can help you if you don't tell us what's going on."

Trying not to sound desperate, I insist, "This is not something that should involve Heather and Tyler."

"Are you sure?" Trevor asks, suspicion clear in his voice.

"Yes, it's the last thing Heather needs right now. She's already under enough stress with Tyler being so far away and in danger every day. Her ability to focus on her wedding is probably the only thing keeping her sane. She doesn't need me to add to her worries."

"With all due respect, Heather has her own ideas about what she considers important, and by excluding her, you could cause her more distress."

"I understand. But, by acknowledging there's a problem, I'm giving it more power than I need to."

Trevor pins me with a narrowed gaze as he advises, "Don't put yourself at risk trying to be a hero. Secrets kill, and there's something about you that I'd kind of like to keep around."

It's not often I'm without words, but I don't really know what to say to his comment. Usually, I'm not the kind of girl that guys flirt with. I am the solid-friend type. I like it that way because I find it hard to trust anyone. I think part of it is the nature of my job because I'm conditioned to question everything — good, bad, or indifferent. The other reason is something I keep much more private. I once trusted a group of friends to keep me safe when I was in college, and my decision came back to haunt me. It's not a mistake I'll make again.

A gust of wind blows through the open area of the barn sending loose hay flying everywhere. Suddenly, Trevor reaches up towards my face. I involuntarily flinch at his touch.

His jaw tightens at my response. "Relax and hold still. I'm just removing some hay that's about ready to poke you in the eye."

I make a conscious effort to relax after hearing his words of assurance. I take in a deep breath and let it out slowly as I try to quiet my galloping heart.

"Easy, take a deep breath. I won't hurt you. I'm not that guy."

"What do you mean?" I snap, feeling defensive.

"Nothing, I just mean what I say. I want you to know I'm not in the business of hurting women and children. I unintentionally did hurt a woman once, and I don't ever want to be in that place again. I guess what I'm saying is, 'You can trust me.' I'm not the same as your ex or whoever is making you act like a skittish mustang in the wild."

So much for the idea that I'm successfully hiding my scars from the world. The man has only known me a few hours, but he seems unerringly accurate in his assessment of me. I'll have to be even more cautious around him because it's clear he's not going to accept superficial excuses. If I'm not careful, I'll end up tipping everyone off, and I'll place my family in the crosshairs.

I decide to pass it all off as a joke. "You want me to just trust you? Isn't that the most clichéd phrase around? I think it must be in the 'guy handbook' or something."

Trevor responds with a quick, crooked grin. "Perhaps, but if I disclosed all of my secrets, I'd have to eliminate you as a threat. I'm not willing to do that," he teases.

It takes me a moment to figure out he just told a joke. But then again, he has no idea I've got my own little personal stalker who scares the crap out of me. I toy with the idea of completely spilling my guts just so I don't have to be in this alone. But trusting the wrong people is part of what apparently got me in trouble to start with. For now, I'll keep my peace.

"Well, I wouldn't want you to have to do anything that drastic," I answer.

———◆———

Heather is busy putting the finishing touches on a German chocolate cake when I emerge from the shower and join her in the kitchen.

"Feeling better?" She hands me a rubber scraper with a generous amount of pecan and coconut filling.

I'm instantly transported back to a time when my life was so much simpler. Before my Grandmother Lydia died, she used to preach that there was never a problem so big it couldn't be made better with a piece of homemade cake. It seems as if Heather has picked up Grandma's mantra and is running with it.

"Much. Thank you. I think the jet lag and my

hunger pains just got the better of me."

"I hope so. Because if this is a new trend in your personality, I'm not fond of it," she chastises gently. I have to laugh at her maternal tone. Sometimes, the five year age difference between us seems more like a couple of decades. In many ways, Heather's been more of a mom to me than our mom could ever hope to be.

I teasingly wrinkle my nose. "Yes, 'Mom'. You're right, I was very rude. If it makes you feel any better, I apologized for my behavior."

"Yes, that does make me feel better. At least someone raised you right." She sticks her tongue out at me.

"Sometimes, I have to wonder who's the big sister here," I jest. "You're not always the best role model for mature behavior."

"You're right," she says with a shrug. "I like to keep everybody guessing — it makes life more interesting."

"Well, it can't be argued that you lead a simple, straightforward life, for sure. You're the only person I know who could end up with a spare hot guy living at your house," I tease.

"He is pretty hot, isn't he? Not that I'm supposed to notice — you know, being married and all. Still, sometimes, the obvious is hard to overlook."

"Just stop! Your efforts to be a match-maker are just pitiful. Just because you found a great guy and decided to marry him, doesn't mean the rest of us have to be in blissful couple-hood."

"Maddie, can you blame me? Meeting Tyler

changed my life. For the first time since I can remember, I'm happy. Am I wrong to want that for you, too?"

"No, I'd like to be happy too. But, I'm not willing to sacrifice who I am and what I do for the sake of a relationship," I respond with more force than I intend to.

Just as I make that dramatic pronouncement, Trevor walks through the kitchen with Ethel and Annie falling close underfoot.

Before Heather can respond, Trevor walks up and places a hand on my forearm as he murmurs, "I learned the hard way if someone is trying to change you to fit their mold, the relationship is doomed. Any guy who's worth it would support whatever or whoever you want to be."

I scoff. "You don't date much, do you? That's nice in theory, but guys seem to have issues with the fact that I've been known to take down powerful CEOs with just the power of my pen."

"I don't know, I suspect there's a lot more to it than just a simple writing implement. It could be the beautiful, smart, passionate woman who's wielding that pen."

"Those are just words, Trevor. The real challenge is finding an honest man who keeps his promises. I think guys like that are a rare commodity. I'm not saying I think they don't exist, I've just never been involved with one. It leads me to question the validity of the premise that supportive gentlemen are alive and well."

"I don't suppose you'll find one unless you start to set the bar higher on what you'll accept for yourself."

"Hey!" I protest. "You've done a good job trashing

everybody else, but I don't see you in a stable relationship either," I challenge.

"You're right," he agrees, nodding his head yes. "I don't have any room to talk. I thought I had love figured out when I dated, fell in love and married the girl I thought was everything I'd ever hoped for. But, then I screwed up big time and pushed her away. I guess I'm a little gun shy."

Once again, I've allowed my mouth to get ahead of my brain. Something about Trevor seems to knock my "polite filter" off course. Instantly, I feel bad about pressing him about relationships. "I'm sorry, I was out of line. I can't even imagine how you move past something like that," I mumble.

"I don't know if I'll ever fully move past it because I don't know what happened to Melinda Jo. Before I got injured, we weren't fighting — or, if we were I was completely unaware of it. I always knew she wasn't overly thrilled I wasn't in the high-powered, corporate world of her parents. When I was sent on back-to-back deployments, she went to stay with them. It wasn't exactly surprising because her parents are well off and adjusting to our newlywed budget wasn't something she did easily. But, I thought we were working through all that. She even made comments about wanting to be a mom."

I try unsuccessfully to curb my curiosity. It's a mixed blessing to be a reporter. "So, what happened then —" I prompt.

"Last I knew, Melinda Jo was working at our local newspaper. She was doing stories about local politics and craft fairs. She had been taking creative writing classes while I was away, and she was hoping to get a bigger assignment. She was a huge sports fanatic. She would always joke with me that even though I was on the football team, I was less passionate about it than she was. For me, football was only a means to a scholarship, not a lifestyle. But, apparently that's not how she was raised. Her goal was to become the only local female sports reporter our town had seen."

"I have to give her mad props. That's a tough beat for a woman. There often isn't anybody rooting for a woman to succeed in that department."

"I know. So, she found it difficult to find a place in our relatively small town in Oklahoma. She decided to move to Worcester in Massachusetts. She figured the Boston market was her ticket to fame. She wanted to be as big as Erin Andrews."

"Did she ever make it there?" I ask, a little taken aback. "I can't imagine having a husband and then leaving him to make it in a bigger market. Then again, what do I know? I'm chronically single."

"In retrospect, it seems odd. But at the time in the context of what was going on with my career, it seemed to make sense. I was just relieved she was somewhere safe while I was stationed in places I couldn't talk about."

"She made it to her parents' house?" I clarify.

"Yeah, she did. She worked at the paper for about two months before they found her car abandoned. They didn't find much blood, but they found a little. So, after about a year of intense searching, her parents did some fancy legal work to get her declared as presumed dead, far ahead of what's typical."

"Why did you tell me you chased her away?" I ask, still puzzling through the problem.

"Toward the end, she was very frustrated with my military career. I wanted to move out of Oklahoma, but I wanted to come to Oregon instead of the East Coast. Tyler made it sound so phenomenal. I respected him enough as my commanding officer to want to switch units when the last deployment ended. However, Melinda Jo felt like I was being disloyal to her. I probably was, but I didn't have the perspective back than I do now. I felt like she was being manipulated by her parents to move back to Boston."

"I'm not married, but it sounds like a common dispute between couples."

"Had she not disappeared off the planet, it would've probably been one of those little spats everyone gets over quickly. Unfortunately, in my case I never got a chance to take back the angry words I said during our last 'discussion' of the issue. It haunts me. I'd been in love with her since the eighth grade and those were the last words she ever heard from me."

"I'm sure you feel horrible. But you had no way of knowing you would never talk to her again."

"I guess so, but somehow I feel like I should've known something. If we were such 'soul mates', shouldn't I have known on some visceral level that she was gone? I never felt what I think I should've felt when they told me she was gone."

"I don't know how I would feel if I were in your shoes."

"I think I'll always feel as guilty about my lack of

emotion at the news, as I did about not being around to protect her when she disappeared. For a long time, I fought the decision to have her declared dead because I figured somehow I would just 'know' one way or the other," he confesses.

"I think that's pretty natural. I don't think anyone wants to believe their family member passed away unless they have solid proof. Look at all the people who go to spiritual mediums even after they know their loved one has passed away."

"You wouldn't believe the number of psychic investigators who contacted me. It was like its own little cottage industry surrounding her disappearance. But, no two of them ever said the same thing. One would be convinced she was alive and well and living on a beach somewhere in Maui, and another would tell me she had been raped and tortured. The emotional roller coaster was so excruciating that I found myself missing the stress of combat. I was glad when they redeployed our unit overseas. Because of the nature of the unit I work with, it made me virtually unreachable. In many ways I felt safer with my unit than I did stateside."

Trevor looks so desolate and alone, I feel compelled to do something radically out of character for me. After I wash the frosting off of my hands, I walk right up to him and hug him. For a moment, he seems confused by my actions. His back is ramrod straight and his arms are held stiffly at his side. But, as I rest my cheek on his chest and slide my arms around his waist, he takes a deep breath and relaxes. He brings his hands up and draws me closer. I can't tell you how long we stood there just silently drawing strength from each other. That simple hug is the single best thing to happen since I can't remember when.

Abruptly, my cell phone starts to buzz. Reluctantly, I pull out of the hug and answer my phone without looking at the screen. I shoot Trevor a look of apology. "Hello?"

I'm surprised to hear my boss, Lyle Beckel on the other end of the phone. I hold my finger up to indicate to Trevor I need to take the call. Even though I don't know what Lyle is calling about, I head back out toward the barn so I can have a confidential conversation. I have a feeling things are about to get worse.

———————•◆•———————

I viciously kick the bale of hay in front of me as I stomp around the barn. I wish we had more hours of daylight left so I could take one of Heather's horses out for a good long ride. I need the perspective now. Just when I thought the stalking situation couldn't get any more bizarre, it does.

Now in addition to a stereotypical death threat, the person who has made it their mission to disrupt my life has added a whole new wrinkle. Lyle me told they were going to place me on temporary administrative leave because whoever the lunatic is who is writing the death threats also wrote into the newsroom to accuse me of wrongdoing with the very charities I investigate. In my head, I know this is just a standard operating procedure they put in place every time they have a customer complaint about a reporter, but unfortunately my heart has a different opinion. I'm completely devastated because Lyle said if they don't get this resolved relatively quickly, he'll take me off all the stories I've been working on for months.

Finally, the reality of that catches up to me and I break down into tears. When I go in search of something to clean up with, I'm surprised to find an old leather executive chair and a fancy office in the back of the barn. I grab a tissue off of the rich walnut desk and sink down into the chair. For the first time in weeks, I sit there and sob. I am scared, sad, angry and indignant my reputation has been challenged. It's hard for me to admit the death threats had become routine for me, but this is a devastating development. Someone knows how to hurt me to the quick; and much to my chagrin they are succeeding.

After exhausting myself from crying, I wander out to the deck of the barn. I look around in amazement. I remember Heather telling me they were going to do this so her friend Kiera could watch her daughter's horseback riding lessons, but I never expected it would look like a fancy bed-and-breakfast. I sit down in a wonderful porch swing and cover myself with a homemade quilt. I'm so lost in my own thoughts I don't hear Trevor come up beside me.

I jump when he touches my arm, but then I manage to smile shyly. "What's up?"

"I was just going to ask you the same thing. I tried to be patient and wait for you come back, but then I got worried about you, so I figured I should check on you."

"That's really sweet, but you didn't have to. There's just been a disturbing development on one of the stories I'm involved with."

"Are you sure that's all it is?" Trevor asks suspiciously.

I'm very tempted to just tell him the whole sordid tale. But even before this latest round of death threats, the authorities cautioned me against telling anyone what was going on until they could complete their investigation.

I shrug as I give him the standard reporter line I use when somebody gets a little too close. "Unfortunately, due to the nature of the story, I'm not at liberty to say."

At first, Trevor looks rather shocked, but then he gives me a look of admiration. "That's probably the most efficient brushoff I've ever heard. I'll have to borrow that some time."

"Thank you … I guess. But, in this case it happens to be true. I'm under direct orders from my supervisor not to talk about this to anyone." I purposefully leave out the part where my boss thinks I'm doing something criminal.

I think that might be the most painful part of all of this. How could my boss, who's known me for years, believe I play any part in what's going on? If Lyle doesn't believe me, what chance do I stand with Trevor?

Chapter Four

Trevor

I'D LIKE TO PRETEND nothing has changed in the weeks since Madison's arrival. Yet, in order for that to be possible, I would have to be the world's best liar. I do many top-secret things in my job as a soldier, but I still haven't mastered the art of applying those skills to my personal life.

It has taken me a while to become comfortable living with the wife of my commanding officer. But, Heather and I have reached an implicit compromise. I'm about a year younger than she is, so technically I guess I would be in the role of the little brother, but I feel more like the responsible big brother. That's why I'm finding it a little awkward that I'm crushing on Heather's little sister. She doesn't seem like the little sister, either. She appears more serious and focused than Heather. Madison seems like she has the weight of the world on her shoulders. I find it a little frustrating that she can't — or won't — talk to me about what's going on.

At the moment, I'm trying to pretend that I'm

reading the newspaper. However, I'm actually watching Madison play with the dogs. She's in the backyard throwing a stick for Annie. As a border collie, Annie doesn't ever get tired of playing fetch. Yet, even Ethel, the pudgy bloodhound is trying to play along. Madison throws her head back to laugh as both dogs try to carry the same stick. The sight is completely mesmerizing. Most of the time, Madison keeps her distance. There's almost a sense of regal-ness about her that makes her seem untouchable. Yet, in these moments where she's totally unguarded, she is breathtaking. I study her silently as I drink the last of my coffee.

"You know, you have my permission to date my little sister," Heather comments with some amusement when she catches me staring a little too intently. "Trust me, you don't want to bother getting my parents' permission because they're not likely to give it to you anyway. They're just weird that way."

"I appreciate that, really I do. Your approval is important to me. Still, I'm not sure if that changes anything. I'm still struggling with the idea of dating. It seems somehow disloyal to the memory of Melinda Jo for me to even be interested in someone else."

"I know it's been a while since you were injured, but didn't you part ways with your wife even before then?"

"Well, yes," I concede, unsure where she's taking the conversation.

"Would Melinda Jo want you to live your life like a reclusive monk?" Heather asks with her hands on her hips.

I smile to myself as I consider the answer to that

question. "Actually, knowing Melinda and her issues with jealousy, I can honestly say I don't really know what she would've wished for me. When we first started dating, we basically lived out of each other's pockets. I never envisioned a day when that would all change. I still can't believe she's not around."

"Let's just pretend that she was a good-hearted, well-adjusted ex-wife, I bet she would want you to pick up the pieces of your life and live, wouldn't she?"

"That might very well be true. But I'm not sure I'm ready to move on. I've been in love with Melinda Jo as long as I can remember. We were envisioning our whole lives together. I'm not sure I can let that vision go, even for someone as amazing as your sister."

"Well, the fact that you can even view her as amazing means you're making major progress. When we first met, it was a few months before I even figured out what color your eyes are because you never looked at me directly."

"That's true. Being around you has helped quash my inner introvert and made me more forthcoming. I wish words could physically form from my thought process. It would make this whole thing much easier."

"Well, you could start by telling my sister how you feel. That might open up the lines of communication between the two of you. I can't imagine that that would be a bad thing."

"In theory, it all sounds well and good for me to try on the role of boyfriend. In my experience, women are waiting for a guy to be totally serious and squared away before they start a relationship. I'm not sure 'squared away' will ever be used to describe the state I'm in."

"One of the things I've learned about living in the country is that you can't get anything done if you try to ride on both sides of the fence."

I glance at Heather with a puzzled expression on my face, "Dare I ask what that means?"

"I'm just suggesting that if you work very much harder to put Madison in your 'friend zone' she might actually take you up on it, believing that you're not interested in anything more. I can tell just by watching you she means a lot more than just nothing to you."

"I do like your sister an awful lot. But, if I can get my stuff squared away, I'd like to be far more than her friend."

"You need to show that because she won't know what you want from her."

"Before I decide the fate of our two families, it would probably be a good idea if we actually went out on a date."

"That's probably a great strategy. As you know, Madison can be a little abrupt and prickly when she's pushed. But, that does not mean she doesn't have a big heart under all that professionalism. I would like to see her end up with a guy as nice as you."

"I appreciate that Heather. If you knew all there was to know about me, you might not think I was such a great catch for your sister. I come with some pretty hefty emotional baggage."

"I can't totally understand, because I've never been

in your shoes, but I wonder how much your injury has changed your ideas about serving in the military."

"At this point, it's not even really all about my missing leg. It's more about what I should have been able to do for my wife and how I dropped the ball."

"I know you haven't said much. But from what I gather, I'm not sure you should be shouldering all the blame. So, I'll withhold judgment."

"If only it was that easy. I'm not really even sure Madison is all that interested in dating. She's made it clear that men are not her favorite creatures at the moment."

"I agree that Madison can be hard to read at times. But, speaking as her sister, I can assure you that she is indeed interested in you. If she wasn't, she wouldn't care so much about holding her own with you."

Madison has been unusually quiet, even for her. I miss our sparring sessions over breakfast. I had forgotten how much I enjoy matching wits with someone, and Madison is one of the smartest, most well read people I've ever met. I wasn't surprised when she told me she had graduated from high school early. She was more reluctant to share that she studied at Oxford University as part of an exchange program with Princeton. I found this odd because most people I know that have gone to prestigious schools like that tend to wear their resume on their sleeve.

When I enter the barn to grab my farrier tools, Madison is in what has become her customary spot. She is balancing her laptop in her lap as she sits cross-legged in the big leather office chair. Ethel is trying to worm her way onto the chair without being noticed, but Madison is oblivious about her antics.

Something is up. She usually goes out of her way to baby Ethel, so for her to disregard the big bloodhound's presence, there has to be something else going on.

I walk over to where she's sitting. In the large echo chamber of the barn, I feel like the sound of my uneven gate is being broadcast through a megaphone, yet she doesn't even seem to notice.

As I pull a cold apple juice from the little mini fridge next to the big antique desk, I ask, "Hard at work on a big story?"

Madison grimaces as she taps away on the keyboard. "I only wish it was so simple. Unfortunately, I've been working on this for two days and I still have no idea what's going on," she answers sharply as she blows the hair out of her eyes.

It's then I glance at the computer screen and notice that she's got some accounting software running.

"Maybe, I could help. I'm pretty good with numbers."

Madison sighs. "You have no idea how much I'd like to take you up on that offer. I've been staring at this for days and none of it makes any sense."

"So, why don't you? It's no problem. In fact, it will give me a chance to brush off my nerdier side. Being a horse farrier is good exercise for me and helps pay the bills, but it doesn't give me the same buzz as solving complex mathematical problems. I miss being with the

National Guard unit where I was solving problems nearly every day."

"That's right, you mentioned that you did some accounting services for your unit. Of all the people in my life who could help me — you seem to be the one most qualified."

"Some accounting services is putting it mildly. I'm actually a forensic accountant. It's my job to help trace the money that goes into terrorist groups like ISIS and Al Qaeda. If we can make them run out of money, it will be more difficult for them to fund terrorism around the world."

"Well, I guess if Uncle Sam trusts you to unravel the banking mysteries of the world, I can too. I don't have much choice because I've tried for several days, but I can't solve this on my own."

"If I can chase down terrorists, I can help you sort out a few issues with your bank," I tease.

"Do you have some time? This is going to take a while to explain."

I pull up my calendar on my cell phone to be sure I don't have any off-site appointments. I stuff the phone back in my pocket and turn to her. "Looks like I'm free all day. I was going to work a bit on Velvet's hooves today, but that can wait."

"Are you sure? I don't want to take you away from your real work just so you can help me sort through the tattered remains of my life and dignity."

"Madison, I wouldn't have offered to help if I didn't think I could find something."

"Nothing we say here goes beyond the barn?" she asks with trepidation.

"No, I promise. If the U.S. government can trust me to keep secrets in a war zone, I can certainly do it here."

Madison sets her computer aside as she looks at me solemnly then does a full-body shudder. "I can't believe I'm doing this; I hope I'm not making a mistake. If this goes poorly, I could lose my job."

"Well, I'm not in the business of ruining your life, so I'll try to avoid that."

Madison takes a deep breath and curls her knees to her chest as she begins hesitantly telling me her story, "This is long and complicated, but you need to know what's going on."

"It's okay, just take your time —"

"I guess it's been nine months or so since all this started. I'm used to people being upset about what I do — after all, I uncover peoples' bad behavior for a living. Some people don't like being exposed. So, I didn't think much of it when the first threat came into the paper. No one else did either — they assigned me an extra security guard to escort me out to my car and put extra virus protection software on my computer. We all thought the first letter would be the last we heard from him or her. When I didn't respond to the threat, it escalated. I didn't start getting truly creeped out until I found a dead bat inside my locked car after I had been on assignment. The note said, 'I may start small, but I finish big.'."

"I can see how that would be unsettling at the least."

"I wanted to pretend like it never happened, so I continued to investigate cases. But, in the back of my mind I always wondered if the next story I did would be my last. Then, I went to a journalism trade-show in New York. No one knew I was going except for the people at the paper. It was meant to be a big roll-out of the paper's new web episodes."

"Web episodes?" I ask for clarification.

"Our paper is hemorrhaging readers as new technology creeps in, so our news director decided to post 'episodes' on a video channel owned by the station. It's a weird mix between print journalism, serious news with a smidgen of public access TV. My area was supposed to be one of the first few featured because it crosses the line between a straight lifestyle story and serious news," Madison explains.

"I take it something happened in New York?"

"Nothing I could definitively prove, but it was enough to make me want to leave town. We had a late night marketing mixer and reception, and when I came back to my room, my laptop had been moved."

"How could you tell?"

"I was having trouble getting a good Wi-Fi signal. So, I went out on the balcony to do some work before dinner. Then I got a phone call, so I came into my hotel room and put the laptop on the small bedside table. I thought it was weird when I got a phone call on the hotel phone. When I picked up the phone, there was a digitized message."

"What was the nature of the message?"

Madison grabs her water bottle and takes a long swig. "It was this super creepy computer voice. I couldn't tell if it was male or female, but whoever it was, called to give me a warning, 'You don't have to be at home for me to find you.'."

"Did the hotel say who the call was from?"

"No, bizarrely enough, they couldn't track down how the phone call got to my room. They couldn't even tell me whether the call originated from within the hotel."

"That is odd," Trevor concedes.

"I was so freaked out I could barely make it through my presentation. When I came back to the room, my laptop was sitting on the top of the television set. The hotel staff swore up and down no one from their organization had been in my room. They even showed me the employee logs. There wasn't anyone that wasn't accounted for and all the housekeeping staff had gone home."

"Did you try to involve the police at all?"

"Yes, the police are involved. But I don't think they believe me. They keep treating this as if it's someone I had a bad breakup with."

"Have you had any bad breakups?" I inquire.

"My last relationship sucked for me, but he was happy to get out of the relationship. He moved on to somebody prettier with a bigger bust than me. Trust me, he's not trying to get me back."

"If he was dumb enough to let a woman like you go, I doubt he has the intelligence to pull off something like that," I respond without censoring my thought process.

The corner of Madison's mouth hitches up into the semblance of a smile. "Careful there, Black. That almost sounded like a full-fledged compliment."

I grin. "I'm not sure how you could interpret my comment any other way. I rarely say things I don't mean."

Madison is silent for a moment, and I wonder if I pushed the boundaries too hard. But soon she mutters, "I don't even have a comeback for that, so I'm going to pretend I didn't hear it." She puts the computer back on her lap and starts to look up a file.

I'm so used to the outspoken, brash Madison, seeing her shy and uncertain is an interesting change of pace.

"What happened after New York?" I ask, getting back to the matter at hand.

"Heather called me and told me she had gotten married and that she was planning to throw a humdinger of a wedding. So, I figured it was a great cover to get me out of town without having to explain all the bizarre circumstances surrounding my abrupt departure."

"Actually, it was a fantastic idea. But what changed — why did you decide to tell me now?"

"My mortgage check bounced," Madison states as if it explains everything.

"That sometimes happens with the way money travels to the banking system."

"Right after I deposited a seven thousand dollar stud fee?"

I guess nothing should really surprise me in the

horse world, but seven thousand dollars is a lot of money, no matter how you slice it.

"That's a little more uncommon, that's for sure. Are you sure it actually made it into your account?"

"Yes, I'm rather anal about these things. I checked my balance before I booked my airline tickets here. It was there. I had almost ten thousand dollars in my bank account. I shouldn't have had any trouble with my mortgage payment or any other bill. I keep so busy at the paper I don't have time to lead an extravagant life — that was enough money to get me through a couple of months at least."

My brows lower with concentration as I consider all the ramifications of what she's told me.

"How are your security protocols on your computer? Is your password sufficiently impenetrable?"

Madison smirks. "Has anyone told you that you talk like a thesaurus?"

I chuckle. "Not this week. But then again, I doubt that the horses mind."

"Oh, I don't mind — it's just a little disconcerting."

"Now, who's using big words?"

"Funny, but I meant my question to be rhetorical. Anyway, because I work on such sensitive documents at the newspaper, I change my password once a week using a special program. No two passwords on my computer are the same, *and* there's a password to get into my computer."

"I'm really impressed. There are military officials who need to take lessons from your protocol."

"I don't really mess around with my job. I take things seriously. I don't want to be vulnerable."

"Does anyone else use your computer?" I probe.

"No, I keep it locked up whenever I'm not using it."

"You didn't mention the fact that it was locked up when you told me the story about the hotel."

"That was one of the few exceptions. I was so thrown off guard by the bizarre phone message with the computer voice that I didn't even think about locking the computer. I just wanted to leave my room because I felt like someone was watching me. Whoever this is has totally gotten into my head. It makes me so angry. I'm smarter than this and I should be able to figure it out."

"Have you told your boss about this new development?"

"No, I haven't. Whoever this is has set out to ruin my career as well. Someone reported to my supervisor that I'm somehow involved with all the charities I've been investigating, and they've accused me of having a conflict of interest. My boss said if they don't resolve this quickly and figure out what's happening, I could very well lose my job."

"That hardly seems fair. You were a victim of crime. Why would you lose your job?"

"I don't know! None of this makes any sense to me. I don't know why anybody would go to such extremes. I have no idea how somebody could get to my bank accounts or why they would even target me."

"I don't really know either without doing a forensic analysis of your bank accounts. It's intrusive. I'm going to need to know what you bought and why. Are you ready for that? I'm going to need to know even the small stuff like where you get your coffee in the morning."

"I guess it's probably a really good thing I haven't really had time to develop a coffee habit." She shrugs. "Seriously, I don't care what you do. I want to know what's going on before I slowly go insane trying to figure it out."

———•———

To be honest, when I told Madison that I would help her, I really thought it would be just a couple days before I found an error in the banking records that would explain the discrepancy. Yet, that's not what's happening. Madison keeps meticulous records about everything. I suppose you would get in the habit of doing that as a journalist, but she not only is reporting every big purchase to me, she's reporting small purchases like soda, candy and gum. When she includes those in her spending diary, she always has a funny anecdote to go along with her purchases.

Though this deep dive has undoubtedly been educational about Madison's own personal habits and obsession with junk food, it's not really getting me anywhere.

I'm really itching for my military clearance and resources. Because I'm not a law enforcement agency, I have to rely on public records to get to the bottom of what's happening. So far, this approach has been unsuccessful. The only thing I've been able to glean aside from her penchant for junk food, her only other indulgence seems to be stilettos. She showed me pictures of her closet, and even though I was warned about the size of her shoe collection, it still takes me by surprise.

I study the spreadsheet I developed when I was trying to follow the trail of Madison's money. She's right, the money was there one day and gone the next, and I really find nothing in her spending habits or spending history to indicate she was involved. After three weeks of carefully reconstructing her financial history, I'm no closer to finding an answer than I was on the very first day. Usually, people who have nothing to hide are not so difficult to chase down. Most people leave a financial trail a mile and a half wide. Otherwise, I wouldn't even have a job with the military.

Almost everything I assumed to be true about Madison when I first met her turns out to be false or at least greatly exaggerated. Given her personality, I thought she would be one of the most ambitious reporters at her newspaper. I was surprised when I did some background research and found out she turned down a more prominent market because she feels so passionate about her current job. She acts as if she's unattached from the rest of society, but she volunteers for a variety of causes, including 4-H. When I asked her about her charitable connections, she explained that if she had children, she would want those programs available for them. She totally downplays what she does outside of her job at the newspaper.

Once again, she shocks me with her lack of attention seeking behavior. Most people I know, male or female would brag that they went to an Ivy League school or that they give to so many charities, yet Madison is remarkably reticent to talk about herself or her accomplishments unless they are tied directly to her reporting. She showed me a national award she won for an investigative report she conducted about a charity that allegedly raises funds to help treat children who've been exposed to HIV. Outside of that she doesn't speak of herself often.

Still, the longer I research her background, the more I question whether there is more involved than a nosy reporter with a gift for finding and exposing unscrupulous people.

CHAPTER FIVE

MADISON

I DON'T KNOW WHAT to expect this morning. Last night as I was rummaging through Heather's junk drawer looking for batteries for my book light, Trevor walked through the kitchen wearing just gym shorts. I tried to disguise the fact that I was openly ogling him, but it was hard not to look. He's more rugged than the guys I'm used to dating, but then again he's more handsome. I saw a lot of him, there wasn't much of him not covered in long sinewy muscles. As he dug through the refrigerator for a snack, I got a wonderful, unobstructed view of his back. He looks like he belongs in an art magazine. I can easily envision someone using him as a model for a drawing class. His body is just that perfect. This is also the first time I've seen his prosthetic limb exposed. I suppose it should look out of place on such a specimen of fitness, but it too is long and lean. Its carbon fiber mechanism is a powerful, yet graceful piece of equipment. So, in a weird way it all fits.

I wanted to step forward and get a closer look at his

tattoos, but I didn't feel like exposing myself, so I stayed hidden in the dark shadow of the kitchen while I just observed him move. If I had given the matter more thought, I would know a trained soldier like him would be alert to my presence. Quite frankly, almost every logical thought in my head disappeared the moment he walked into the kitchen. Consequently, when he tossed a question over his shoulder, I was not prepared to hear his deep, hypnotic voice.

"Do you have plans tomorrow?" he asked quietly.

After I caught my breath and dislodged my heart from my throat, I answered, "No, not really. Most of my plans have been shot by my stalker."

"Would you like to spend the day with me? I've got some stuff to do tomorrow you might find interesting."

I'm not sure what I found most embarrassing, the fact that he caught me drooling all over him, or that he felt like he needed to entertain me like a kid who can't be left unattended. Yet, the thought of spending the day with him was incredibly enticing.

I tried for nonchalance. "Sure, it's not like I have anything better to do."

"Great, be ready by 07:30. I want to get an early start. By the way, thanks for the great show."

"What show?" I asked, puzzled. If anyone had been putting on a show, it was Trevor.

"Your nightgown is gorgeous, especially when back-lit," he responded with a wink.

I looked down at what I was wearing and realize the utilitarian cotton and lace gown which is demure enough

Laura Ingalls Wilder could have worn it, probably wasn't so concealing once Trevor turned on the hallway light.

"I'm sorry for putting you in such an awkward situation," I uttered as I grabbed a quilt off the back of the couch on my way through the living room.

Trevor took it from me and gently wrapped it around my shoulders. "It didn't feel awkward to me, Madison. In fact, it was the prettiest thing I've seen in a good long while."

Not knowing what else to do, I stammered my good nights and agreed to meet him bright and early in the morning.

I found it difficult to sleep last night because I was replaying the scene from the kitchen in my head over and over. In my dreams, I was smooth, articulate and flirty. But, in reality, I was none of those things. I still feel like the awkward sixteen-year-old who found herself on a college campus without any friends. I don't know if I'll ever outgrow my awkwardness.

This morning I'm trying to soothe my frazzled nerves with some tea and toast. I'm scared to eat anything else because my stomach is already clenching with nerves.

Trevor is out feeding the horses, so I take a few breaths to calm down and start to unload the dishwasher. Just sitting here waiting for him with nothing to do is driving me crazy. I suppose I could pretend to read my Kindle. Lord knows I have enough unread books on there to keep me busy for a couple of years. Yet, I know even if I had my Kindle in front of me, I couldn't pay attention to it.

After I finish, I head out to my favorite porch swing

to wait. Soon, Trevor rounds the corner with two large thermoses. "I know you don't drink coffee, so I took a gamble on hot chocolate."

"Oh, you didn't have to. I could've just dealt with the coffee. I'm not allergic to it or anything; I don't like it."

"But you like hot chocolate, right?" He holds up the second thermos.

"Does a bear hibernate in the winter? I adore hot chocolate. In fact, I pretty much like anything with the word chocolate in it, hot or cold."

"Then we're pretty much set."

He lightly lays a hand on my shoulder to escort me to Tyler's beast of a truck, I noticed there's a horse trailer attached. "Did we pick up a passenger for this trip?" I ask as I nod toward the trailer.

"Just temporarily. I'm dropping her off for a client. She got adopted, so I'm the escort," he explains.

"I thought this was a date," I admit sheepishly. "But, I can see now there might be a more practical reason you had me come along."

"Never fear, this is definitely going to be a date. I just have to get some business out of the way first."

<hr>

"Well, that went smoother than I expected. Madame Frog is going to make a great little riding horse," I comment as I double check the lock on the horse trailer.

"Is it wrong for me to hope that you might go on all of my deliveries? We did this in about half the time it usually takes me. How did you get so good at driving a truck with a trailer?"

"I ended up taking a break from college during my freshman year, so I went back to my grandmother's ranch in Texas to help out. Her long-term foreman had a heart attack and he wasn't able to work the ranch. I discovered by accident I have an affinity for farm equipment and trailers. My dad just about blew a gasket because he believes all women should be demure and proper. Helping my grandma out and becoming like one of the ranch hands was not in his plans for me."

"Has he ever seen you work the ranch? If he did, he would see without a doubt it's your natural environment."

I laugh at the thought of my dad and his three-piece suits on any sort of ranch. "No, farming was never his thing. He always felt as if it's somehow beneath me. Although I own several horses now —thanks to my grandma's generosity when she passed away — my dad still thinks I should be a proper lady and hire someone to do all those tasks. Although I have a great foreman, I still like taking care of the horses, and I can tell more about their breeding prospects if I'm hands-on with them."

A hard, lethal look crosses Trevor's face. "That makes perfect sense to me. Something tells me your dad and I aren't going to see eye to eye."

"I doubt anybody sees eye to eye with my dad. So, you'll have to join his anti-fan club. Tyler is pretty much the president of the club, so you'll be in good company."

"How do you feel about it all?"

"Oh, I long ago came to the conclusion that my

parents and I were meant to just coexist on the planet. We have an unspoken agreement: they don't support anything I've ever done, and I try to stay off their radar. As dysfunctional as it is, it works."

"I take it none of your family knows about your current situation," he asks with concern marring his features.

"No, I didn't figure it would be productive to even tell them. You already know the reason I haven't told Heather, but it's a different thing from my parents."

"Madison, you know you're going down a dangerous path, right? The people who love you should probably know you're in trouble."

"Trevor, really — we're not close. I don't know what good it would do to tell them. They would just try to convince me to give up reporting. There's really no point."

"Okay, I guess I get it. I just wish there were more pairs of eyes looking out for you, that's all."

———◆———

I'm trying to be patient, I really am. It's a struggle for me to do things on other people's schedule. But, despite my repeated pleas for more information about the day, Trevor refuses to divulge any clues. Usually, I have no problem getting people to tell me almost anything. At first, I'm not overly concerned, I usually excel at wheedling information from all sorts of people. But, after we've been on the road for nearly an hour, I'm starting to get discouraged.

"You know you're driving me crazy …" I exhale a

frustrated breath.

Trevor looks smug. "Yep. This might be a convenient time to remind you I've had extensive training in counterintelligence and I'm pretty much immune to your efforts. But, trust me. I think you'll like this. It's a very Oregonian thing to do."

"You suck at playing Twenty-Questions," I pout.

"Uh-huh, tell me something I don't know," he quips with a wide smile. "Why don't you take a few minutes and rest? It will take us a bit to get there. There's no need for us both to be up this early on a Saturday."

Finally, the hypnotic rhythm of the tires combined with the bass-heavy music coming from Tyler's speakers lulls me to sleep.

Trevor wakes me up by tickling the end of my nose with the end of the string from his University of Oregon sweatshirt. "Wake up sleepyhead. We're here."

I sit up so fast, I nearly knock him out when we butt heads. "Sorry!" I exclaim as I sit up straighter to look out the window of the truck.

I can tell that Trevor is getting a kick out of my excited reaction, which at the moment, rivals a five-year-old on his first day at kindergarten. "Oh my gosh! I've seen this place on the Travel Channel."

Trevor smirks at my remark. "You actually watch the Travel Channel? It hardly seems your pace."

"Hush! It's not like I'm the Energizer Bunny all the time. I like my down-time. Besides, they have some interesting programs. It's good for background research on stories," I add defensively.

"Just so you don't miss the point of today, I'm declaring this an officially sanctioned goof-off day. If you're not familiar with the concept, thinking about work, planning for work, and waxing poetic about work are blatant violations of the rules governing goof-off day."

"Isn't that an oxymoron? Who has rules for goofing off?"

"I do. I have a hunch if I don't tell you we're here to have fun, you might treat this as a scouting trip for one of your stories."

"As much as I'd like to argue, you have a point. I'll try to mentally put on my bathing suit and flip-flops and just go for it."

"Normally, I would argue it's a great plan, but it's pretty cold out here. I don't want you to think about anything. I just want you to relax."

"I've had way too much to think about recently, so a mental vacation would be a relief."

Trevor grabs my hand and interlaces his fingers with mine. My eyes must've betrayed my surprise because he shrugs. "It's a date, remember? Chivalrous guys do this kind of thing."

I want to bury my face in embarrassment. It seems everything I do comes across as cranky and witchy. "I knew that. It's just been a while since I have had anyone treat me decently. I've forgotten the rules of normal dating."

"Well, I'll just take great pleasure in reacquainting you with how you should be treated."

I have to admit, it feels fantastic to be pampered.

The Portland Saturday Market is insanely crowded, but whenever someone encroaches into my personal space, Trevor places a protective arm around my shoulders and calmly steers me through the chaos. It's almost as if he can see the boundaries I've put up around myself even though I haven't really mentioned them.

If I was expecting Trevor to be serious, I was sorely mistaken. As we travel from booth to booth, he is making this an experiential outing. First, we sat and had a cartoon artist make a sketch of us. He makes a big production of romantically posing with me sitting across his lap. Then, we had our picture taken at one of those old-time photography booths. At first I pose in a long prairie dress with lots of ruffles, and he poses with a Davy Crockett style cap. But, then he ups the ante and strips down to just buckskin pants and a leather vest. I figure if he can be brave, I can too. While he's looking at picture packages, I go behind the dressing room wall and put on a bustier and fluff up my hair. Fortunately, I still have a tube of bright red lipstick in my purse from a standup interview I did. It's not usually what I wear, but in this setting, it's so much fun. Although I'm psyching myself up for the reveal, I'm still really nervous about his reaction.

I had nothing to fear. His reaction is everything I could've hoped. In fact, it's rather amusing. I swear I heard him growl in appreciation.

"I'm not sure if I should give you a standing ovation or cover you up with my coat," he comments with a surprised scowl on his face.

My confidence wavers a little when I hear Trevor's

remark. "I guess I deserve that for trying to dress sexy. I don't have the body to pull this off," I mutter to myself.

Trevor's eyebrows raise in shock. "I think you misinterpreted what I said. The only reason I want to cover you up is because you look so sexy that I don't want to share you with anybody." He walks over and gives me a searing hot kiss.

I'm still a little breathless when the photographer admonishes us, "Hey now! If you're going to turn up the heat, you need to wait until I position my cameras."

My coloring usually hides my habit of blushing pretty well, but there's no disguising this degree of embarrassment.

Trevor just grins as he turns to me. "You heard the man. I have a perfectly legitimate excuse to kiss you again."

"Something tells me you probably don't need an excuse to do exactly what you want to do in life."

"No, not so much any more. There's something about being blown to pieces which encourages you to be more spontaneous and live for the moment."

Hearing him talk so casually about what had to be a devastating time in his life is a little odd.

"I'm not so sure I want to be just another spontaneous fling in your life."

"Nobody said I wasn't completely serious. I'm just less likely to wait around for it to be my turn any more. My near-death experience taught me life is too precious to just passively take it as it comes."

The photographer interrupts us. "All right you two

love birds, I'm all set up here now. But, remember to keep it somewhat PG because there are kids wandering around."

Trevor grins at the photographer. "Okay, I'll try to control myself. But, it's going to take all of my military discipline because my date is so hot."

Much to my chagrin, I turn red again. Something about the fact that he finds me sexy is incredibly embarrassing, yet titillating.

The photographer chuckles and gives Trevor wink. "Take it easy on your girl. It looks like you picked a shy one."

"Don't worry, I'll take great care of her," Trevor assures him.

I know he means that as a joke, but I can't help but think there's more than just a kernel of truth in his statement. I do feel very protected in his presence.

"That's good to hear. I don't see very many men come through here with that attitude anymore," the photographer comments as he tests the flash. He carefully leads us through several quasi-suggestive poses. When he announces it's the last pose, Trevor cups my face and delivers on his promise to kiss me again. Vaguely, I can hear the camera snap in the background as I pull away with a dazed expression on my face. True to his word, Trevor grabs his sweatshirt and drapes it over my shoulders.

He kisses me on the forehead. "Go on and get dressed. I'll just be over here trying to collect myself."

I can't stop grinning as I dress in my street clothes.

It's been so long since somebody thought I was sexy, I've forgotten what it feels like. The look of appreciation in Trevor's eyes makes me feel like I'm a high-fashion model instead of the plain Jane I am.

When I emerge from the dressing room, Trevor is negotiating with the photographer. I'm shocked when I overhear that he not only plans to buy the cheap promotional picture, but he's buying all of them.

"Madison, we'll have to stop by here in a couple of hours. He is framing one of the prints for me and it's going to take a bit for him to finish." He turns to the photographer and says, "Thank you for making this so much fun. It's not often I'm happy with pictures of myself, but these are great."

I smile and add my thanks. Then, Trevor wraps his large hand around mine as he escorts me through the crowds. After a bit, I realize he's searching for something. Just as I'm about to ask what he is looking for, we stop in front of a booth with homemade fruit pies. "This is great. They moved their booth from where they were before and I was afraid they closed down. What flavor do you want? I'm partial to peach with some vanilla ice cream on the side, but they also make a phenomenal cherry pie here."

Without trying, my thoughts go back to the stories Heather tells about her girlfriend, Kiera, and all the history surrounding the relationship-saving peach pie. Part of me wonders if Trevor knows that story or if it's just coincidence. Once again, I blush at the thought.

Trevor notices and asks, "What did I say now? I didn't mean to embarrass you."

His honest question makes me even more embarrassed about my train of thought. "Oh, it's nothing. It's just a little family folklore."

Trevor chuckles and shoots me a mischievous grin as he replies, "Oh, that's right. Your sister makes magic pies. I haven't hung out with her friends too much, but I understand several of them put a lot of stock in the relationship building powers of her cooking."

I swallow hard. "… or so the legend goes."

"In that case, I think we should eat as much pie as possible. I don't think we should tempt fate," Trevor responds with a wink.

We collect our pies and head over to a table with an umbrella. Just as I'm setting the food down, I hear a voice with a Boston accent. A chill travels up my spine. Oregon is about as far away from Boston as I can get yet. I can't seem to escape reminders of home. Much to my surprise, she turns around to address me, "What's wrong? Are you so ugly that you can't land a real man?"

I spin around to look at her with a horrified expression on my face. You don't want to know the words rushing into my brain. I've worked really hard to clean up my vocabulary since many of my interviews are taped for the web cast now, but who the world is this chick? Her stringy blonde hair and bright green eyes look strangely fake, but there is something about her seems familiar somehow. Maybe she's a crazed fan. What in the world does she have against me? Is this related to the rest of the craziness in my life?

My thoughts are interrupted by a sharp command from Trevor. "Watch yourself," Trevor instructs brusquely. I'm not exactly sure who he issued the warning to. I'm still in shock someone would have the nerve to say something like that.

The woman faces Trevor and snarls, "You going to do something to stop me, Gimpy?"

Everyone within earshot just gasps at her comment. Trevor shakes his head as if to clear it. "Pardon? I don't think I could've heard you correctly."

"Oh you heard me just fine. I have to know, do you still pass out at the sight of blood? I bet you do. If you wimped out when they took out your teeth, I bet you positively fainted when they chopped off your leg."

Trevor freezes at her words, but I don't have the sense to do the same, so I respond, "You know, my grandma used to say, 'If you don't have anything nice to say, don't say anything at all.' I don't know who you are or what you want, but go away!"

"Don't talk to me like that! You owe me more respect. You don't know what you've started," she huffs as she disappears into the crowd.

I sink into the chair beside the table as my knees buckle.

Trevor brushes the hair out of my eyes and tucks it back under the floppy felt Fedora he just bought me. "Are you all right?" he asks with an anxious expression on his face.

Honestly, I'm a mess. Yet, the worry on his face compels me to try to hide my fear. "I'm fine. It's not the first time someone's been witchy to me and it won't be the last."

"Madison, that was more than just being mean. It was personal. Do you know who she is?"

The serious tone of his question combined with the steely look in his blue-grey eyes reaffirms all of my fears. I take a deep breath and peel the label off the water bottle in my hand, but, it's too late for any self calming rituals. I shake uncontrollably. "Trevor, I think I recognize her from Boston. Please tell me this is some bizarre coincidence."

As soon as he hears my words, Trevor's body language goes on high alert. "Where? Where do you know her from?"

"The p-p-paper," I stammer. "I think she works in my industry."

"How in the world could she work in your field without you knowing who she is?"

"I believe I met her once at an office party. If I remember correctly, she covers what we call 'Home Ec.'. But, it's been almost two years since I've seen her. I can't imagine what business she would have with me."

"What do you mean, 'Home Ec.'?"

"It's the light and fluffy lifestyle section. You know, like home economics projects — 'One Hundred Crafts You Can Do with Pinecones' or 'How To Decorate With Throw Pillows Just Like Martha Stewart.' I only met her once, but I remember it because she asked me a bunch of questions about how I got to be a 'serious' reporter. I thought the questions were a little heavy for an office party, yet I answered them anyway. Then, she seemed super angry when I told her I have a degree in journalism. That was the last time I saw her."

"So, how does she know who I am?" Trevor demands impatiently.

"I don't know. I didn't even know you up until a few weeks ago and I haven't told anybody about you." I feel more unnerved by the second.

"Well, you would've had to say something to somebody. What does your boss think you're up to?"

"As far as Lyle knows, I'm just here for Heather's wedding. He's not letting me work on any stories anyway, so I might as well be."

"Are you sure you didn't tell anybody about us?" Trevor asks again.

"Yes! I'm positive," I answer with a bit of snark in my voice. "It's not like I've been checking in with the folks back home. After Lyle accused me of stealing money from the charities I investigate, I haven't been real motivated to turn to him for help. Besides, I don't even know where she got her information."

"Exactly! She has to have some secret, internal source to be able to share that kind of intimate detail," Trevor insists.

Now, his accusations are just getting my hackles up. How many different ways do I have to tell him I haven't said a word? "Well, her source isn't me. I don't even know you that well," I answer shortly.

Trevor sighs. "That's what I was afraid you were going to say. If you didn't feed her information, who did?"

"A lot of people have a bad reaction to anesthesia. Maybe she was just guessing," I venture quietly.

"I thought about that. But how does she know about my sensitivity to blood and the fact that I'm an amputee now? I know my gait has improved to the point where most people can't even tell I have a prosthetic limb."

"I don't know, Trevor. It's creepy. Can we go home now? I don't want to stay here anymore. I don't know who else is watching me."

"Okay, I understand. I hate that she ruined our date. Let's go back and check with the photographer. Maybe he's got our stuff done," Trevor says with a weary sigh.

Chapter Six

Trevor

My head is spinning as I check out the rearview mirror. Fortunately, it doesn't look like anyone's following us. Still, I'm thankful for the defensive driving courses I received, complements of Uncle Sam.

I look over at Madison. The smile she's been wearing all day is nowhere to be found. She is pensively chewing on the end of a pen and furiously writing notes. So much for my plans for this to be a stress-free weekend.

"What are you doing?" I question, somewhat afraid of the answer.

"I'm writing all of my impressions about what happened. They might be important someday. I'm also trying to remember all I can about 'Barbie-Light'."

I snicker at her description of the shouting woman. "Are you sure you don't want to call her Deranged Barbie?"

"Don't tempt me. But, seriously I'm trying to figure out how she's connected," Madison answers with a furrowed brow.

"What if the incident isn't related to you at all? What if she's connected to me? Everything she knew about you she could find out from your Facebook page. But, that's not true of the things she knows about me. Trust me, I was not bragging about nearly passing out at the dentist's office. If the Army knew about my aversion to blood, they might have disqualified me from service. So, I've never told a single soul. It's a weird thing for somebody to know about me."

"How in the world did she know we were dating? Today was like our first official date. I didn't even understand it was a date until you held my hand and kissed me."

"I don't know the answer, but I'm not going to take any chances with you until I can figure out some answers."

"What do you mean?"

"Do you have anything to do for the rest of the weekend?"

"No, not really. Since Lyle took away my official work, I'm not even supposed to be working on my stories. But unfortunately, my brain won't shut off; I keep having story development ideas."

"I guess I'll have to work hard to keep your mind off of work. I hope you don't mind, I've developed a contingency plan for this weekend. I'm relatively sure that no one's following us, but I don't want to take any chances. I'd rather not lead a crazy person to Heather's house."

"I don't know. It seems there's no place where I feel safe," she confesses, twisting her hair with her fingers.

"Lucky for you, I have training in this kind of stuff. I don't take any of these threats lightly," I state boldly.

Madison looks around Tyler's truck with a thoughtful glance. "I definitely feel safer when I'm with you. I don't think I could handle staying by myself tonight."

"Relax. I've got this covered," I respond with more confidence than I feel. But, she doesn't need to know my doubts.

As soon as I can, I make a U-turn and head down a dark, unused road. A few minutes later, I look over at Madison. She has stopped writing, and the pen is dangling from her fingers like body jewelry. I'm glad she's sleeping. That means she won't be able to tell anyone where we went. It's hard for me to completely trust anyone these days, but I'm ninety-eight percent sure I believe her when she says she isn't the person who spilled the beans.

If you would've asked me if Madison knew the ins and outs of camping, I would've laughed in your face. She seems like she would be much more at home on the runways of Paris than standing over the kitchen stove making stovetop popcorn.

"This is a cool little cabin, how did you know it was here?" she asks.

"You're the only person who knows about it. I haven't even told Heather and Tyler," I reply.

"What do you mean?" Madison asks with a look of confusion on her face.

"Tyler got a performance bonus, so, he asked me to invest it for him. He wanted me to do something fun with it. That's why I got this cabin so they can both go fishing or whatever," I explain. "He told me not to tell Heather because apparently they like to one-up each other when it comes to pranks. Tyler is so paranoid, he didn't even tell his own family."

"This is charming. You could have done much worse," she says as she pours melted butter over the popcorn. She looks up at me. "Lightly salted or movie theater salted?"

"Movie theater salted. Is there any other way?"

"I don't think so, but I thought I'd ask just to be polite."

I take the popcorn bowl from her and escort her into the living room area.

Madison looks around and spots the beat up leather couch. She grins like a kid at Christmas. "Oh my gosh! I swear I had the same couch when I was in college. I totally loved it, but my prissy roommate did not. She had some guys haul it away when I went home for a weekend. I was so sad."

Once again, Madison has thrown me for a loop. Based on her elegant appearance, I would've guessed she would have been the roommate with the classier taste. But, as she hops onto the couch, tucks her legs up under her and leans her head back against the overstuffed cushions, it is clear she is very comfortable in these surroundings.

When I sit down beside her, she grabs a handful of popcorn and throws pieces in the air and catches them. She is getting some rather impressive height, so I have to ask, "That's an interesting skill to have, when did you learn to do it?"

"Well, it might be endemic to the role of little sister to be able to perform weird and strange talents. I don't know, I think I was about five or six when my brother Carlton first showed me how to do this. He was in junior high and used to have a lot of friends over. I think one of them dared him to teach me. He thought it was funny until I turned out to be more skilled at it than him. He was not amused."

I shake my head and shoot her a quick grin. "I guess the list of things I miss because I'm an only child keeps growing."

"Oh, I have plenty of stories to tell. I think that's why I became a reporter. I always had commentary on what was going on in my life, but no one ever wanted to listen. I would always write stories to explain my feelings and reactions."

"Did you always want to be reporter?"

"Yes, I was even editor of the student paper when I was in elementary school. At first, my parents thought it was cute, but then as I railed against our lifestyle and started championing the rights of others, they discouraged my talent."

"That's too bad. A parent should not react that way

to their kids' success. If I'm ever a dad, I'll be the one cheering on the sidelines of peewee sports or academic all-stars."

Madison contemplates me carefully as she comments, "It sounds like you've given this an awful lot of thought."

"I suppose I have. When Melinda Jo disappeared, it was like she took all of my hopes and dreams with her. I had always dreamed of being a dad with lots of kids because being an only child was pretty lonely for me. Melinda Jo and I married right out of high school. I thought she was on the same page as me when it came to kids, but after we got married, she told me she wanted to wait until she was in her mid-thirties."

"That must've been quite a surprise. Did you guys argue about it a lot?"

"No, there was no real arguing. Melinda Jo just decided. I had little choice but to go along because I loved her so much. I also thought once she settled into married life, she might change her mind. But, it got no better. She was always driven to succeed in a career, and she figured kids would get in her way."

"I guess some women feel that way, but I think there can be a balance."

"That was what I always thought, too. My mom is a successful executive assistant to the President of the University of Oklahoma. She's worked there for years and they always were supportive of her family commitments, even when my dad had a stroke and she had to take time off to take care of him."

"Oh, that must've been hard. How is your dad

now?"

"He's much better. He still has residual weakness on his left side and he sometimes has a hard time finding words. He finds the speech thing the most frustrating side effect of the stroke. He owned his own accounting business, and after the stroke he felt like he needed to give up actively working with clients because he simply couldn't find the words anymore," I explain.

"As someone who relies heavily on words to earn a living, I can sympathize. Do you ever think about getting remarried so you can have the family you've always dreamed about?"

"Not until recently," I admit. "For many years, I didn't want to admit Melinda Jo was gone. Then, after the IED, survival became the theme of the day and I've had little time for anything else."

"That's understandable. You had other priorities in your life."

"What about you? Any kids in your future?"

Madison snickers at me. "It's a little hard for me to envision having kids when I don't even have a guy in my life right now. Given the caliber of guys I've dated in the past, that's probably a good thing."

"What if you had an honorable guy in your life; would you be open to having kids then?"

"Yes, I think so. It just hasn't been a realistic option for me, but I think kids are adorable and I've always wanted some."

A comfortable silence falls over us. But, my brain is still stuck on the mental image of Madison as a mom doting over her own kids, teaching them silly things like catching popcorn with their mouth.

Finally, I ask, "Would you like to watch a movie or something?"

"No, I'm enjoying the peace and quiet of sitting in front of a real-life fire place."

"It is nice, isn't it? Chilling here sounds like a brilliant plan. Let's make ourselves comfortable."

Madison looks at me skeptically. "Just how comfortable are we getting?"

"Whatever makes you feel comfortable works for me," I respond.

"You might regret your words. Beneath all this outside packaging, I am a pretty earthy gal."

Unbidden, thoughts of Madison free from social restraints pops into my mind and my groin tightens. I shift on the couch to disguise my reaction. But, apparently I'm not the only one affected. Madison's hand is shaking as she tucks some loose hair behind her ear.

"Relax, I won't bite unless you want me to," I quip. Much to my surprise, heat flares in Madison's eyes. This is getting more interesting by the second.

As I shift to get closer, pain shoots up what is left of my leg, reminding me that I've done far too much walking today. I curse my body's bad timing as I voice my thoughts out loud, "I'm sorry for the disruption, but I need to take my prosthetic off. I need to give myself a break."

Madison looks a little startled but recovers quickly. "Okay. Do you need me to leave?"

Her question causes me to pause for a moment and think about my options. I realize this is the first time I'll be taking my prosthetic off in front of anyone except my combat team or a doctor, but then I reason that my reservations are just silly. If Madison is in my life, she is going need to know it all, even my frailties.

I shrug as nonchalantly as my rapidly beating heart will allow. "It doesn't matter. Do whatever makes you feel most comfortable."

Madison appears to be weighing her options. "If you don't mind, I'd like to stay."

I shrug. "That's fine. Knock yourself out. It's not really all that exciting." Fortunately, I'm already wearing shorts, which makes it a little easier. I guess if you could call losing a leg lucky, I was one of the luckier ones. My amputation is right below my knee joint. This gives me a little more flexibility when I'm walking. I reach down and pull the straps which help create the suction holding the prosthetic to my stump. After I remove it, I examine my leg to see if there any new red spots. My stump has been healing nicely since returning from the Middle East.

Madison is watching with rapt attention, but there is no judgment or revulsion in her expression. I breathe a sigh of relief, I wasn't sure what her reaction would be, but her non-reaction reassures me.

"I thought it would be more complicated than that," Madison comments thoughtfully.

"Yeah, the technology surrounding prosthetics is slick these days. I've even got a different leg for running."

"Does it hurt?" she asks as she reaches out to touch my thigh.

"Most days it doesn't bother me much. If I do too much walking or running, it gets a little tender. But, the most disconcerting thing is that I still have phantom pain. Sometimes, I swear it feels like I've stubbed my toe even though my foot isn't there anymore."

"That must feel really odd," she says.

"You have no idea. It makes you feel like you're a little crazy. Fortunately, I had a really good rehab doctor who let me know this is entirely normal. If they hadn't warned me in advance, I really would've thought I was going crazy."

"To be honest, most of the time I don't even notice your leg isn't there. It's hardly noticeable when you walk."

In some ways, it's the biggest compliment she could have ever given me. I've worked hard to even out my gait and to improve my balance. It's part of the reason the Army's decision to put me on leave rankles so much.

"Thanks, I appreciate that. I try hard to look as normal as possible. Now that I've taken care of my leg, is there anything else we need to do to get comfortable?"

"Not that I can think of," Madison responds as she takes off her hat and shakes out her thick mane of hair.

I've gotten adept at hopping around on one leg and I go out to the porch to gather more wood for our little fire. I wish I would've thought ahead and brought ingredients for s'mores. After I tend to the fire, I sit next to her and gather her close to my side.

"Mmm, we fit together nicely," Madison observes. She turns her face toward me and arches her neck placing her in the perfect position to kiss.

I'm a good guy, but I'm not a saint. I cave into my desires and capture her mouth with mine. I start by kissing her lightly. Madison reaches out to clutch my shoulders. Her fingers knead my muscles through my T-shirt as she pulls me closer. I take the hint and deepen the kiss. Her soft mews of pleasure are addicting.

When I pull away to catch my breath, she sighs and whispers, "Wow."

Wow is right. I've never been so turned on by just a kiss. "I'd say we've got a little chemistry," I reply, resting my forehead against hers.

"If we had any more, I think I'd spontaneously burst into flames. I didn't want to stop."

Her simple admission sends a fresh wave of desire through me. I pull her hair to the side and kiss the soft skin between her neck and shoulder. She draws a sharp breath and moans softly. Her unfiltered response is like pouring gasoline on a campfire. I thread my fingers in her hair and pull her head to the side so I can have better access to her arching neck. When my fingers reflexively tighten in her hair, she practically purrs.

Madison turns and grabs the bottom of my T-shirt. As she pulls it over my head, she hisses in dismay. At first I'm confused, but then I remember she hasn't seen the scars left by the shrapnel. She pauses to kiss the particularly vicious one left by a piece of barbed wire. It had become infected, so the scar is raised and jagged. Her tender attention is almost my undoing.

"How could someone do this to you?" she whispers harshly.

"It's the price of war, Sweetheart. Some of us just

pay a higher price."

"It's not fair!"

My mouth quirks up in a crooked grin. "War rarely is. I knew what I was signing up for."

"It's still too much to sacrifice." She continues to kiss my chest. Breathing heavily, I pull away and study her. Her lips are parted as she too fights to steady her breath. When I see the open want in her face, I groan softly and murmur, "I should stop before I can't. You are too much of a great thing."

"Honestly, even though the traditional rules say I should stop, I don't want to. I feel safe, protected and desired in your arms. I'm a big girl and I can set my own rules. I'm tired of this cat-and-mouse game we've been playing for the last few weeks. I don't want to do the smart and logical thing for once. I really want to keep going and see where this takes us."

If I thought things were hot before, her words raised the heat to a whole new level. I struggle to fight my need and think rationally.

"Madison, if we keep going, there is only one place where this is ending," I whisper hoarsely. "If we don't stop, I won't want to."

She gives me a searing hot kiss, before she answers softly, "Maybe that's exactly where I want you."

I feel like I'm about to explode. But, I try again to be logical. "Mad, I didn't bring any protection with me."

She shrugs. "I'm on the pill for endometriosis. After my former fiancé left me for the office bimbo, I had every test known to mankind. I'm safe."

"Are you sure? I don't want to rush you," I say, unsure why I'm fighting so hard to be honorable.

Madison chuckles. "Yes, I'm sure. Who would've thought it would be so hard to proposition a cute guy? I kind of thought these things happened a little more naturally. Would you rather stop?"

"No, I don't want to stop. I thought I made it clear I like you a lot. You are the best thing to happen in forever. I just want you to be on the same page. If we decide we're all in — so to speak —there won't be any going back."

Madison swallows hard and blinks. "I wasn't expecting anything less, Trevor."

I nod slowly as I hold my hand out to her. I cringe as she has to help me off of the couch. I have to laugh at myself as I'm hopping down the hall with her. So much for suave and debonair.

CHAPTER SEVEN

MADISON

I'VE ALWAYS HEARD THE warning to watch out for the quiet, serious guys. I never really understood what that meant until now. But, as I stretch in the shower and feel muscle twinges all over, I am thankful I took a gamble on Trevor. Part of me is horrified by my brazen behavior, but the rest of me is celebrating. Trevor definitely put his fine body to work pleasing me. He seemed to worship every square inch of me. I've never been so thoroughly loved. I'll never forget the expression of reverence on his face as we made love — just as he promised. It's probably the same look of wonder I had on my face.

To say it was unusual is the understatement of the century. I don't consciously remember much about the time I was raped in college because of the GHB, but my body has never forgotten. It takes me forever to actually feel any sort of desire. My experience with Trevor was so much better than I could have imagined. Trevor has no idea he's given me such a gift. For the first time in years, I feel sexy and powerful.

Trevor is so thoughtful. It never ceases to amaze me when he does little things to make me happy. This morning, he left a pair of sweats and a new T-shirt for me to wear. The sweats are a little on the long side, so I roll them up and put on the pair of thick socks he's provided for me.

When I pad into the kitchen for breakfast, I notice he is hunched over his cell phone, studying it intensely. He looks up when I accidentally bump the table. "Morning Sweetheart. I love your sense of style, but I have to say this outfit is my favorite."

I blush. "Thank you, I think."

"Oh, I definitely mean it as a compliment. You look all soft and well-loved. You look like you're mine."

I suppose I should be incensed about being claimed. But, I can't seem to muster an objection because I like the thought of being Trevor Black's woman.

"It's likely I look that way because I am. Well-loved doesn't even begin to do how I feel justice," I concede, blushing hotly.

"I want nothing more than to spend the day wrapped up in you, but unfortunately your brother-in-law has the worst timing in the world."

My eyes widen in surprise. "What do you mean?" My heart feels like it's beating out of my chest.

Trevor sees my panic and hastens to reassure me, "Don't worry, it's good news. Colton just showed up at the Portland airport. He sent me a text message not knowing we're up here already. He wants me to go get him so he can go home to Heather."

"What are we waiting for? Heather will be beside herself with joy."

"I know. But Tyler wants to surprise her. That's why he sent me a text message instead of Heather."

"That's rather mean. If Heather knew he was coming, she would fix him a royal feast. She going to feel like she let him down if she doesn't have his dinner cooked."

"You and I know that, but Tyler has a reputation for being a stubborn romantic. He'll have a different interpretation of it all. I hope Heather forgives him quickly."

I start to throw all of my belongings into a duffel bag, but then I catch a glimpse of myself in a reflection in the pane window. "When Tyler sees me, he'll know exactly what we've been up to," I say over my shoulder.

"I don't have a problem with that, do you?" Trevor asks with a raised eyebrow.

I have to think about it for a minute because I'm usually the cautious one who thinks these things through for months before I make a move. But, as I weigh the pros and cons of my relationship with Trevor, I am having a hard time figuring out any negatives. Finally, I shrug. "No, I guess I don't have a problem with it either."

"Good, I'm glad we don't have to hide the fact that we're a couple. What do you suppose Trevor will say about us?"

I laugh softly. "If I know my sister and her husband, they'll both be turning cartwheels. Since they are so blissfully in love with each other, they think the whole world should be coupled up."

Trevor brushes a kiss against my temple. "Nothing wrong with that. Meeting you has changed my life. I want everybody to feel as happy as I feel right now."

Oh my gosh! Why can't I stop blushing. It's like I've never had a boyfriend before. "You say the most romantic things at the most random of times."

"It's not random. It's the way I feel."

As we're riding in Tyler's truck on the way back to Portland, the conversation turns serious. "I haven't seen anybody following us, so maybe the day and a half we've been off the grid was helpful. I wish we had more time."

"I don't know what to think about Barbie Light. It seems like she knows secrets about both of us. I don't even know how she came up with all those details about you," I say.

"I don't know either," Trevor comments. "I'm a little worried that she knows both of us. She seemed to have a lot of intimate information. Maybe I have been added to her stalking list by now."

I shudder. "I hope not. It's frightening to live like you don't know when the other shoe will fall."

"Well, I've replayed the conversation in my head about a million times and it seems like she was as fixated on me as she was on you."

"Sadly, I think you're right. I'm not sure what to make of it all. I had no connection to you at all before I showed up at Heather's. It seems inconceivable someone would be after us both."

"How did Deranged Barbie know personal

information about me?" Trevor asks pointedly.

"I don't know. Have you ticked anybody besides the terrorists off? Do you have a vengeful ex around?"

"Not that I know of. My only ex has been declared dead," Trevor answers dryly.

"Seriously? You've only had two partners and I'm one of them? I suddenly feel like the Queen of Debauchery."

"Don't feel bad. I was a willing participant in any of the aforementioned debauchery. If I have my way, there will be much more to come."

"Gosh, I hope so! You've spoiled me for anyone else."

Trevor looks about ready to choke on his tongue at my bawdy comment. Yet he recovers quickly and responds cheekily. "Thank you Sweetheart, I try."

———————◆●———————

"Madison, please come and sit down. Pacing in front of the window won't make the plane arrive any faster," Trevor declares.

"I know. I'm just worried. I'll feel better when he's home in one piece. I thought you said he was already here."

"I must've misinterpreted his text message. But, I'm sure he'll be here soon. Since you bolted this morning without eating, do you want to grab a bite to eat while we wait?"

I swivel around at his suggestion. "I guess I should eat. It's not like standing here is doing any good."

After I scarf a chocolate filled croissant and what seems like half a gallon of hot chocolate, I hear Tyler's name being paged. "O. M. G! I think he's here!"

"Should I be jealous you're so excited to see another guy?" Trevor teases.

"Oh yuck! He's practically my brother. That's gross!"

"You can't blame me for checking. Colton is pretty handsome."

"Not as handsome as you," I reply. "I'm just excited for my sister. She'll be so surprised."

"Gidget better be surprised. I'm going to be supremely disappointed if she's not," a deep voice from behind me says.

I turn and run into his arms. There is only one guy on the planet who is brave enough to call my sister Gidget.

After Tyler releases me from a bear hug, he holds out his hand for Trevor to shake.

He examines Trevor carefully. "I'd ask you how you are, but the smile on your face tells me everything I need to know."

"Maddie, I hope you didn't make it too tough on this guy. I know you LaBianca gals can be hard to convince." He turns to Trevor. "I had to wait forever and a day for her sister to come to her senses and marry me."

I stick my tongue out at him. "Funny, that's not the version of the story I heard. I understand it took you that long to figure out my sister was worth the risk."

Tyler looks a little sheepish. "Okay, you busted me.

I did take a while to come to my senses and admit my true feelings for Heather."

"What were you thinking?" I tease. "She is the best thing to ever grace your life."

"I won't disagree with you, for sure," Tyler answers with a wide grin.

Trevor looks at Tyler intently. "Mission accomplished, sir?"

Tyler nods tightly. "Affirmative."

Trevor sags so abruptly I'm afraid he's going to fall. I place my arm around his waist to steady him. "Thank heavens!" he breathes. "One less thing for me to worry about when I rejoin the unit."

"How's that going?" Tyler asks with a serious expression.

"I'm still waiting for them to put the official reason they discharged me in writing. Right now, it's a spitting war between us. No one wins."

"Doesn't your DD215 spell it out?"

"No, it doesn't; it states I have medical issues incompatible with service."

"B. S. and they know it. The team isn't as strong without you in it."

"I appreciate your vote of confidence, Colton. But unfortunately your voice won't hold much weight, especially when a brief tour of social media demonstrates we're friends."

"Also a bunch of B. S. We serve together — of course we'd be friends. What do they expect? I know better than anyone else how you operate as a soldier."

"Like I said, I can prove next to nothing without official paperwork," Trevor responds.

It distresses me I haven't bothered to fully understood the stress Trevor has been under until now. Some girlfriend I am. I pretty much suck.

"I have faith it will work out the way it's supposed to," Tyler asserts.

"Thank you." Trevor mumbles.

The ride home is slightly awkward since Trevor is not allowed to talk to any of the team members about the mission. I can tell he has tons of questions to ask, but doesn't want to break protocol.

I don't know how much to share with Tyler about my life. I'm afraid he might be angry with me for potentially putting Heather in danger. Trevor and I decided that it might be safer to let other people know what's happening. When Tyler asks how much vacation time I have to spend with them, I take a deep breath and disclose, "I'm not sure. I'm on indefinite leave at the moment because a reader claimed I have a financial stake in the investigations I've been conducting."

"That's bizarre," Tyler exclaims. "You are one of the most ethical people I know. There's no way you would cross any lines."

"It's true, I wouldn't. But my boss doesn't really believe me," I reply. "I wish Lyle had as much faith in me as you do."

"If he doesn't, he should. Can you appeal his decision?" Tyler asks, his frustration clearly reflected in his voice.

"Not really, Lyle Beckel has full editorial control. He's the one who sets our boundaries and makes assignments."

"That bites," Tyler answers.

"Tell me about it, it's only my career at stake. Nothing major or anything," I retort sarcastically. "I can't believe they would take the word of an anonymous reader over mine."

"I still think it ties into your other problem," Trevor responds.

Tyler swings his head around to look at me. "What other problem?"

I blush slightly. "It seems as if I've picked up a stalker who is fond of issuing death threats."

"If you're in danger, why is this the first time I've heard of this?" Tyler asks with narrowed eyes.

"I didn't want to worry everyone. I thought maybe it might all blow over."

"Has it blown over?" Tyler asks.

"Umm, not really," I concede.

Trevor addresses Tyler. "As nearly as I can tell, things seem to be escalating. Whoever it is got close enough to Madison to move her things."

"Please tell me the police are involved in this," Tyler comments.

"Yes, they have been informed, but I don't think they care much. I think some of them don't even believe there is a real threat."

Tyler pivots toward Trevor. "In your professional opinion, does she have a reason to be worried?"

"Personally, I believe the police are brushing this off a little too quickly. Especially in light of what happened at the Portland Saturday Market," Trevor responds.

Oh Crap! I really didn't want to hear this. I was hoping I'd overblown it all in my head. Hearing the two of them discuss it so calmly sends a chill up my spine.

Tyler pins me with his sharp gaze. "Maddie? Do you have something you'd like to share with the class?"

I sigh. "I don't even know if this is related, but this platinum blonde bimbo who I call 'Barbie Light' singled us out and started making fun of Trevor. She seemed to know a lot of personal information about us both. It was creepy because prior to this trip, I'd never met Trevor. This lady seemed aware we were a couple even though it was our first official date."

Tyler flinches. "Yep, that would be enough to make your hair stand on end. Trevor, was it somebody you knew?"

"I don't know for sure, but it's not somebody I recognized right off the top of my head."

"I agree with you. It sounds like things have gotten really personal. Are you going to go to the police with this one?"

Trevor shakes his head. "I don't think that there is enough to bother with the police. They'll want to know if any threats were made. This person didn't make any overt or incriminating threats. It's just her general presence which made us feel uncomfortable."

"I agree that's creepy. Black, make sure you watch her six. Heather would kill me if anything happened to her baby sister," Tyler instructs.

"Roger that," Trevor agrees.

It isn't long before we're back at the farm. It has started pouring down rain, so Trevor and I make a run for it, leaving Tyler in the car for the moment.

We arrive in the mudroom and take off our shoes. Heather comes around the corner wiping her hands on a dishtowel. "Oh, it's you."

"Yeah it's me," I answer with a snicker. "Who were you expecting; the Queen of England?"

"No, I'm wondering why Tara called and told me to go grocery shopping and to make a big dinner."

I want to slap my forehead. I totally forgot about Tara. She's Heather's friend who has a knack for seeing things yet to happen. I probably should've called her and given her a heads up that all of this was supposed to be secret.

"I don't know, maybe she figured we'd be hungry after all the walking we did yesterday," I suggest. But even I can recognize that I sound lame.

"Okay, it seemed like more. But maybe I'm misreading things. Dinner will be ready in a few minutes."

"Do you need my help with anything?" I offer.

"You could dress the salad greens for me," Heather says as she starts to cut an amazing looking roast.

"Let me wash my hands, I'll be right back."

As soon as I reach the safety of the bathroom, I pull out my cell phone and text Tyler.

"I'm afraid we've been outed by Tara," I text, my hands shaking with adrenaline.

My phone beeps as I receive a reply from Tyler, "Oh no, I forgot about the power of T. I'll be right in."

I quickly wash and return to the kitchen. I surreptitiously set up my cell phone camera on the table and hit record.

Just then, there's a knock at the back door. "That's weird, I thought I heard Trevor come in with you," Heather says as she dries her hands on a dishtowel.

It's all I can do not to grin as I shrug. "I don't know where he is. Maybe he went out to take care of the horses and forgot something."

As Heather goes to check the back door, Trevor sneaks into the kitchen. He stands behind me and puts his arms around my waist. I glance up at him and notice he's wearing an ear to ear grin. It's a really good thing Heather can't see him right now because she'd know for sure something was up.

It's too bad I can't get into a position where I can see Heather's face when she opens the door. But, I don't have to wait long because I hear a high-pitched squeal and the sound of Heather sobbing. This was not the reaction I was expecting because Heather always seemed so calm about Tyler being gone. But, I guess his deployment has taken more of a toll than I knew.

My brother-in-law comes around the corner

cradling my sister to his chest and murmuring, "Gidget, it's going to be all right now. I'm fine. I made it back in one piece like I promised."

"I still can't believe it! Why didn't you say something the last time you were on the phone with me?"

Tyler chuckles softly. "That would've ruined my surprise, and what fun is that?"

"Cowboy, you almost gave me a heart attack. That wouldn't have been so fun, now would it?" Heather responds as she playfully bats his arm with the dishtowel she was holding.

"I don't know, a little mouth-to-mouth resuscitation might be exactly what I need," Tyler quips as he winks at Trevor and I.

"You're so bad!" Heather exclaims with a giggle. "True to form, you're here just in time for dinner."

"Don't get me wrong, I missed you more than my next breath, but I really, really miss your cooking. Did I mention most M.R.E's taste like dog food and there's not enough hot sauce to disguise the flavor?"

"Well, you can thank Tara for today's spread. Otherwise, you might've been eating a TV dinner."

Tyler looks at Trevor. "Is the mission a go?"

Trevor nods. "Affirmative, sir."

Tyler claps Trevor on the back as he announces, "Great! We've got some work to do. Heather's got four table leaves behind the laundry room door." Tyler looks at me and continues, "Hey Madison, set nine more places please."

"Nine more places!" Heather exclaims. "I didn't

make that much extra food!"

"Gidg, I know you well enough to know you probably did. There's no stopping you when you're in the mood to cook. But, never in the history of our get-togethers has anyone ever gone hungry. I suspect everyone will have your back and we'll probably have leftovers."

Trevor and I look at each other in confusion. He shrugs. "Come on, Mad. We have orders to carry out."

Tyler grins at Trevor. "When we're not on base, I'm not your commanding officer, I'm your friend. So, knock it off with the Sir stuff." He turns to Heather. "I'm beginning to have a little more sympathy for William now. Oh wait, make that ten place settings."

Heather looks down at her worn blue jeans and checkered flannel shirt as she chastises Tyler, "You did it again didn't you? How many times do I have to explain to you that it takes me a bit of time to look presentable? I'm a total mess! I wasn't expecting to see anybody today, not even Maddie. I certainly wasn't expecting to entertain the whole gang."

Tyler walks over to Heather and kisses her gently. "Trust me, you look totally amazing. These are our friends; they won't care what you wear."

Heather sighs. "You're probably right. But this is not how I envisioned our big reunion. I was planning to wear something phenomenally cute."

Tyler kisses her again. "Darlin', you know I don't give a rat's patootie about how you're dressed. I'm just happy to have you in my arms again."

Kiera wheels into the kitchen from the living room. In all the chaos, I didn't even hear her arrive. "I would tell you guys to go get a room, but seeing as this is your house, it would probably be inappropriate," she teases. "How are you doing, Tyler?"

"I'm doing much better now, thanks for asking," Tyler answers as he puts his arm around Heather's waist.

Mindy comes barreling into the room. When she sees Tyler, she gives a little scream of excitement and jumps into his arms. "Uncle Tyler! You're back! I prayed for you every day while you were gone."

"Well, Princess Mindy, your prayers must have worked wonders. I'm back and so is every member of my team. We even got the bad guys."

"I knew you would," Mindy states confidently. "You know … I know these things."

"Where are your braces?" Tyler asks, noticing Mindy's grin.

"Uncle Tyler!" Mindy says with exasperation, "You've been gone for months and months. The orthodontist took them off. He said I'm one of the best patients he's ever had."

"I can believe it," Tyler says with a gentle smile. "Your new smile is stunning."

"Do you think so? One of the boys at school said I had a pretty smile, but I couldn't tell if he was teasing."

"Oh man! Do we really have to talk about boys? Didn't I tell you that you're not allowed to date until you're thirty-five?" says a voice from behind me. I know from pictures Heather has shown me the person speaking is Jeff, Mindy's dad.

"Daddy, you're so silly! Mom told me if I keep getting good grades, I can date when I'm fifteen," Mindy counters with her hands on her hips.

Jeff walks up behind Kiera and places his hands on her shoulders. "She did, did she? I can see we'll have to discuss it a little more. I don't remember giving you permission to grow up."

"You can't stop kids from growing up! It doesn't work that way. Look at Becca, she's already in preschool," Mindy argues.

"Oh man!" Jeff groans. "You just had to remind me, didn't you?"

I hear Trevor snicker behind me. "With all due respect, I think your goose is cooked."

Jeff sighs. "You're probably right. I guess I'll have to console myself with all the pie Kiera brought."

Tyler pipes up. "Jeff, have I mentioned how much I love your wife? But, I wonder who she's playing matchmaker for this time. Everybody here is married."

"Nuh-uh," Mindy says, pointing at us. "Aunt Maddie isn't married yet. But, they're going to be next after Grummy and Papa." She walks up to Trevor. "Can I be in your wedding? I have lots of practice now, and I'm almost big enough to wear high heels."

Trevor looks like he just went on a parachute jump and landed awkwardly. He takes a deep breath and answers, "I don't know yet. There are a lot of things to be sorted out before I can think about getting married."

"Well, don't wait too long. Aunt Maddie gets

impatient about these things," Mindy advises.

Her statement shocks me, not because it's not true, but because it is. I have no idea how she would even know. I've only been on a couple Skype calls with Heather when Mindy was baking at her house.

Tyler comes to my rescue. "Wait a minute! Gwendolyn and Denny are getting married? I must've missed a whole lot while I was gone."

Mindy shrugs. "Well, it's kind of a no-brainer they're going to get married. Papa fell in love with Grummy a long time ago. But, she doesn't know it yet. I think it's a secret. Anyway, Papa's gonna have to do some convincing because Grummy's a little scared because she was married to somebody mean before."

Tara walks up behind Mindy. "Hey Mindy Mouse, are you spilling everybody's secrets again? Remember when I told you about the responsibility which comes with our gift? You need to keep information private until someone absolutely needs to know — you know, like it's a matter of life and death."

Mindy looks puzzled for a moment and then answers, "Oh, I get it. It's a secret between me-n-God until I have to tell, like I did with Aunt Heather and Uncle Ty."

"Exactly Mouse. Not everybody appreciates having their business spread all over. Some people aren't quite ready for all the things you know, so you have to pick and choose carefully. It's a big responsibility," Tara explains.

"Aunt Tara? Should I tell them about the TV station? It seems kind of important."

"I don't know, that's up to you. Does it seem like it might be a matter of life and death?" Tara asks.

"I don't know yet. I just get an icky feeling in my tummy when I think about it," Mindy replies somberly.

"In that case, I might keep that knowledge to myself until I could figure it out. When you tell people things you know, they sometimes want to find out the small details and you don't have those yet."

"Okay, I'll think on it a little more," Mindy responds.

Trevor and I are so watching this conversation unfold as if it's a tennis match. If it's confusing to me, I can't imagine how confusing it is for Trevor. I don't know if he knows the back story of Mindy and Tara. Both of them seem to be able to predict what will happen in the future. It's a little too good to be true if you ask me, but Heather is a true believer in their skills.

"Mr. Trevor?" Mindy says as she turns toward us. "I'm supposed to tell you to watch out for a lady who looks like a Barbie doll. She's just pretending."

A chill goes up my spine. I can see now why Heather believes. I haven't even had a chance to tell my sister about the creepy lady, and I know Trevor and Tyler haven't said anything to anyone.

"Black, you need to take note. I don't know how she does it, but usually Mindy's spot on."

"Duly noted." Trevor looks a little shell-shocked.

"Does you mean you're going to pay attention to me?" Mindy asks. "This is super-duper important."

I nod in agreement as Trevor responds, "Yes, it

does mean I'm taking you seriously. A good soldier always uses all the information they have."

"I'm sorry I didn't know you yet when the bomb went off and hurt your leg. I could've told everybody not to drive down the road. Maybe your friends wouldn't be dead and Uncle Tyler wouldn't have terrible nightmares," Mindy declares sadly as a big fat tear rolls down her face.

Trevor pulls out one of the kitchen chairs and sits on it so he's eye to eye with Mindy. "Princess, stuff happens all the time. No matter how helpful your gift is, you won't be able to save everybody. All you can do is your best. Sometimes, we find out things too late. Sometimes, it's just a better plan. If my friends and I had not been hurt, I would've never gotten to live at your Uncle Tyler's house. If I hadn't come here, I wouldn't have met your Aunt Madison. She's pretty important in my life. I would be much sadder if we'd never met. So, I guess it all works out in the end."

"I like you, Mr. Trevor," Mindy announces. "You're super nice. I'm glad you'll be my uncle someday — I mean, you won't really be my uncle, just my pretend one like Uncle Tyler and Uncle Aidan."

"It would be an honor to be related to you, even if it's pretend." Trevor gives her a little hug.

My heart is so mushy right now. I'm near tears. The exchange between Mindy and Trevor was so sweet. It's odd to me Trevor doesn't have any kids. He seems to be a natural with them.

Mindy turns her attention in my direction, "Aunt Maddie, you're going to be really scared and angry, but try to remember how much you like Mr. Trevor."

"Thank you Mindy, I'll do my best to remember," I respond, feeling shaken by my emotions.

"Dinner is ready. I don't want everything to get cold," Heather interjects.

In all the hubbub surrounding dinner, the heavy conversation is mostly forgotten.

* * *

Two days later, as I'm coming back from my morning ride on Jacques, I see satellite trucks parked out in front of the barn. I tie the big horse up to one of the posts in the corral and try to quietly investigate. I find Trevor working in Velvet's stall. "What's going on?" I whisper.

"Some feel-good piece about returning veterans. I guess they want to show the Captain in a family environment. They've already interviewed me because I used to be in Colton's unit, but I think they still need to talk to you."

"Why would they need to talk to me? I barely even know what went on over there."

"I guess they want some information about the impact on the family of soldiers who have served."

"They'd be far better off to interview Heather," I suggest.

"I think they've done that already. They want some additional footage of Heather and Tyler's tight knit family."

"Okay, I guess I'll do whatever Heather wants me to do," I acquiesce.

Eventually, the producers get to me. It seems like

this will be a little PSA campaign to encourage people to support soldiers who are serving in the military. Heather thinks it might increase support for returning veterans, so she asked me to participate. After the reporter asks seemingly thousands of questions which I feel like I stumble through, Trevor comes onto the set and gives me a huge hug and a bouquet of wild flowers.

We're standing together in a loose embrace as he murmurs against my temple, "Sweetheart, you did so well. I'm so proud of you."

"It wasn't really a big deal. I've gotten used to being on camera. It doesn't freak me out the way it used to."

"Still, you are amazing." Trevor brushes a soft kiss across my lips.

"Thank you. I think you're awesome too. Not everybody would give me flowers just because I talk about how much I love my sister and brother-in-law."

"I don't know about that. I think you were brave wearing your emotions on your sleeve. I really wish I would've known you during the time I was on active duty. It would've been so amazing to come home to someone like you."

Once again, I'm floored by his unflinchingly honest musings.

Later that night, I'm sitting in the office in the barn when an old fax machine starts to spit out papers and scares me a little. I didn't realize anybody still uses faxes anymore. When I glance at them, I notice they have Trevor's name on them. I head deeper into the barn to let him know they came in.

Trevor scans the documents, reading through them quickly. "It's just as I suspected," he mutters under his breath.

"What? What did you suspect?" I prod.

Trevor sets me down on his knee as he points to the computer screen. "See? These are the IP addresses you normally use to do your banking."

"Yeah, so?" I ask, struggling to follow the conversation.

Trevor hands me the fax. "See these numbers, these are the deposits associated with the charities you've been reporting on They match each other, but they don't match your current IP address or even the one you use at work. You didn't write those checks."

I grin with a watery smile as I remind him, "I think I told you already I didn't write the checks. Didn't you believe me?"

"Of course I believe you. But believing somebody based on a hunch and having a hard evidence to prove it, are two different things. Now, there's a trail of paper to follow to figure out who took away your Cheerios."

"Now that's an interesting way to put it. But, it's true. All the changes this year have left me with a little emotional whiplash. I'm excited I'll have something to show Lyle. You are phenomenal."

"Don't get too excited yet, I haven't actually figured out who the perpetrator is, I've just proven who it isn't."

"I, for one, hope this is enough to convince the bank to give my money back."

"It's not a perfect investigation, but it should pass

any scrutiny. I'll keep working on trying to find the details."

"Thank you Trevor, you have no idea how much this means. I love having you in my corner."

CHAPTER EIGHT

TREVOR

NOW THAT TYLER IS home, the wedding preparations have ramped up to epic proportions. This is harder than I expected. I thought I'd done a pretty good job of compartmentalizing my memories of Melinda Jo, but she's popping up in my mind in the most random of places. Some days, I feel like almost every conversation I have with Madison involves dredging up a memory of her. Some of them are fun memories, but a lot of them are painful. Even my spooky conversations with Mindy are an odd reminder. Melinda Jo and I were not much older than she is when we first met and fell in love.

At the moment, we're standing in a tuxedo shop trying on clothes. This brings back a bittersweet memory of Melinda Jo. While we were still in high school, we used to go to the bridal shops and men's clothing stores and try on the clothes we planned to wear when we got married. But sadly, by the time we actually got married, Melinda Jo had become estranged from her parents and she decided we should go to Lake Tahoe. I scraped together enough money to fly us there, but the rest of it was about as low budget as you can imagine. We ended up getting married in our street clothes because the airline lost our luggage and we couldn't afford more clothes. Maybe it was an omen of things to come, I don't know. I just know she was furious with me for ruining the wedding.

As I'm lost in the past, Tyler snaps his fingers in front of my face. "Are you done day dreamin'? We're ready for you to try on your tux."

"Aren't you getting married in your dress greens or your dress uniform from the Sheriff's Office?" I ask.

"Gidget isn't really sure what she wants us to wear, so she wants us to explore all possible options before she decides."

"You are a brave man. All possible options is a very wide directive," I observe.

"Well, what can I say? I promised Heather the wedding of her dreams. So, if it means I have to try on a few monkey suits, so be it."

"What are the women wearing?" I inquire.

"Can you believe she's keeping it all secret from me?" Tyler says with a smirk. "I tried to tell her since we're already married, the superstitions don't apply. But, she's not buying my logic."

"You guys are too funny. You would give a standup comedian material for years."

"Yep, my Gidget is one-of-a-kind. They broke the mold when it came to her. I still pinch myself every morning I wake up next to her. I can't believe she settled for a guy like me," Tyler gushes.

"I agree. You're one lucky guy."

"Speaking of lucky, how are things with Madison?" He raises an eyebrow.

"Are you sure you want me to answer? She is your sister-in-law, after all."

"It depends. Just how much are you planning to share?" Tyler quips.

"Enough to tell you I'm eternally grateful you allowed me to crash at your place."

Tyler grins. "That good, huh? If it was just a fling, you'd be telling me tall tales."

"When have you ever known me to have a fling?"

"Come to think of it, never. The guys in the unit were beginning to wonder if you were some sort of non-pacifist monk or something."

I chuckle. That explains a lot of the very weird conversations over the years. "Hardly! I was just hung up on my wife."

"Was?" Trevor probes, watching me closely.

"Yes *was*. Madison has given me some real incentive to place the past in perspective."

Tyler nods thoughtfully. "I hear you. It's funny how the love of a good woman will do that to you. I was all kinds of buried in the past when I met Gidget. I almost let it ruin everything."

"I'm dying to know why you call her Gidget," I ask.

"Well, I could tell from the moment I met her she outclassed me in every way. She was shiny and perfect.

She reminded me of the fresh young girl next door your dad always tells you is too good for the likes of you. She reminded me of the perfect life so often depicted on the cover of *Life Magazine*. As a result of those impressions, 'Gidget' was born. At first I didn't trust the attraction between us because I'd been royally burned. Still, it didn't take me long to discover her sweetness goes through and through. But by then, I had almost scared her off by being a complete jerk."

"When did you finally decide she was your 'one'?" I ask, suddenly curious to hear the rest of the story.

"That's hard to describe. I think my heart and my head fell at different times. For my heart, it was almost instantly. It took my head a few months longer to trust what my heart already knew," Tyler explains.

"I don't know if I'm quite there with Madison yet. I know she makes me happier than I've been in years."

"Well, that's something," Tyler says philosophically.

"I don't know if it's enough. After what I went through with Melinda Jo, I feel like I'm waiting for the other shoe to drop."

"How does Madison feel about all of this?" Tyler asks.

"I don't know. She has been open in some ways but closed off in so many others. She gives a great show of staying strong and in charge. But, I can't shake the feeling she's been hurt deeply before. It's like she holds the most tender part of herself in check, so she doesn't get truly hurt."

"It's entirely possible. Her parents are a piece of

work. I don't know if Madison got as much of their wrath as Heather did, but I'm still trying to fix the damage they caused to Heather."

"Hmm, that's interesting. I get the feeling this was a guy. She seems to have terrible luck with them. I guess she was engaged to a lawyer who decided it was more fun to sleep with his receptionist than his fiancée. That's a decision I can never understand. Madison is as hot as they come, and she's wickedly bright and funny. In my book, there is no better combination."

"I hate to tell you this, buddy, but it sounds like you've been good and snared by a LaBianca woman." Tyler grins widely.

As I think back over what I've said in this conversation, even I have to admit he's probably right.

"So, how do I trust this?" I ask, anxiety filling my voice. "My first wife left without a trace and I thought things were going pretty well for us. I'm not even sure if she's alive or dead."

"First of all, you're a lot older now, and you've been through more hell than most people face in a lifetime. That makes you wiser whether you want to be or not."

I chuckle at the truth in his statement. "I can't argue. Almost dying in the field makes you grow up fast."

"Right? Sometimes I feel like an old man. Nothing like having teammates die in front of you to help you decide what's important," Tyler interjects.

"Having half your leg chopped off will speed up the process some too."

"Look how far you've come. In the beginning, you

were so sure your life was over, I couldn't even imagine you'd be joking about it a few years later. You need to remember you don't know what happened to Melinda Jo. She may have had her own issues."

"I'm not sure that makes me feel better. I feel like I should have been able to tell if something was up, or I should at least be sensitive enough to know if she's dead."

"I have a bit of a different take. I think each person has different gifts. People like Mindy and Tara are exceptionally gifted in reading people and their motives. Other people like you and me are gifted with animals. I mean, I think my horses prefer you over me, even though I rescued them years ago. There had to be some internal drive which drove you away from three-piece-suits. The information you can massage out of a few random numbers is astonishing. You could make it big in the business world, but that's not what you turned to in a crisis."

"I don't know. I just feel more at peace around animals. It's always been that way for me. I used to drive my mom crazy rescuing all the neighborhood pets — whether they needed it or not. Animals have always been my passion."

"How in the world did you end up as an accountant?" Tyler asks with open curiosity.

"Well, I've always been gifted in math. I was always several grades ahead and teachers had a hard time staying up with me. Then when I was almost fourteen, my dad, who owned his own accounting business, had a debilitating stroke."

"Oh Geez! I'm sorry, that's rough."

"At first an old school buddy of my dad's stepped in to take over his clients. But, then several of them called my dad to tell him their money was suddenly missing from their accounts. I had to deal with the complaints because my dad couldn't even speak intelligibly yet. My dad was heartbroken as he watched his business that he spent two decades building go down the drain. I felt helpless when I saw my dad cry, so I promised him I would help."

"Wow, that's a lot to pile on a kid," Tyler comments as he fiddles with the bowtie.

I shrug philosophically. "It was what it was. I made a deal with my guidance counselor. He allowed me to take accounting classes at the high school instead of more math classes since I was so far ahead. I was so desperate to help my dad I worked my way through two years worth of class material in a couple of months."

"What did your mom say about the plan you made with your dad?"

"If we had actually told her, she probably would have been horrified. Mom was always big on letting me be a normal kid even though I was an only child. She thought it was a normal part of the Talented and Gifted program and I never said anything to correct her."

"Wow! That's amazing! I remember being completely focused on the skate park when I was that age."

"It turned out to be a good thing I took all of those classes. A trusted friend of my dad's was skimming money from Dad's clients, and then tried to doctor the books to cover it up. He might have gotten away with it, except he failed to notice my Dad had this odd habit of adding an extra little line on his nines. My dad doesn't trust computers, so he always input the data on traditional ledgers before he input them in the computer. My dad was also super paranoid about fire because he witnessed his childhood home burn down. Dad kept handwritten copies of all of his files in a huge fire safe vault in the den of our home behind a bookcase. It was all very cloak-and-dagger, and I always thought it was a stupid habit to do extra work. At least I did until I used those same redundant records to catch a slimy embezzler. My dad was so impressed and grateful. From that day on, I was hooked on forensic accounting forever. I love putting the puzzle pieces together."

"What happened to your dad's business?"

"I helped him keep it afloat for a few years, but by then people started to use home accounting software and we couldn't afford to stay in business. So, my dad took early retirement. I got married and joined the National Guard. Originally, I had planned to go to college, but multiple deployments took care of that plan. When Melinda Jo disappeared, my CO gave me some leave to deal with the situation, but eventually I had to go back to the war zone. I was transferred to your command, and you know the rest of the story," I reveal with a ghost of a smile.

"I can't believe we've been friends this long and you never told me the whole story."

"I don't tell many people because my dad is still embarrassed about his stroke. He thinks it makes him look weak if he acknowledges my role during those years.

After I almost died, I was forced to examine my life and decide what was important to me. I made the decision to follow my passion."

"I've always wondered why you fought so hard to get back into the Guard after you lost your leg."

"That's simple. I have enough of my father's OCD to never want to leave a job half done. I didn't want the terrorists to beat me. So, I refuse to quit."

"Hooah!" Tyler cries as he high-fives me.

His loud antics attract the attention of the other shoppers, and they scowl at him. Aidan and Jeff come out of the dressing rooms. Aidan is signing something to us. When Tyler laughs out loud, I look to him for translation.

"Aidan told me to pipe down because even though he's deaf, he could hear me all the way in the dressing room," Tyler explains. He turns to Aidan. "Of course you could, Mr. Rock Star. You probably have your implants turned on high. You should probably use your voice though. I haven't used my sign language in months; it's pretty rusty. I could put some interesting words to your signs if I'm left to my own devices."

Aidan's next sign needed no interpretation. "Nice," I quip. "Colton, I've known you for years and I'm not allowed to call you an asshole."

"To be precise — he called me a *Funny* Asshole. I'm rather fond of that moniker, so I'll let it slide. Aidan, this is my best friend from the unit, Trevor. Mindy says someday he's going to be my brother-in-law."

"It's nice to meet you. I'm Aidan, his best friend in

the civilian world. I guess we'll be seeing a lot of you then because the odds of Mouse being wrong are about the same as they are with Tara — next to none. Welcome to the family."

"Are you sure? It's a big prediction to come from such a young girl. At her age, it could be fanciful thinking."

Jeff steps forward and sticks out his hand for me to shake. When I do, he says, "Hi, I'm Jeff, Tyler's best friend from college. I used to be a skeptic, too. Tara and Mindy have been right so often, I don't even bother to apply logic to the situation any more. I just brace myself for what they have to say and react accordingly. Mindy may be only a pre-teen, but she has been through so much garbage, she is far wiser than her years."

"Garbage?" I ask, seeking clarification.

"You didn't notice the scarring on her hand?" Jeff responds with surprise.

"I saw it, but I figured it may have been a birth defect."

"No, I only wish it was that straightforward. Her deranged grandmother tried to boil the 'evil' out of her. Then a few months later she threatened to harm Becca. Even though Mindy was only six, she tried to use the city's bus system to rescue Becca. When the bus wouldn't pick them up, some creepy pedophile offered her a ride then tried to kiss her. She fought him off and kept her four-month-old sister safe throughout the ordeal."

"Wow!" I exclaim with admiration. "How did you and Kiera become their parents?"

"I had just started dating Kiera when it all went down, but I was already head over heels in love with her. When Kiera decided to adopt the girls, they became a package deal in my mind. I've never regretted my decision. My little makeshift family is flat-out amazing. Kiera taught me to forgive myself and how real love works."

"That's a wild story. No wonder conversing with Mindy is like talking to a full-grown adult," I muse.

"She is smart as a whip and intuitive as heck. If she has taken the time to give you her forecast, you best sit up and take notice because I've never seen her be wrong," Jeff replies.

I shudder. "This is a lot to absorb. Your daughter made some pretty sobering pronouncements."

"I'm not surprised, things are rarely simple with Mindy Mouse," Jeff states.

Although the rest of the afternoon was light hearted — I think we really did try on every suit in the store while Tyler snapped selfies — I couldn't shake my feeling of unease as I replayed my last conversation with the young heroine.

As Tyler drives up his long winding driveway, I scan the field for Madison. She said she would be riding this afternoon. I'm alarmed when I see all four horses calmly standing in the pasture with their blankets still on. Usually by this time of day, Madison has removed all the blankets so they can sunbathe in the late afternoon sun.

I pull on my barn boots and battered hat and head to the barn to grab a few sugar cubes so I can round up the horses. I'm stunned when I find Madison curled up in a ball in her favorite chair. Although she is wrapped up in one of Heather's vintage quilts, I can tell her teeth are chattering. I walk over and place my hand on her forehead. *Oh crap! She's burning up.*

This is one of the occasions that I absolutely hate what happened to me. Before I was injured, I would've thought nothing of picking Madison up and carrying her back to the house. But, I'm not sure that I trust my walking skills on the uneven, muddy ground enough to carry her. As I'm debating my next move, Madison's eyes spring open. At first, she has a blank, confused look on her face, but when she recognizes me, she smiles weakly. "Oh hi. I thought you weren't coming back until this afternoon," she croaks, sounding a little bit like a bullfrog.

I stroke the hair out of her face. It is damp with sweat. "Sweetheart, it's five thirty in the evening. I've been gone all day."

"You're kidding!" she exclaims, but the brief exertion causes her to start coughing with a deep rattling cough. When she finally stops coughing, she continues, "I got dizzy around ten o'clock so I came in here to rest a little."

"How long have you been sick?" I gather her hair up into a ponytail and grab a rubber band from the desk drawer.

"I'm not sure. I wasn't feeling great last night. I had a bad headache and was a little nauseous. When I woke up this morning, my throat felt like it was on fire. I was hoping it might just be allergies since I'm not used to all this greenery in Oregon. But, I guess it's something more than that since I slept for over seven hours."

"Do you think you can walk to the house if you lean on me? If not, I could go get Tyler to carry you," I offer, embarrassed at my inability to fully help her.

"No thanks. I think I can make it with your help." As she stands, her clothes stick to her body because she's drenched with sweat. "Ugh, I'm so gross! I need to go to the bathroom and take a shower."

"Do you want me to ask Heather to help you?"

"No, don't. Tyler just got home and I don't want them to get sick. I figure you've already been exposed since you're not shy about kissing me."

Immediately, my thoughts travel back to our hot little picnic we had yesterday. She's right, neither one of us were exactly shy. "How do you want to handle this? I don't think you're steady enough to be by yourself."

Another round of vicious coughing overtakes Madison. My heart aches for her because it sounds so incredibly painful. When she can speak again, she says, "As much as I'd like to argue with you, you have a point."

"So, what are we going to do about it?"

"Could you help me?" she asks shyly.

Every logical thought I ever wanted to have goes flying out of my head as I envision her wet and naked. My next thought is that I must be a sick pervert to want to make love to Madison when she's so sick. I guess that I'm silent and lost in my fantasies for a few moments too long because Madison backtracks. "Oh, never mind. It was a stupid idea. I'll figure something else out."

"Madison, I haven't said no. I'm just trying to collect my thoughts," I reply, my voice rough.

Madison studies me intently. I can tell the moment she notices my predicament. "Oh —" she breathes as her eyes widen.

"Oh is right. I can't help it. This seems to be my usual state of being when I'm around you. I am trying to get my priorities straight so I can help you. My baser needs are fighting with my logical brain."

Madison chews on her bottom lip as she searches my face. "I'm sorry I put you in such an awkward situation," she whispers. "Let's just forget the whole thing."

"No," I state firmly.

"No?" Madison questions with a look of astonishment on her face. It's clear she wasn't expecting me to argue.

"No," I reiterate. "You shouldn't have to pay the price because I have a vivid imagination. I want to do this for you because it's something I can do to help you feel better."

"What about you?" she asks softly.

"What about me? So, I'll be a little uncomfortable. It certainly won't be the first time," I admit.

Madison takes a deep shuddering breath. "For reasons which escape me at the moment, I trust you. Can we please get this over with? I am so sore and tired I can barely hold my eyes open."

I brace my good foot against the chair leg and hold my hand out to Madison. "Let's get this going. I'm sorry I can't carry you. I wish I could, but in this weather, I think you'll be safer with your feet on the ground."

"It's okay, Trevor. I don't know if I would let you carry me even if you could. I'm a little oversized to be carried like a baby." She takes my hand and pulls herself up to a standing position. As she sways a bit, the quilt pools around her feet. She leans against my side as she steps over it. "Is that too much weight?" she asks.

"No, it's fine. Technically, I can even carry you if I need to. I was required to demonstrate I could rescue a teammate before they let me back into the Guard."

"Oh okay. I don't want to be a problem."

"Madison, you're a lot of things to me, but a problem is not one of them."

She snuggles a little closer to me as we carefully make our way down the ramp and through the yard. However, by the time we make it to the back door, she starts coughing again.

"Darn it! I wish I could stop doing that. Heather might overhear me and want to get involved," she mutters half under her breath.

"Tyler mentioned something about going out to eat, and I don't see her Bel Air in the driveway. I think you're safe."

"That's a good thing. It means we'll have privacy," she comments absentmindedly.

Normally, I cherish my privacy. However, right now privacy might be more than I can handle.

———◆———

After I load the last dishes in the dishwasher and press start, I breathe a sigh of relief. The last time I checked on

Madison, her fever had dropped three degrees and her nagging cough seems to be taking a break.

As I look around the great room to see if I've missed anything I need to clean up. I notice an official looking envelope. As I walk closer, I can tell the Fed-Ex package probably contains the official results of my military appeal. I toy with the idea of waiting to open it until Tyler is awake. But, let's face it, I'm too impatient to wait.

I sink down on a kitchen chair and gingerly open the cardboard envelope. There are only two pieces of paper inside. You'd think something that's going to impact the rest of my life would be a little more impressive. I quickly scan the ruling. I have to read it two more times for it to sink in.

It appears that I technically won my appeal. But, somehow it feels more like a loss. Yes, I can go back into the military, but there will be new restrictions. I can only operate in theaters that are pre-approved by the medical board, and I'm no longer able to travel outdoors with my team where exposure to sand and grit is possible. In other words, I can serve my country if I'm willing to be a desk jockey.

My only coherent thought is, *Frickin' Insurgents! I'm glad Colton blew your heads off with a .50 millimeter.*

Big fat tears run down my face as I climb the stairs so I can keep watch over Madison's breathing — it's a little rough for my comfort. A random thought crosses my mind, *I wonder if Madison will still be interested in a glorified file clerk.*

CHAPTER NINE

MADISON

THESE FLOWERS DON'T LOOK so bad if you ask me. I know my skill level doesn't even begin to match Heather's, but I've decided making flowers out of molding chocolate is rather fun. Heather received an emergency cake order from one of Aidan's band mates, so I'm helping her with Donda's birthday cake.

Heather walks through the kitchen holding a lethal-looking blade she uses to level cakes. When she spots what I've made, she comments, "Wow Madison! Those are really great. Are you sure you don't want a job at the bakery?"

"Yes, I'm sure," I respond, giggling. "I like being a journalist, assuming I can get back to my old job."

"How are you feeling? Did you finish your antibiotics? Walking pneumonia is nothing to mess around with."

I roll my eyes. "Yes, 'Mom', I finished all of my medicine like a good girl. Between you and Trevor, I'm the best cared for patient on the planet."

"You can't blame us for worrying. You were really sick there for a while."

"I know, but I'm feeling much better now. The only time I cough now is if I'm riding and I get my lungs full of freezing air."

"That's good. I'm not sure Trevor could handle it if you relapsed. He seems so easy-going. I was shocked to find out what a worrywart he can be."

"He definitely decided to go on an anti-germ crusade. I've never seen anybody do so much Internet research. He asked my doctor so many questions the doctor assumed he was my husband."

"I'm not sure Trevor doesn't see himself in that role anyway. Have you guys talked about the future?"

"Heather!" I exclaim. "I've only been here for four months. It's a little early to be shopping for wedding invitations. Besides, the future is a bit of a touchy subject right now."

"Is he any closer to making a decision?" Heather asks.

"I don't know. He seems really torn. On one hand, he wants to stay with the unit and accrue credits for retirement — but he doesn't want to merely ride a desk. If he had wanted to have a desk job, he could've kept his dad's accounting business, but he signed up for the military for the adventure and to work in the field."

"What do you want him to do?" Heather asks as she continues to level cakes.

I fiddle with a piece of molding chocolate as I formulate an answer. I sigh heavily. "This is going to sound like I have a double standard and it's totally un-PC, but I don't really want him to reenlist."

"Why?" Heather probes.

I sigh again. "I wish I could say I have only altruistic motives — that I want him to be as fulfilled as possible in his career. I know he'd never be happy chained to a desk. He's worked too hard to overcome his amputation to be penalized."

"True," Heather says.

"Though, the more selfish side of me realizes the biggest factor in my decision is the fact that he would be going away. It seems like we just found each other; I don't want him to leave. I feel so much safer when he's around. It's nice to be able to truly breathe. I don't want to give up the feeling of comfort and trade it for worrying about him every single day like you did when Tyler was gone."

"Oh Maddie, I can completely understand what you mean. Even though I'm proud of Tyler and his military service, before he left I wanted to call his commanding officer and beg him not to make my husband go."

"Really? You always seemed so calm about his deployment, I would've never guessed you were that nervous."

"Nervous doesn't even begin to describe it. I was petrified every day he was gone. I didn't dare let it show because I've discovered Tyler has a need to save the world. If I stood in the way, he wouldn't be as happy. So, I sucked it up and dealt with my anxiety."

"I'm proud of you for being able to. I don't know if I'm strong enough to do the same. I'm having enough problems dealing with my own life."

"How is the investigation into the stalker going? No one is saying much of anything."

Her question catches me off guard — I wasn't even aware my sister knew anything about my situation. "You know? You got enough stuff going on in your life right now. I didn't want to bother you with it."

"I figured something like that was going on in that head of yours," she replies. "For the record — you should've told me. I am not happy some creep is after my little sister."

"I'm not thrilled about it either, but there's not much I can do about it. That's one of the reasons I don't really want Trevor to leave. He is so much better at staying calm and objective in these situations."

"I take it he hasn't found anything?"

"I guess he's figured out that the bank accounts are all linked, but he hasn't gotten to the bottom of who owns the IP address. I guess it's been registered under a dummy corporation within another dummy corporation. He says he's getting close, though."

"I hope you guys get to the bottom of this quickly. I don't like the thought of either one of you being in danger."

"For once, I hope God is listening. I'm so over living scared," I mutter.

I can feel the beat of the bass traveling through my feet as I sit on the balcony of the restaurant where we're having a combined bachelor and bachelorette party for Tyler and Heather. They decided it would be silly to have separate parties. I feel sorry for the other people who are here for open mic night. Aidan is trying to be like an average everyday person and blend in. However, when you are as striking a couple as Aidan and Tara, it's difficult to fly under the radar.

Trevor is more relaxed than I've seen him in weeks. He has his arm casually draped over my shoulder in the booth as he chats with Tyler. Aidan and Tara come back from the dance floor and join us in the large round booth.

Tyler taps Aidan on the shoulder and asks, "What do you say we go dazzle the amateurs a bit? My fingers are itching to play the guitar."

Trevor sits up straighter and asks Aidan, "Need someone on skins?"

"I don't know. Are you any good?" Aidan answers.

"It's been a little while since I've played, but I spent three years in jazz band. They used to call me Thumper."

Tyler shrugs. "Sure, we could use a third."

Heather turns to me. "I feel like one of the popular kids now. The rest of the women can eat their hearts out, we're with the band."

"Yeah, I feel like my seven years of piano lessons have been totally and completely wasted. There's not much call for Bach or Beethoven," I quip.

"Geez, I guess that leaves Kiera and I out since I have no appreciable musical talent, and as far as I know Kiera doesn't play either," Jeff says as he dishes out some of the nachos we've been sharing. He turns to Kiera and asks, "Will you still love me if I'm not in the band?"

She pats him on the hand and replies, "Of course dear. Someone has to help them negotiate their multibillion-dollar record deals."

Aidan laughs and nudges Jeff. "I'll admit, it's handy to have my attorney as a close personal friend." He turns his eyes to me. "It's kind of loud in here. Did you say you play piano?"

Tara scowls at Aidan. "You should've said something. I'm sitting here with my hands idle." I notice she's signing with lightning speed. I know a few signs in ASL because one of my roommates in college was deaf.

"Yeah, I play piano. I mostly play classical music, but I can pick my way through a pop song pretty decently."

Heather scoffs. "*Pfft*, don't let her fool you. She used to win the talent portion on the pageant circuit more times than not when we were little."

"What do you say? Are you going to play with us?" Tyler asks.

This is not how I thought today would go. I'm not sure I'm brave enough to be so spontaneous. "I really play much better when I have sheet music," I stall.

"No problem, I have a bunch in my guitar case because I've been arranging a few songs for a cover album. Is *Imagine* in everyone's range?"

Everyone in the group nods. Inexplicably, so do I. I can't remember the last time I preformed publicly. I hated competing in the pageants so much that as soon as I could stop, I did. I never looked back. I swallow hard as

Trevor slides his arm around me and escorts me to the stage. I turn and face Heather. "What am I doing?" I mouth.

Heather winks and gives me a thumbs up sign. Trevor leans over and murmurs, "You've got this," as he pulls out the piano bench for me. He kisses me behind the ear before he sits behind the drum set.

Trevor sets the beat and I start the introduction, then as if we've rehearsed a million times Aidan and Tyler come in with their guitars. I can hear the din of noise in the restaurant as patrons socialize, but as soon as Aidan opens his mouth to sing, it becomes instantly quiet. I hear a woman to my left screech, "Oh my Gosh! It's Aidan O'Brien!" Suddenly, the room lights up with dozens of flashes as people in the restaurant whip out their cell phones to document an unannounced performance by the pop star. Since Tara is one of Heather's best friends, I'm used to hanging out with Aidan. To me, he's just the guy who is patiently teaching Mindy to play the sax and guitar. Sometimes, I completely forget Aidan and Tara are famous. If I had pondered all of this for a moment, I would never have set foot on the stage.

Before I know it, we finish the song and the audience erupts in applause. The guys pull me to center stage for a bow. Although I'm embarrassed, I have to admit this feels completely different from my pageant days.

As soon as we leave the stage, Trevor pulls me close for an embrace. "Madison, you were phenomenal; I'm so proud of you."

Aidan winks at me. "If I didn't already have a full-time band, I would hire you in a heartbeat. You can accompany me anytime." I'm touched by his compliment because I know Aidan started out as a semi-professional piano player when he was a kid.

"I appreciate your confidence in me, but I would just as soon stay behind the cameras. I don't think the life of a star is for me," I reply as we all sit down at our table.

Tara kisses Aidan and then turns to us. "I'm already Aidan's number one fan, but you guys made him sound even better."

A waiter appears at our table with another round of drinks. Heather looks at him quizzically. "We didn't order those."

The waiter nods toward another table across the room as he explains, "I know you didn't. But, these are from the gentleman over there. His instructions were to 'Drink up and enjoy yourself.' These drinks are on him."

The words are like ice water thrown into my face. My vision grays around the edges and I have to gulp for air. I start trembling uncontrollably, but before I can say anything the world turns black.

The next thing I know, I'm laying on a couch in what must be the break room of the restaurant. "I didn't see her drink anything, so I don't think it's that," Tara comments as she strokes my hand.

"Maybe she's getting sick again. I know she rode the horses pretty hard today," Trevor suggests.

"No, I don't think that's the problem. I think it's a little more complicated," I hear Heather add.

"Do you think this has something to do with her

being stalked?" Tyler asks Heather.

"No, I don't think it's related because we've all been sharing appetizers," Heather reasons.

I force my eyes open and struggle to sit up. Trevor rushes over to help me. "You scared the crap out of me. What happened, Sweetheart? Are you all right?" he asks as he tenderly kisses my temple.

I shut my eyes again as humiliation sets in. Trevor moves my hair out of my face as he urgently calls my name. "Madison? Are you in trouble again?"

I gather my courage and answer, "No, I'm fine now. I just had a really bad flashback to when I was in college."

"Oh, Madison, I'm so sorry. Those can sneak up on you at the most random times. It happens to me too," Tara offers sympathetically. "Do you and Trevor need some privacy?"

I draw in a shuddering breath as I look around at my friends and family. Although they started out as Heather's friends, they've warmly adopted me. The other day, Kiera told me I had been inducted into the Girlfriend Posse. I know from talking to Heather if anyone would understand, it would be Tara.

Trevor is still studying me with a look of distress on his face. I realize he probably has no idea about my past. It's not something I discuss very often. I try to push it to the back of my mind and pretend it didn't happen. I squeeze Trevor's hand. "Tara, I appreciate your concern. But, I consider everyone here to be closer than my family, so there's no sense in hiding what happened." I turn to Trevor and reveal in a halting voice, "I'm sorry Trevor, I probably should've told you this when we first met—"

"Whatever you have to say isn't going to change how I feel about you — you know that, right?" Trevor interjects.

"I know none of you are going to judge me for this, but I really thought I had put the rape behind me."

Trevor looks like I've physically punched him. A look of pure pain crosses his face and is quickly replaced by rage. "What happened to the lowlife?" he asks with a lethal tone in his voice.

"As far as I know, nothing. I was in a bar. It was a lot like this one, in fact. I was one of the youngest people at the university, and I was trying to prove how mature I was. So, I went out drinking with some girlfriends even though I was underage. The bartender gave me a drink and said one of the guys bought it for me so I could 'drink up and enjoy myself'. I was really flattered, so I let my guard down and drank it without thinking."

Trevor just grips my hand and absorbs each word like a physical blow.

"The next thing I remember, I woke up on a bench in front of the dorms," I continue. I never talk about this, so it feels a bit like I'm confessing a deep, dark sin. I have to draw in a deep breath to continue, "At first, I thought maybe I drank too much and passed out. But, then it became clear someone had done something terrible to me."

"The administration at the college didn't do anything?" Jeff asks.

"There wasn't much they could do. I was so afraid of getting busted for drinking, I didn't tell anyone for a few days. By that time, they couldn't do a rape kit or collect DNA from me. It became a matter of my word against a group of guys who were several years older than me. I never knew exactly who attacked me," I explain as tears roll down my face.

Kiera offers me a tissue. "Madison, I'm so sorry that happened to you, and I'm even more sorry someone was not held accountable for what they did."

I swallow hard as I admit my weakness. "I know. I kick myself every day that I wasn't brave enough to go to the police department right after it happened so they would have the evidence they needed to convict someone. I wonder all the time how many other girls have been attacked because I didn't do the right thing."

Tara pats my knee. "I struggled with guilt in my own life for years. Finally, I had to just let go of all the shame and guilt because the only person I was hurting was me."

"Maybe if I had done something sooner, what little evidence they collected would have been tested. I'd like to think I didn't go through all that just so the experience can be reduced to a potentially jizz-stained crumpled up pair of bikinis stuffed into the corner of an evidence locker somewhere."

Trevor cups my face and gently raises my chin so I have to look at him directly. "Madison, do you understand none of this was your fault?"

"Intellectually, I know that. But, sometimes — like tonight — it comes back to haunt me. I'm sorry I upset everybody."

Tara leans over and gives me a hug. "When Aidan and I first got together, one of the first things he said was that I had to tell him what hurts because he couldn't see the scars on my soul. I've never forgotten that. You may not want it to, but anyone who's gone through this experience will tell you it changes who you are. You need to let us know if you need any help."

"Tara, I appreciate the offer, but it was a long time ago. I'd really like to forget anything happened. Can we go back to having a good time? I'd like to remember today for something positive. We're supposed to be celebrating Heather and Tyler's marriage. I don't want to give my attacker the satisfaction of knowing that night still haunts me."

Trevor helps me off the couch and envelops me in an embrace. "Madison, I'll do anything you need me to do. If you want us to forget it, I'll do my best to honor your request. But, just so you know, if we figure out who did it, Tyler and I — and a few close friends from the Army — might dish out our own justice."

That thought makes me smile. "I guess what I don't know won't hurt me," I quip with a watery grin.

"Come dance with me, Madison. I can't dance as well as I used to, but I can still slow dance," Trevor says as he gathers me in his arms.

I brush a kiss across his sexy lips. "I'd love to."

Aidan and Tyler take the stage again as Trevor and I head to the center of the dance floor. The crowd applauds when they see Aidan. He blushes as he grabs a microphone and addresses the audience, "Thank you so much. I'm here tonight to celebrate the love of strong women. My best friend is getting married, I have wonderful friends who are falling in love and I have an amazingly strong wife who holds my world together. This song is for them." Aidan sits down at the piano and starts to play *You Are So Beautiful* by Joe Cocker as Tyler plays the acoustic guitar. Randomly, I wonder if Aidan knows *Modern Romance* is one of my favorite movies.

Trevor pulls me close and gives me a long, hot kiss. By the time he's done, I'm the one having difficulty staying on my feet. I always thought "weak in the knees" was a cliché, but I'm practically melting in his arms even before he whispers, "I love this song, it describes you perfectly. You are the most beautiful woman I've ever met — inside and out."

I sigh and lay my head on his shoulder as we sway to the music. As the song ends, I kiss his earlobe and murmur. "You're beautiful to me, too. I'm so glad I found you. Thanks for the most romantic dance I've ever had."

"My pleasure, Madison," he answers in a low, sexy growl.

My mouth goes dry in response to his words. "Do you suppose anyone would mind if we ducked out early?"

"No, I think they would totally understand," Trevor replies with a knowing grin.

———•———

The atmosphere in Trevor's truck is so charged, I think both of us are having a hard time coming up with things to say. Finally, I break the silence. "I like your new truck," I say as I look around at the restored Ford from the '50s.

"Thanks, I bought it from Denny. I guess it used to be Jeff's, but they wanted it to go to someone who would actually drive it."

Trevor makes an abrupt turn on to a narrow forest road. "Where are we going?" I ask, not expecting the detour.

"It's a beautiful night with a full moon. I want to take you to one of my favorite places and make love to you under the stars," Trevor explains as he laces his fingers through mine.

The image that pops in my head is so erotic I have to take in a deep breath. I wish I had something sexy or clever to say, but all I can come up with is a breathless, "Okay. I'd like that." Based on my current conversational skills, you'd never guess I make my living with words. Yet, Trevor doesn't seem to mind.

After a few more minutes of driving, Trevor has to stop and open a gate. He makes a turn onto a gravel road. "Almost there," he promises in a low voice.

The anticipation is intoxicating. He hasn't done more than kiss me while we were dancing and hold my hand, but I feel like a single touch might send me over the edge. I am already breathing hard.

Finally, he drives to a clearing and stops his truck. As he grabs a heavy sleeping bag and some bottles of water from the truck, he hands me a flashlight. He arranges everything in a backpack and shrugs it on. He takes the flashlight back and slides his arm around my waist. Side by side, we walk through a little outcropping of trees and up a small hill. When we reach the top, I have to catch my breath for a whole new reason. As far as I can see, there are bright twinkling stars highlighted by the full moon. "This is the prettiest thing I've ever seen," I whisper.

"You're the most gorgeous thing here. The stars pale in comparison."

It's a good thing he can't see me blush in the dark. I give a full body shiver.

Trevor sits me down on an old stump. "Sit tight. I'll have us warm in a minute."

He takes off his backpack and removes some newspaper, crumples it up and places it in a ring of stones. I notice there are already partially burned logs in the center. He takes a lighter and lights a piece of newsprint. He unrolls the sleeping bag and takes off his jacket and shoes.

I lick my lips in anticipation as I watch Trevor strip off his shirt and sweater as the fire roars to life. He silently walks over and removes my boots. He kisses my ankle and then helps me stand in front of him. "I plan to make it beautiful. Ever since I saw you playing in the backyard with the dogs, I've been fantasizing about what it would be like to love naturally."

"Love naturally?" I repeat.

"I know it sounds corny, but this is one of the most peaceful places I've ever been. I wanted to bring the woman I've fallen in love with to a place I cherish. I want to make love to you in the firelight under the stars because there is nothing artificial about us — our love is as natural as this place."

His words make my heart skip a beat. "You love me?" I stammer.

He kisses me deeply. It's almost as if he's trying to show me what he can't express in words. He pulls away and leads us to the sleeping bag. After we lay down, he zips us in.

When we're laying face to face, he resumes speaking, "Yes, I love you. It's not something I expected. I wasn't even looking for love, but minute by minute, day by day, it got harder for me to imagine my life without you in it. Then I reached a point where I knew I didn't want to even try."

His honest, heartfelt words are too much. A tear rolls down my cheek and Trevor wipes it away with the pad of his thumb. "Oh crap, I've made you sad. I should've known to keep my mouth shut until you were ready," he frets.

"No, that's not true," I insist. "I'm emotional because I realize I've spent a lifetime making love complicated. But, you just described love in the simplest, most straight forward terms I've ever heard. If that's how you define love, I love you too because I don't ever want anyone except you by my side. I guess love doesn't have to be as hard as I've made it."

"Life is complicated enough, love doesn't have to be. I promise to be by your side and give you whatever you need for as long as you want me in your life. It's as simple as that."

"That sounds like a perfect definition of 'love naturally'. I will do the same for you. But, don't plan on getting rid of me anytime soon. I consider true love to be a lifetime deal."

"I'm more than willing to make that deal. I love you, Madison."

"I love you too, Trevor Black."

"Now, I believe I made some other promises tonight I need to keep."

"I like this falling in love stuff," I quip as I roll Trevor on his back and kiss his muscular chest.

When I wake up, my nose is ice cold. It takes me a moment to remember where I am. I stretch and rub my sore hip. I must've been sleeping on a rock.

I look down at Trevor. He's still sound asleep. He looks so peaceful, I hate to disturb him. But almost as soon as I have that thought, the decision is taken out of my hands because my phone rings. I scramble to the backpack to silence my phone before it wakes him.

I shiver as the cold morning air hits my bare breasts.

"You should've told me the fire went out," Trevor says in a sleep-roughened voice.

"I just woke up myself. Somebody called my cell, but I missed the call."

Trevor looks out at the sunrise. "As much as I'd like to stay here with you, there are four hungry horses back at the farm who would probably like me to feed them."

"I need to check out some stuff for my job that's not officially my job right now, too. Yet, I don't want to leave this magical place. I'll always consider it the place I discovered the true meaning of love," I respond as I kiss him softly.

Trevor groans. "Madison, please don't make me forget I have responsibilities because, if you keep that up I might just give into my less-than-honorable intentions and call in sick."

Reluctantly, I back away and put my hands down at my side. "Okay, I'll be good as long as I get a rain check."

The corner of Trevor's mouth hitches up. "Somehow, I don't think it'll be a hardship."

After Trevor steers us on to the main paved road, I pull my cell phone out of my pocket and check my messages. I can't disguise the gasp that comes out of my mouth while I listen to Lyle talk. My hands are trembling when I finally collect myself enough to hang the phone up.

Trevor looks at me with an expression of stark terror on his face. "Madison? What is it? Talk to me."

"That was my boss. There's been another threat." My voice shakes like I'm a rookie reporter doing her first shoot.

"What was it this time?" Trevor tightens his grip on the steering wheel.

"Trev, they had pictures. Pictures of us on stage singing and then dancing together."

"Anything else?"

"Just a note. 'Always watching. Don't think hanging out with a washed up ex-soldier will protect you.'" I quote. Repeating the ugly words makes me sick.

Trevor fumes, "That's Bull! I don't know where that person's getting information, but my separation from my unit was supposed to be private and confidential with no press coverage."

"I don't know the answer. I don't understand any of this. Now this person seems to be more focused on you than me. It doesn't make any sense. The stalking started before I even met you, but maybe they are after you, too. Maybe this has something to do with your military service."

"I doubt it. Our unit is secretive and not many people know who's in it." Trevor pulls the truck over to the side of the road and examines me intently. "Mad, I don't want to freak you out or anything, but do you think any of this has to do with your rape?"

"I don't see how it could. I didn't have a chance to pursue any criminal charges. All I did was report it to the school's medical clinic because after it happened, I thought maybe I should get tested for STDs but, I don't think they did anything. They didn't even want me to talk about it with my friends. The administrator in charge of the dorms suggested that if I said anything or admitted being a victim, it would put me in more danger. For years I didn't tell anybody except my sister. Heather helped me find a counselor to deal with the aftermath. But, my counselor was from off-campus. I'm not even sure my parents know about what happened."

"What happened to your roommate from college? She would've had to know something happened, right?" Trevor asks.

"I'm not sure. After the incident, I became even more of an outcast. I think a lot of the women thought I should've been able to handle my alcohol. One of the meaner girls on my floor started calling me La B-baby as a play on my name. I guess LaBianca was not good enough for her. Because she was popular, a lot of the other girls followed suit. I finished that term in college —

just barely, and then I took a break and went back to my grandma's farm for a few months. I was planning to transfer to the University of Texas, but Grandma Lydia convinced me I didn't want to give up my Princeton education just because someone was a prick. I thought it was so funny at the time because she actually used that word. So, I don't know what happened to all the girls who lived in my dorm because they moved ahead and I didn't for those few months. My move put me behind the rest of my class."

Trevor intertwines his fingers with mine as he holds my hand. "Madison, that should've never happened to you, and I'm sorry Princeton didn't do more. That really sucks."

"Oh, I didn't mention I was actually on a student exchange when it happened, I was actually at Oxford University in England."

"Your parents sent you off to another country when you were only sixteen? Were they nuts?" Trevor asks incredulously.

I chuckle at his extreme outrage. "Maybe I should explain. It wasn't so much that they 'let' me do anything. I was so intent on getting away from the constant barrage of criticism that is my parents' favorite mode of communication, I would have joined the circus to get away from them. Fortunately, I was advanced enough and my SAT score was high enough Princeton admitted me with virtually no questions asked."

Tyler looks at me quizzically. "If you have a big fancy degree from Princeton, why aren't you some high-powered executive or partner in a law firm? I thought that was pretty much standard practice for all of you high achievers."

I laugh out loud at his confusion. "You sound exactly like Heather. She could never understand my career choices either. The short answer is that my dad used to hang out with a bunch of attorneys and I was never impressed with them. Besides, I'm not the type of woman who fits in well in a corporate environment. I like fighting against the system too much to be part of it. I'm not a big fan of conforming. Besides, when I'm allowed to do my job, I do a lot of important work. Everybody underestimates me because I don't have a big famous name or position. I'm a plain looking reporter who works for a little backwoods paper, so they never think to look out for little old me. They have no idea I got almost a perfect score in my SAT when I took it at fifteen, or that except for the one term of college when I was coping with the rape, I had never gotten below ninety-five percent on a paper or a test during my entire academic career. I think I prefer it that way. It was annoying to be known as the perfect brainiac. I wanted to be social and outgoing like Heather."

Trevor squeezes my hand. "Well, I didn't know any of that about you and I still think you're perfect just the way you are. I really wish you could see yourself through my eyes. If you could, you'd never call yourself plain again."

I lean over and kiss his cheek as I declare, "I'm so glad you love me because you're great for my ego."

CHAPTER TEN

TREVOR

THE EXCITEMENT OF THE day has proven too much for
Madison — or maybe it's because we spent the night
making love. Whatever the cause, she has fallen asleep.
As much as I enjoy driving Tyler's decked out truck, I
prefer this old-fashioned one because it's big bench seat
allows Madison to be curled up next to me as she takes a
nap on the way home. She shifts in her sleep to snuggle
even closer.

Last night was the single greatest night of my life. I
feel guilty even thinking that because I loved Melinda Jo
for so long. She was my first everything. She was my first
crush, kiss and sexual partner. Until I met Madison,
Melinda Jo was my measuring stick. I realize now we were
probably more in love with the idea of being the perfect
cute couple than we were with each other. Neither one
of us coped well with the idea that we would change and
grow. I never understood her blind ambition, and she
never understood my patriotism. I guess I didn't do a
great job of communicating my need to be needed.

Maybe I failed to tell her how much I loved her until it was too late.

I hope I've learned my lesson now. Madison is too important to lose through my own stupidity. I'm trying not to freak out about the outside forces that may come between us. I need to get to the bottom of what's going on. Our safety may be at risk, for all I know. Since I don't know who the stalker is, I have no way to evaluate the true threat level.

As I pull up to the farm, I notice Tyler appears to be waiting for me. I gingerly leave the truck and quietly close the truck door. "Good morning," I greet.

"Black, you are a brave man," Tyler declares.

Something in his tone makes me stand up straighter as if I'm still under his command. "Sir, is there a problem?" I ask reflexively.

"Yes, but not in the way you think," Tyler smirks. "What were you thinking? My lovely wife is beside herself with worry. The next time you decide to sneak off like a horny teenager, send out a few text messages first. You may get an earful from Gidget, so be prepared."

A blush creeps up the back of my neck. I was so tied up with Madison last night, I forgot to account for family politics. It's a weird dynamic living with my boss — especially, since I don't know if he'll still be my boss soon. "I'm sorry, Captain," I answer, uncomfortably. "I should've planned ahead and kept Heather better informed. I apologize for being rude."

"Hey man, don't worry about it. We've all been there. I take it things are going well?" Tyler responds with a smile.

"As well as it can possibly go with a stalker dogging our steps. I wish we could catch the creep. Whoever it is sent another email with pictures of all of us last night. I guess the underlying message was we aren't safe anywhere."

"Have the FeeBees been brought in yet?" Tyler inquires with a scowl.

I shake my head. "I don't think so. I think she's having problems getting even the local police where she lives to take it seriously, let alone the FBI. I guess they're treating it as if she just has an overzealous fan. Personally, I think it's a lot more serious problem. There's the weird thing with her banking stuff. I believe her when she says she didn't donate to those charities. She has far too much integrity to involve herself with an organization she's investigating."

"Do we need to enlist William? As a former Oregon Supreme Court Justice, that man has contacts you wouldn't believe."

"Would he do something like that for us? He doesn't know us all that well."

Tyler chuckles. "I always forget you don't know everyone's back story because I've been your friend for so long it feels like we've shared the same past. But, I'm sure William would be happy to help out. He has essentially adopted Kiera, Heather and Tara as his honorary grandchildren. He would move heaven and earth for them. He's pretty much extended the privilege to anyone Kiera knows and loves."

I shrug. "I guess it's worth a shot. If nothing else, it would scare the crap out of people."

"It sure would. It sounds like these folks need a good scare," Tyler agrees.

"Do you have a big white board? I feel like there's something I'm missing with this and I want to plot it out. There has to be some clue about the stalker. I need to put on my analytical hat and find the sucker."

"If you need any help, let me know. I believe Heather has a huge board she used to use on her food truck before she opened the bakery. I think it's up in the attic. You're welcome to it."

"Thanks, I appreciate that. I need to go get Sleeping Beauty in the house. I think she's still feeling the effects of the walking pneumonia because she's really tired."

Tyler makes an odd face as he looks over at my truck. "I don't mean to criticize, but shouldn't your woman be smiling? She looks like she's ballin' her eyes out."

"Crap! Let me go see what's wrong —" I exclaim as I run toward my truck.

I throw open the door of my truck, only to find Madison curled up in a ball and sobbing. I can't imagine what happened. We were fine before she fell asleep, but she's definitely not fine now.

"Sweetheart, what's wrong?" I ask, unable to completely erase the worry from my voice.

Madison points to her phone as she explains between hiccups and sobs. "I'm being freaking terrorized that's what! I got another stupid fraud alert from my bank, and now they're freezing my money. I don't know what the heck I'm supposed to do. I can't live on nothing." Her panic is evident in her voice.

"Madison, we'll be okay. We're in this together. I've got you covered until we figure this out; don't worry about money. I'm getting close to cracking the identity of the person who has taken your bank account hostage."

"I'm sorry Trevor, I'm beginning to wonder if you actually have any expertise tracking anything. It's been months, and I still have to sleep with my pepper spray. I gotta tell you, this sucks," Madison tearfully complains.

I know she's upset, but her words still feel like a slap in the face. Does she really think I can't help her? I don't know how to prove to her I'm making progress. This conversation is pushing my buttons like nobody's business. When I had to stop doing my job for the military, it was like I had lost my sense of identity. As much as I enjoy working with the horses as a farrier, it's not what I was trained to do. I'd like to pretend otherwise, but I have real issues with being considered 'less than'.

I'm having flashbacks to the way I used to feel around Melinda Jo. For the most part, our relationship was good, but every time she was under any sort of stress, she would run back to her parents' house. It always made me feel like I could never measure up to what she was used to. Her parents were richer, smarter and more cultured than I could ever imagine being. I felt like I never fit into Melinda Jo's world.

This could get ugly in a hurry if I let my past influence how I feel about this; I take a few calming breaths before I even start to talk. I'm relatively sure she didn't mean it the way it sounded. Still, I just don't know.

"Madison, I'm sorry you feel that way, but I am

getting much closer to solving what's going on. I apologize that it's taking so long. Whoever this is, is pretty sophisticated; their online banking transactions are bounced all over the world and funneled through several dummy corporations. But, I'm getting close to finding an actual name."

"Trevor, how close are you really? I might be dead by the time you figure it out," Madison laments.

I reel from the direct blow. I know that she can't possibly know how much her words impact me — but being too late to solve this mystery is my biggest nightmare. I find myself compulsively checking on Madison throughout the day to make sure she's okay. But, if she can't believe that I'm doing my best work for her, I might need to reevaluate my relationship.

"I'm sorry I'm such a disappointment to you." I say tightly through clenched teeth. "I'm going to go feed the horses," I say as I start to leave the barn.

"Trevor, are you coming to dinner with Gwendolyn and Denny tonight?" Madison asks quietly.

I turn to look at her. I'm sure she can read the hurt and angst on my face. Eventually, I gather myself to respond, "Madison, I don't think it's a good idea. I've got some things I need to work out."

Reaching the driveway, I walk around my truck and pull out my work gloves. As my anger grows, I slam the truck door. I hitch the backpack Madison used last night as a pillow up on my shoulder. I can still smell the fragrance of her. My heart breaks a little as I stalk away. I knew this was too good to be true.

Insomnia is a pain. I know I need to crash because Madison and I got very little sleep last night. Yet, I can't turn my stupid brain off. Instead, I'm standing here staring at a whiteboard with a hastily drawn flowchart. No matter how I look at it, the fact that apparently we're both being stalked at the same time doesn't make any sense. I can't figure out how this person knows about my medical background. Unless I have shorts on, most people can't even tell my leg is gone and there's no way this person should know about my dispute with the Oregon National Guard.

The puzzle pieces just aren't fitting together. Madison and I live on two different coasts, have completely different occupations and friends. The only thing that ties us together is our romantic relationship. However, when the Deranged Barbie confronted us, it was on our first date. I have no idea if that's related to the bigger stalker issue or if it was an isolated event. I've even gone as far as emailing Madison's supervisor to see if anyone else at her newspaper is receiving the same sort of threats. He assures me no one else is receiving threats. He claims he's been in the newspaper business for thirty years and never seen anything like this. It was clear in talking to him that he doesn't fully believe in Madison's innocence. He didn't come right out and say, but he strongly hinted if this isn't resolved soon, Madison's job might be in jeopardy. I'm not impressed with his management style. I can't believe he's holding the fact that she has a stalker against her.

I pull up the spreadsheet I've been working on.

Madison provided me with a whole year's worth of financial information. It's clear that someone has taken over her banking identity at least. Prior to six months ago, Madison's spending habits were ridiculously predictable. I teased her about her record keeping prowess, and she shrugged and replied she didn't have much choice since she's the daughter of a CPA.

As I study the list of charities which have received bogus donations from Madison, I can't dismiss my hunch all of this is tied to the specific nature of the charities she investigates. Most of the charities she's looked into are related to family or women's issues. She has spent a lot of time investigating adoption agencies and social service agencies which serve women. There was one particularly ugly story where a convicted rapist ran a bogus sexual assault hotline just so he could receive sexual gratification from hearing women's stories of rape. I can't ignore the possibility her stalker might be one of the CEOs she's ousted. Many of them were making wages that made my head spin. But, if that's the motive, why go after me?

Tyler walks into the office and peers at the board. "I guess my wife still loves you, she sent me to ask you what kind of sandwich you want for lunch," he quips. He tilts his head at the board and asks, "Making any progress?"

I concentrate on the board for a few more moments before answering him, "I don't know — maybe. What if we're looking at this all wrong? What if Madison's tormentor is a woman? Maybe even Deranged Barbie."

"It's statistically unlikely, but it might fit in the

situation," Tyler concedes. "Did Madison recognize the woman who approached you?"

"No, not really. I thought she had a Boston accent, but Madison says she isn't sure if she is familiar. I guess that's the weakness of this theory. This is so frustrating!" I pace the floor. "Nothing fits. There is no one theory that covers everything."

"Well, I guess I would ask Madison if she knows of any women who have an issue with her."

"Yeah … about that … it might be a little awkward. We're not exactly on speaking terms right now."

"What in the heck did you do, Black?" Trevor demands.

I rake my hands through my hair, making it stand on end. "I wish I knew, but as nearly as I can gather — it's what I didn't do. I haven't found her freaking stalker," I confess. "I have to admit, I was a little blindsided by it all. Things seemed so perfect last night, but this morning everything's a huge mess. I don't know what to think, my head is spinning."

Much to my surprise, Tyler laughs out loud at my predicament. "Welcome to the world of loving a LaBianca woman. You'll never know whether you're coming or going," Tyler teases. "Seriously though, you can't let one fight ruin your relationship. Our women are headstrong and stubborn, but they're also smart as whips. The challenges are never ending, but it keeps life interesting. Gidget does a great job at keeping me on my toes. Personally, I wouldn't have it any other way."

"I hear you, but that doesn't mean she's ready to talk" I remark as I turn back to the white-board.

"Well, you'll never know until you try. Come on into the house and eat some lunch. Heather is making panini sandwiches and soup. You can't go wrong with that. Everything will look better on a full stomach."

———•———

I'm still puzzling over paperwork when I hear Madison come into the barn. I look up expectantly, waiting for her to speak. I'm not sure how to predict what she'll say. I wait, trying to seem causal. She looks a little embarrassed. "Fanny threw a shoe while we were out riding, so I thought I should bring her back."

"That was a good call because Fanny has ongoing issues with her hooves. Can you please put her in her stall? I have a few questions for you before you leave."

Madison looks pensive. "Umm — okay I'll be back in a few."

A few minutes later, Madison returns. I stand up so she can have her favorite chair. Ethel's tail wags uncontrollably when she sees her. Madison smiles and snuggles the dog. "Oh, you're such a sweet puppy. I'm glad to see you too!"

She's so much less reserved around the dog than she is in any other situation. It's fun to watch. Finally, I address the elephant in the room. "How do you feel about seeing *me*?" I ask softly, bracing myself for a negative comment. Her answer is so important, a sweat breaks out on my spine. I'm not sure if I've had a more critical conversation. Her decision about us means everything. I've thought a lot about Tyler's advice over the last few hours. He's right, my relationship with Madison can never be categorized as boring. I hope she's as invested in the idea of us as I am. I hope last night wasn't a fluke. I swallow hard as I wait for her answer.

Her eyes mist over as she looks at me. "I don't know what to say. I shouldn't have been so harsh. But, I'm so scared. I'm not sure what to think right now. I don't know if I can make any logical decisions until this situation is resolved. But, I'm sorry for lashing out at you. There was no call for that."

"One thing I've learned in the military is stress makes people do strange stuff. I won't say your words didn't hurt because they did. But, I'll live," I answer with a shrug. I'm trying to act nonchalant, but it worries the heck out of me she isn't sure where she stands. I thought we had resolved all that last night.

"Did you need something?" she asks.

I turn my attention back to the whiteboard. "Yes, I've done a little more analysis on your situation, and I have some follow-up questions."

Madison pales and pulls her knees to her chest defensively as she stammers, "O-okay, I guess I might as well face the music. What do you need to know?"

"I looked at what's been going on from every single angle I can think of. There is no simple explanation, but it got me thinking about whether or not we're approaching this correctly."

Madison tilts her head at me. "What do you mean?"

"Is it possible that your stalker is a woman? Is there someone at work you don't get along with or maybe in your neighborhood?"

Madison looks a little shocked, but she recovers and says, "No, not really. I work with guys mostly. Moses has been my cameraman since I started, and I get along fine with his wife. Lord knows, I probably single-handedly keep her Pampered Chef business profitable. I buy a ton of stuff from her. She goes to Zumba class with me, too. I'm pretty sure we don't have issues. Lyle Beckel's wife had a debilitating stroke a few years ago. Any time he's not at work, he's at the nursing home with her, so I doubt that it's her. Aside from Moses and Lyle, I don't interact with anybody else at work very often. It's important for me not to involve the rest of the paper in the stuff I do. I don't want the paper to be sued because someone doesn't like what I found out about them. I used to run my own undercover stings of the charities, but since I become more well-known, I'm not really able to do that anymore."

"What kind of feedback do you get from fans?" I ask as I clean off a spot on the white-board for her answers.

"Well, they used to be all about the typos in my articles. Now that I've found my way to the web-based shows, I'm more likely to get feedback like, 'I hate the new haircut'. I always find it funny. Why should they care what I wear or don't wear or how my hair is? It doesn't impact my ability to cover the story accurately. But, unfortunately, the public seems to think it does. Therefore, I have an army of classic suits in every color and weight."

"Have you ever felt like any of those threats were concerning?"

"No, until recently they've been benign. Some people try to sell me on their home-based businesses, and I can't tell you how many times I've been approached to sell for Amway. Some fans are just strange that way. They don't see our relationship for what it is."

"Is it possible one of your fans feels rejected and is seeking retaliation?" I ask cautiously.

Madison purses her lips thoughtfully. After she thinks for a moment she responds, "The only person I've had any conflict with over the years has been our former entertainment news director. He wanted me to cover one armed bandits in Las Vegas and report my findings to him. His questions were bizarre and all focused on cheating, and I thought he seemed pretty unethical. He was upset I wouldn't do the story, but that was years ago."

"Well, that's a thought. What was his name?" I ask, pulling a cap off one of the whiteboard pens.

"His name was Brad Hackshaw. Last I heard, he had gotten a job in a small town in Texas. I'm sorry I don't remember the name. It's been a long time since I worked with him, and it didn't seem important for me to keep tabs on his whereabouts."

"Don't worry about it. With a name like that, it shouldn't be hard to track him down. It's not like his name is Bob Smith or something," I reply.

Madison grins as she comments, "I don't know, it could be. He fancied himself to be a real ladies' man. He thought he looked like Brad Pitt. I'm here to tell you he didn't, and the man had no game with women. Being pinched in the butt at the coffee machine is not as sexy as it sounds."

"Seriously, who does that? I thought we'd come further as a society."

"One would think. I don't think dear-old-Brad ever got the memo."

"All right," I mumble, writing a notation by his name. "Can you think of any women?" I ask.

Madison sighs. "No, I really can't. I am not much threat to women. I'm pretty ordinary, and I'm awkward as a baby giraffe."

Her self-assessment takes me by surprise. "You'll pardon me if I respectfully disagree. I happen to think you're extraordinary."

"Thanks, but I think as my boyfriend, you are required to say nice stuff. That doesn't mean the rest of the world thinks that way," she deflects my compliment wryly.

"It doesn't mean they don't either. You graduated from an Ivy League school at twenty-one with honors, you are tall and thin with amazing eyes and hair. There's a lot to be jealous of," I counter.

"Believe it or not, most people have no clue about my academic background. I don't really share it much because when I was younger, people thought it made me weird. Now, I don't share it because everyone acts like working at the newspaper is a 'waste of my talent'. I won't even go into the knock-down-drag-out verbal altercations I've had with my parents over this. That's what I love about Heather. She gave me the guts to disregard the family expectation and follow my bliss."

"I am so glad you're doing something you're

passionate about. I will work my best to make sure you can get back to it," I assure her.

From the distance I hear a shriek. Madison and I both take off running toward the house. I reflexively reach for my sidearm — which of course isn't there because I'm a civilian now. Crap!

Madison catches up when I slip a bit in the muddy corral. "Wait!" I yell. "It may not be safe."

"Duh! Why do you think I'm running? I have MMA training. That's my family in there. I'll kick butt if I need to," she responds as she kicks it up a notch.

"Son of a bit —!" I breathe under my breath as I tweak my knee. I've been up on my leg too long today to be sprinting under these conditions. What's left of my leg aches.

I hear Heather exclaim, "Stupid Sicko!" as we round the corner to the front porch. When she sees us, she says, "Don't touch anything! Tyler got called into work at the Sheriff's Department. I'll have him send out Javier and the rest of the team. This jerk needs to be caught. I'm tired of him threatening my family."

"I am so used to seeing Colton as a soldier I forget he's also a cop," I remark as I step closer to see what upset Heather so much. I now understand her reaction. It's stomach turning, for sure. There look to be a dozen dead roses decorated with several decapitated rats.

When Madison gets close enough to see, she sways a little as she turns away. "I'm going to throw up. What did I ever do to anyone to deserve this?"

I walk up behind her and put my arms around her

and murmur against her temple, "Not a darn thing, Sweetheart. No one could possibly deserve that."

Much to my relief, Madison relaxes in my hold and rests against me as she pleads, "Trevor, please do something. I can't handle this much longer, and I can't endanger my love ones."

CHAPTER ELEVEN

MADISON

IT'S BEEN HOURS AND I'm still shaking. What kind of deranged person does that? Trevor about had an apoplexy when Javier, the lead evidence tech on Tyler's team, found a note under all the roses which simply read, "You can't hide."

I still have fingerprint ink on my hands from the exclusionary prints Javier took. It makes me feel like a criminal — like I did something wrong. I'm so confused because all I've done is live my life the best I can. I go to the bathroom to wash it off. When I finish, Trevor meets me in the hall with a mug of hot milk laced with honey. I can't believe he remembers. I once made an offhand remark about soothing rituals, never thinking I would have to put them into practice.

I take the mug from him. I will my hands to stop shaking so I don't spill milk on Heather's beautiful wood floors. When Trevor notices I'm having difficulty, he takes the mug back from me. "Madison, I want you in my bed tonight," he instructs, gruffly.

"With all due respect, I'm not really in the mood, Trevor," I respond sarcastically. There. Anger and self-righteous indignation are better than abject fear.

Trevor seems to understand my response as he cups my face with his free hand. "I know Mad. I need you there for my own sanity. I need to touch you to know you're safe. I've been around too much death and destruction. Call it my own little quirk, but I need to feel you in my arms tonight."

Trevor is so circumspect about his military service I often forget he lived through the same hell that gives Tyler nightmares to this day. I study Trevor closely and see open anxiety in his face. There is a tension knot in his jaw as he unconsciously clinches his teeth. It occurs to me that this might be even harder on him than it is on me. I take a deep breath to calm my nerves and lean into his palm which is resting on my face. I finally admit the urge I've been fighting all day, "There's no place I'd rather be."

"For that, I'm thanking my lucky stars!" Trevor says in a rather tortured whisper. "I need you so much."

"I love you, Trevor. I'm sorry for earlier. I guess I let my fear get away from me."

"In light of what happened, I think you had good cause. I wish you'd let me take you to a hotel or something. I think you'd be safer since whoever has a beef with you knows exactly where you live."

"I understand what you're saying, but I can't. If I let them run me out of my home, what's next? Are they going to stalk me at work, the grocery store and everywhere else I am, just to prove a point? I can't let them have the satisfaction."

Trevor exhales before he responds, "Okay, we'll do it your way for now. But, if the threats increase, we may need to look at this again."

I shudder as I contemplate what an increased level of threat would be. Dead rats and black roses are enough for me, thank you very much.

I'm always surprised when I enter Trevor's room because it's so stark. As far as I can tell, even though he's been living here for months, he still treats this place is if it's a hotel. There isn't a personal memento anywhere, and it's as neat as a pin. It seems nothing has changed since Heather set this up as a guest room. As I sink down into the featherbed, I'm grateful for Tyler's extravagant tastes in mattresses. "This bed is positively decadent," I remark.

There's a ghost of a smile on Trevor's face. "Yes it is. But, it's so much better now that you're in it."

As I prop myself up against the headboard, Trevor turns the TV on to cable news. "Do you mind if we turn it off? I don't think I could face any more bad news today, and as a news insider, I'm forever evaluating the side of the news they don't tell you. It's just too much to think about today."

Trevor shrugs. "Sure, no problem. Do you mind if I read a little?"

"That's fine. Would you get my Kindle for me? It's on the bedside table."

"Okay, I'll be right back," he replies.

When Trevor returns, he's laughing. "Somehow, I didn't expect this case from you," he comments.

I grin at him as I take my Kindle, complete with it's Hello Kitty case from his hands. "You like that? I got it from Moses, my cameraman. He got tired of me complaining about not being able to find my Kindle when we were out on shoots. So, he figured the bright color would make it easier for me to find. Since it does, I left the goofy case on it. It also serves another purpose — now I can read all the *Harry Potter* and other young adult fiction and no one will judge me because they think it's my child's Kindle."

Trevor laughs and says, "What you read is your own business. I won't judge you for your taste in books if you don't judge me for reading cheesy crime novels."

"To each his own, I suppose. That's why there are millions of books out there. Everyone has different tastes," I reply with an easy smile.

I'm really surprised by our lighthearted conversation. I thought nothing would make me smile today. Yet, here I am grinning like a loon, settling down to read beside Trevor like we're an old married couple. Sometimes, my life changes so quickly my head spins. If you had told me a few months ago I would have a new boyfriend who allows me to let my guard down, I would've thought you were crazy.

I sigh deeply and snuggle up next to Trevor as I comment, "This is so nice. I want to shut out the rest of the world and stay here like this with you in our own little utopia."

"I promise, I'll do my best to make your world safe again. We shouldn't have to hide away in the bedroom to feel safe. That's just nuts. You should be able to go back to work busting charities and Heather should be able to accept packages from the mailman without completely being visually assaulted by the contents of the package."

The amount of responsibility Trevor feels for my life is humbling. But, instead of fighting it like I usually do, I'm just going to go with it. I lay my head on his shoulder as I murmur, "I know. I trust you. We'll catch this guy. I'm sure of it."

———•◦•———

On our way home from the feed-store, I spilled soda on my shirt when Trevor had to brake suddenly, so I go to my room to get clothes. A chill travels up my spine when I notice my computer is ajar. I know I didn't leave it that way. Heather and Tyler could not have touched it since they are out of town in Portland at a food trade show.

"Trevor!" I bellow.

Trevor comes flying in to my room. "Are you okay?" he asks breathlessly.

"Stop! Don't touch anything."

Trevor stops so abruptly he almost throws himself off balance. "What happened?"

"Don't think I'm crazy, but I swear someone moved my computer."

"If you're sure, we need to call in Tyler and Javier."

"Yes, I'm sure. See, it's open. I ran a virus check this morning, and when I was done, I shut the laptop. Since Heather and Tyler are gone, there's no reason it should be open."

"Oh geez! Someone was actually in the house!"

Trevor exclaims. "Remember when I told you things might change in the future? This is what I meant. I'll make arrangements for us to stay somewhere else tonight. Whoever this is — is too close."

As a wave of nausea passes over me, I run to the bathroom to throw up. When I'm finished, I close the lid and sit on the toilet. I bury my head in my hands and cry until I get the hiccups. I hate being weak like this, but I feel like there's no safe place. If this person was in my bedroom, how long have they been stalking me. What do they want from me? Am I going to be raped again? The thoughts spin and spin in my head.

Trevor hands me a wet washcloth to wipe my face and a toothbrush with toothpaste on it to brush my teeth. When I finish brushing my teeth, Trevor collects me in a warm embrace. "I'm so sorry. I don't know why we can't catch this guy. But, hopefully whoever it is will have left behind some forensic evidence on your computer. That forensics guy, Javier, seems pretty skilled. If anyone can do it, I bet it's him."

"Yeah, he seems to know what he's doing. Javier left me a card the last time he was here. I'll just call that number because there isn't really an emergency. If the person was still in the house, Annie would be barking her head off."

Trevor nods. "She is possessive of you and intolerant of uninvited visitors. She would give my parents' German Shepherd a run for his money."

———•———

True to his word, Trevor arranges for us to stay at a bed-

and-breakfast a few miles out of town. He takes the added step of renting a car so our vehicle isn't identifiable.

As far as the proprietors of the bed-and-breakfast are concerned, we are newlyweds who don't want to be disturbed. Trevor told them this to minimize interaction with the outside world, they left us a huge congratulatory basket of goodies.

"Just so you know, I'm removing all the chocolate from this basket. If you want any, you need to speak now or forever hold your peace. I'm so stressed out, I could eat all of this plus the whole candy aisle in the store."

Trevor looks up from his computer and smiles at me. "If it makes you happy, knock yourself out, Sweetheart."

I reply, "Thank you. I'm not a big fan of Skittles, you're more than welcome to them."

"Duly noted," Trevor quips. Suddenly, he sits straighter and points to the laptop screen. "Holy smokes! Now were getting somewhere."

"What? What did you find?" I ask, impatiently.

"I have a name on the bank account. Now hopefully, we'll figure out what's going on."

"Who? Who in the world is it?"

"Some chick by the name of Mysti Winter, do you know her?" Trevor asks.

"The name sounds vaguely familiar, I think I met someone with that name a few years ago at a trade show, but I don't know much about her."

"Well, now we have a name. Maybe Javier can come

up with the match on the DNA. I'm totally stoked about the possibility. It's about time for a concrete development in this case."

"Does the name sound familiar to you, Trevor? I still can't shake the feeling that this is somehow related to you too, even though I can't figure out how in the world it would be."

"I was hoping her name would give us some clues. I've never heard of her. I wish I had because it would make this easier."

"I just don't know how somebody could have such a big grudge against me without me knowing why. I mean, come on Trevor — somebody sent me dead animals. That's a massive amount of rage right there. You'd think if I inspired something so disgusting, I'd actually know what I did "

"Some people are so twisted you can't figure them out," Trevor mutters as he furiously taps away on the laptop. His fingers are flying, and I half expect to see flames shooting out from them like a special effect. "Holy smokes!" Trevor bellows after a few seconds. "Her LinkedIn profile says she worked at your paper!"

"What? At the moment, I'm the only female reporter except for Aunt Bea, who runs our advice column. But, she is like seventy," I answer with shock in my voice.

"Just a minute and I'll see if I can find a picture of her," Trevor offers as he keeps pounding on the keyboard.

My fingers are flying across my cell phone. "I'm already looking — but I don't see anything. That's odd.

When you're in the news business like me, they plaster your picture everywhere — even if you don't want them to. You can even track all of my bad haircuts by my publicity shots. It starts being ridiculous."

"Right, if she is really a reporter, why would she want to hide her appearance? It seems like the more exposure you have, the better your chances of attracting readers. Isn't that the way it works?"

"Yes, something is off. I searched the work email database and I don't see her name anywhere."

"I'm not finding her either. I'm beginning to think I've hit another dead end."

"Let me call Lyle and see what he says," I say grabbing my cell phone. "Oh crap! It's like one o'clock in the morning Boston time. I probably should wait until the morning to call. This is so frustrating. Is there anything we can do?"

"I'll contact Javier. He said to call day or night if we found out anything, so I don't think he'll mind."

"Okay that sounds like a good idea. While you do that, I'm going to take a bath in your decadent bathtub. I love old deep tubs. They keep the water hot for so long. Lord knows I have some tension in my neck," I respond as I dig out some pajamas from my suitcase.

My phone rings and I recognize the number as Heather's, so I pick it up and greet her. I briefly tell her Trevor has a name. We talk for a few minutes, and then she tells me the report I printed out is on the printer in the den. Chills race up my spine as I tell her I printed nothing. She tells me the name on the report and I about faint. Shakily, I hang up the phone.

Trevor is watching me with concern, so I explain what happened, "That was Heather, she called to tell me the report I printed out was on the printer in the house instead of the one in the barn. She didn't think it was any big deal, but the problem is I never printed a file. Since I'm not officially working, there's no point in me printing out stuff and wasting their paper. The particular file I was working on is extremely confidential. It could bring down some big players at a local university and cause them to be fined by the NCAA. Even Lyle doesn't know about this file. It should've been heavily encrypted and unable to be opened, let alone printed on Tyler's printer."

"Are you telling me no one knows this file was on your computer?" Trevor asks with alarm.

"Yes!" I exclaim, "I came across this story right before I left home. I haven't had a chance to even talk to Moses, my cameraman, about it or brief Lyle on the way the story was unfolding. No one even knew about the tip I got, except me."

"What is your investigation about?" Trevor inquires.

"I got a tip that the local alumni association of a university a couple towns away from me was paying an escort service to entertain football players — they were using it as a recruitment tool. Apparently, the alumni association has paid them several thousand dollars for the services. I did some preliminary research and found out the allegations might be true. I was about to run down all the receipts and interview the escorts when I was abruptly called out of town because of the threats."

"Is there anything juicy in the report which was

printed? Have you worked on it since you got here?" Trevor asks as he finally stops typing for a moment.

"I haven't worked on that specific file at all. I have a code to open encrypted files, but I left it back home. Even if I wanted to, I couldn't open it."

"You don't have it memorized?" Trevor asks.

"No, the code changed right before I came here. It changes randomly. Sometimes, it's multiple times a day and other times it's a few months between changes."

"No wonder you're freaked out. This must've had something to do with the break-in the other day."

"Yes, that's the only thing I can think of. But I still don't know how my stalker would've gotten into the file to print it."

"I don't know, either. But I guess you'll have to hand your laptop to the real forensic technicians to figure it out," Trevor advises.

"Oh Geez, functioning without my computer will be like someone chopped off a limb." As soon as the words fly out of my mouth, I want to retract them. I gasp as I utter, "I am so sorry. That was thoughtless and rude. I apologize." I cover my face with my hands in shame.

As I peek through my fingers, I notice he's chuckling as he responds. "Don't worry about it. I say stuff like that all the time. I will call Javier about the computer for sure. Go take a bath. This will probably take a while," Trevor instructs as he picks up his phone.

I let out a heavy sigh. "I guess I will; there's not much more I can do here. My life is crumbling around me and I'm helpless to stop it."

"Try to relax. You have a team behind you now. We will figure this out, I promise."

CHAPTER TWELVE

TREVOR

THE MORE I TALK to Javier, the more concerned I get. According to him, it would take extraordinary computer skills to be able to do what was done to Madison. The good news is he was able to get some DNA off of the computer. Whoever it was wiped down the keyboard but forgot to wipe off the screen. Eventually we'll figure out who this is. Javier said it would be about a month before the DNA analysis came back because the lab is backed up.

Out of reflex, I call Tyler and fill him in on what's going on. This is one time I could use my whole team. I do all right on computers, but Matt is the expert. He knows computers on the programming level. I'm pretty good at navigating my way around social media, search engines and accounting software, but beyond that, I need to call in expert help.

By the time Madison finishes her bath, I've made a critical decision. We need to bug out. It's no longer safe here for Madison, even though we're staying at a bed-and-breakfast away from Heather and Tyler. It's not far enough away from her stalker. I've run it by Tyler and he thinks my plan is solid. He willingly gave me the time off. At least that part is settled. Now I have to figure out where to go. I don't want the stalker to be able to trace our movements.

I wait anxiously for Madison to get in bed so I can talk to her. She has no idea I've made a decision, so she's in no hurry to get back to bed. She spends a few minutes brushing her hair and painting her fingernails. I'm trying to be patient and wait for her to be finished. But, it's not going very well. Finally, I can't wait any longer to share my plans, so I just blurt them out. It's probably not the smartest decision I've ever made, but it is what it is.

"Madison, we need to leave town as soon as possible. I've made arrangements to visit my grandfather's old hunting cabin outside of Boise, Oklahoma."

"Don't you mean Idaho?" she asks.

"No, it's definitely in Oklahoma. I used to go fishing with him every summer," I insist.

"Trevor, we talked about this. There is no way I'm going to pick up my stuff and leave again. I moved clear across the country to get away from this and they still found me. There's no need to go gallivanting around the country just to hide from whoever the heck this is."

"I understand — but in this case, they actually got close enough to touch your things. This isn't merely cyber-stalking. You're in extreme danger. I think this is more than a fan run amok, I think this is personal and lethal. I don't think they'll stop until they hurt you."

"They can try. But I have years of self-defense and MMA training. I can counter any attack."

"Can you counter bullets? I wouldn't put something drastic past this person. Clearly, they are out to hurt you. It wouldn't be surprising if they resort to weapons, legal or otherwise."

"Can't you run a background check on Mysti Winter and see if she owns a concealed weapon permit anywhere?"

"It's a good idea to run a background check, but I doubt the person who sent you dead rats through the mail is going to be a stickler for rules and regulations. I suspect he or she is a little deranged and a lot dangerous. We need to get out of town as soon as possible."

"Trevor, I thought you understood my career is important. I have safety protocols. I've been in the field for a long time, I'm not stupid. You said you would support anything I wanted to do, whatever way I wanted to do it. I don't want to leave. This person has disrupted my life enough. I'm not a wuss. I am a professional reporter. I will not turn over control of my life to some crazy stalker. I did it once, and it didn't work. So, I won't do it again."

I have to consciously relax and unclench my jaw as my frustration builds. "Madison, for Pete's sake, don't be stupid," I practically bellow. "Didn't you get the message from the decapitated rats that this person is bent on hurting you? I don't know how much clearer they could have been. They can get to your bank accounts, they can get to your computer, and they can get to your front porch," I continue, raising my voice and underscoring every word by slapping my fist with every point. "Are you planning to be a sitting duck and let them get to you? Because, make no mistake that's where they're headed. Pardon me for giving a care and trying to keep you safe. What was I thinking?" I ask sarcastically.

"Don't call me stupid!" she shouts. "I'm not dumb. I'm just tired of running. Like you said, this person can get to me anywhere. What makes you think running away will make any difference at all?"

"I don't know! All I know is I can't let you sit here with a target on your back. Maybe leaving will buy us some time. Maybe the person will do something stupid and Tyler and his force will track them down. Maybe I can find this person's real ID instead of their fake name. Because, quite frankly I don't think Mysti Winter exists. I think it's another bogus name just like the shell corporations. Whoever it is still has control of your banking and probably everything else in your life right now. I'm beginning to think this Mysti Winter is our stalker. Think of it as regrouping instead of running away. It's not even a lie — because that's what we'll be doing."

"Well, it sounds like you don't support what I do. I'm in dangerous situations all the time as a journalist. I know how to handle myself. Why can't you trust me?" Madison asks with her hands on her hips and her eyes lit with fire.

I feel like roaring like an injured lion. But, I make a concerted effort to lower my voice, as I remember we are in a bed-and-breakfast.

"Madison, it's not that I don't trust you." I rake my

hands through my hair in anger. "I don't trust the deranged, psychopath who is after you. It almost seems like he wants to become you and take over your life. His behavior is crazy dangerous. I don't know why you can't see the risk" I counter.

"What makes you think I don't see it? Like I said, I'm not stupid. I don't want her to win. If I run away like a dog with my tail between my legs, she'll know she won. I don't want to give her a victory. Besides, Heather and Tyler are getting married in two weeks. I've got to do a bunch of stuff as the maid of honor and Tyler needs you as a groomsman. We can't take off right now!"

"Well, Tyler didn't have any problem when I told him. He knows what's going on and he agrees that I need to get you out of here. We need to get you the hell away from the rest of your family. I believe staying here might put them in danger too. Do you want that?" I reply.

"No of course not! But, Tyler's a cop. He can help protect us. I can't desert my sister right now. That would be beyond rude."

"And, I can't let you stay here," I state matter-of-factly. "So, it appears we're at an impasse."

"I can't believe you went behind my back and told Tyler we were leaving. You know he's probably already told Heather. This is going to totally stress her out, and it's not fair. She's been planning this for months and months and *months!* I'm supposed to be helping her, it's my job. I'm her sister, for Pete's sake."

"I can't imagine Heather would want you to stick around if she knew how much danger you were in. I'm not talking about missing the wedding, I'm just talking about getting out of town for a few days to give Javier a chance to process the evidence and see if there are any more clues," I argue.

"I'll think about it," Madison concedes. "Do you know how going behind my back makes me feel? I thought we were a team in this. I don't like it when people make decisions about my life I'm not involved in. It's kind of a hot-button issue for me. You would have to know my family to understand this, but you can't simply tell me what to do. I don't operate that way."

"Well, when your safety is on the line, I *do* operate that way. A while ago, you told me you love me. That should mean you trust me enough to do what's best for you. Trust me, this is what's best for you right now. When the threat is eliminated, I won't act this way, but I'm a trained soldier. Protecting people is what I do — right now, I'm protecting you."

"I understand that you're a soldier — but Trevor, I'm not in the Army. I'm a civilian. I'm just trying to do my job, and I don't want some crazy person to interfere. My job is to get information to people. Uncensored and unfiltered. If I let her decide what I'm going to do and when and how I'm going to do it, I've lost all sense of integrity. Do you understand?"

Madison is not the only person who has buttons. I take a deep breath and answer as calmly as I can, "I do understand. You might need to take a break from your job for now to protect your own safety. You can't cover stories if you're dead."

Madison bristles. "Trevor, that was a low blow. Of course I don't want to be dead. I guess I just don't see the point of moving away from a place where we have police backup at our beck and call — police who finally have faith in me. Do you know how frustrating it was to have this threat looming over me and have absolutely no one on the planet believe me? That's the reason I left Boston."

"It may be the logical approach, but my gut tells me I need to get us out of here. I ignored my gut once and now my wife is nowhere to be found. Some crazy stalker probably killed her too. Please, Madison, do the smart thing here and don't put your ego before your safety," I plead.

Madison comes over and climbs into bed. She rolls up into a tight ball with her back facing me. This is so not how I anticipated spending our night away from the world. I had visions of making love to my girlfriend all night, not having to fight to keep her safe.

Madison sighs deeply and then mumbles, "I said I will think about it, I can't promise you any more right now. Now, I'm tired and I want to get some sleep," she snaps.

Her anger is like a blow. I don't know why this has to be so hard. I struggle to keep my voice even. "Okay, we'll talk in the morning. Please remember I'm doing this because I love you and I want to protect you — not because I doubt you're smart or strong. I've seen bad things happen to strong, smart people before. I don't want to have to face the idea of you not being in my life. Don't make me face that choice, please."

"Okay, fine," she answers shortly. "I'll think about it and tell you my decision in the morning. Right now I want to stop thinking about it and go to sleep. Is that too much to ask?"

I squint as the morning sun hits my face. I didn't think I was ever going to get to sleep last night, so I'm shocked I've slept in this long. I'm relieved when I look down and I find Madison wrapped around my body. Apparently, her subconscious mind isn't as angry with me as her conscious mind.

I suppose she can sense my scrutiny because her eyes open while I'm studying her body language.

"Morning," she mumbles as she stretches.

"Good morning, Sweetheart. Can I get you some coffee or tea or something?"

"Yeah, I'd like some hot chocolate, please. I scoped it out last night and there's a couple packets by the coffee machine."

"That sounds perfect," I reply as I brush a kiss against her cheek and hop off the bed.

While Madison dresses, I set out to make her chocolate. When she comes back, I pull out the chair in the little kitchen area of the bed-and-breakfast. She sits down and wraps her hands around the hot chocolate. She takes a sip and pronounces, "This is perfect. It's just the way I like it, thank you," she offers graciously.

"You're welcome," I answer as she takes a sip and gets little miniature marshmallows on her upper lip like she's a kid. The image makes me smile. Yet, I know I have a serious question to ask, and given our heated discussion last night, there are no easy answers. I'm dying of curiosity to see what she's decided. "I hate to break the relaxed mood, but I have to know what our plans are for today," I venture carefully, not wanting to upset her again.

Madison shrugs and pulls up the sweater which drooped over her shoulder. "I'll go," she answers simply.

"Really?" I clarify somewhat incredulously. I totally expected her decision to go the other direction. The about face completely shocks me. "What changed your mind?" I can't stop myself from asking.

"Well, I got to thinking about what you said about Tyler and his team. If they're busy protecting me, they can't focus their full attention on finding whoever this is. I have done most of my duties as a maid of honor. One of the other Girlfriend Posse members will have to take over for me."

"From what I can tell, planning weddings in a hurry seems to be their specialty. I wouldn't worry about it. Besides, Heather and Tyler are already officially married, so this is just for show."

Madison's smirks at me. "I wouldn't say that too loudly, Heather might be a little upset. Have you seen the cake she's planning? She's been making little sugar and fondant doodads for it for months. Don't even get me started on the flowers, Gwendolyn is planning to practically empty out the local flower warehouses."

"Don't worry about it, I'll do my best to get you back here for the big day."

Madison gives me a soft smile. "Believe it or not, I trust you. I'm furious this person has completely taken over my life. I know you'll take good care of me and I'll be fine. I needed to get used to the idea. I know you think

I'm a total witch, but I'm really not. I take a little while to adjust to ideas which aren't mine. What am I talking about? I take forever to adjust to *my* ideas too. I'm the kind of a person who likes routine."

"I was frustrated by your decision making process, but I never thought you were a witch. I just thought you were scared. I've decided your defensive reflexes are just that — reflexes. I can tell by the way you treat Ethel you are not, at heart, a cold person. I only have to worry when your porcupine quills come out. I've decided to just duck," I explain.

Madison chuckles wryly at my character assessment. However, she doesn't appear angry, so that's good.

"I guess you are not far off target. But, you're not the only person who will have to do some adjusting. I'm going to have to remember to stay calm, cool and collected when the big, bad overprotective soldier shows up and tries to take over my life."

"Touché, I'll try to tone down my over-protective nature, but can I do that after we catch this creep?"

"Okay, I concede. I need you to be a little overprotective at the moment. The more eyes I have on me, the better."

"Madison, Sweetheart … trust me, I have no problem watching your six day in and day out." I grin.

CHAPTER THIRTEEN

MADISON

"I STILL CAN'T BELIEVE you chartered us a private jet. This is insane!" My jaw drops as I look around the richly appointed plane.

"Actually, this was all Heather and Tyler's doing. I guess there are certain perks to being close, personal friends with a huge pop star. I guess Aidan is always asking them how he can share the wealth. Apparently, they took him up on his offer."

"I can't get over the thought of having a private plane at my disposal. That's some life he must lead."

"I know, right? But, I've hung out with Aidan over the last few months and he's a surprisingly normal guy. I guess he struggled for many years before he made it big. So, he remembers what it's like to not have much," Trevor shrugs.

"How did we get out of here without someone knowing who we were?"

"Well, being a huge pop-star has taught Aidan a few

things about clandestine travel. He booked the private flight under his bodyguard's name. That's what the FAA paperwork says if anybody bothers to look at it."

"Wow! I'm used to cloak-and-dagger stuff with my job, but I don't have any resources like this. Heather is always going on and on about how wonderful her friends are. I must say, I completely agree. I'm so glad they consider us part of their clan now."

"Now you know why I followed Tyler to Oregon. He's the most stand up guy I've ever met in my life."

"That's right, you're an Oregon transplant. I always forget you're from somewhere else. You've done a good job of disguising your Oklahoman accent. I hardly ever notice it. It only comes out when you're upset or very happy. Although, I have to admit I love the way you say, 'Sweetheart' — it's almost as endearing as the way Tyler calls Heather Darlin'."

"I'm pretty sure there's a compliment in there somewhere. So I'm just going to take it," Trevor responds with a raised eyebrow.

"Oh, I didn't mean to suggest an Oklahoman accent is bad, I just forget you're from there," I answer apologetically.

"Sweetheart, I'm kidding. I've worked hard to tone down my accent. Everybody thought I was a dumb country hick if I let my accent show. When I was dealing with all of my dad's accounting clients, I developed a professional voice as free of an accent as I possibly could. I guess it's carried over to my personal life. It's not something I consciously do anymore. It just happens."

"Some days, I wish I could do that too. Everyone

makes all sorts of assumptions about my eastern accent. Some people even think I'm from New York, which is a little crazy — because I sound nothing like someone who's from New York. People on this coast don't know what Eastern accents actually sound like," I respond in a rush of words, sounding very much like I'm from the East Coast.

Trevor salutes me with his coffee cup. "Here's to boring Midwestern accents where no one can tell where we're from."

"Speaking of that, are we going to pretend to be somebody else when we get on the ground? Won't people in your own hometown know who you are? Do we need to be that secretive?"

Trevor smirks at me. "I'm not sure we need to go that far. Unless, of course, you really want to role-play, and then we can talk about it."

"I thought you didn't play any of those kinky games Mr. Black," I tease.

"Well, I don't usually, but you've given me powerful motivation to try new things," he responds with a wink.

I know he meant it as a joke, but the idea makes me a little breathless.

Trevor pokes me in the thigh with his finger. "Did I lose you? You've got a strange look on your face."

I blush at the idea of being caught with my dirty thoughts. "Mmm? Oh no, you didn't lose me, I was just thinking."

"If your thoughts are going in the same direction as mine, we're going to have some fun tonight," Trevor promises as he gives me a slow, hot kiss.

"You know, Trevor Black, you may be just the thing I need to get my mind off our problems. That sounds like a wonderful game plan to me."

———•———

I'm not sure why I was so resistant to going on this trip with Trevor. It was exactly what we needed. A week and half in the woods with someone you absolutely love is an amazing gift. We've had a chance to talk about anything and everything that's ever bothered us and share our goals in life.

There aren't any phones or computers to interrupt us because we don't have internet service at the cabin. At first, I was completely frustrated about my phone not working. After a few hours, I realized what a gift it was my cell didn't work. We have to take the conversation deep or whither away from boredom.

I've gotten pretty good at campfire cooking. Trevor shared with me ways they modify MREs and other food in the field to be able to survive. It's been fun to adapt those recipes to my own and surprise Trevor with the outcome. I've always been intimidated by cooking because Heather is so gifted in the kitchen. Out here, there was no competition and Trevor makes me feel like I am the best cook on the planet. I could do with more ego strokes like that.

Trevor takes a bite of stew as he studies the Scrabble board. "You once told me I sound like a walking thesaurus. My skills are weak compared to yours. Quixotic? I'll have to take your word for it that it's an actual word. I'm tempted to think you might be randomly placing tiles on the board just to win."

I place my hand over my chest in a gesture of innocence. "Quixotic is a wonderful word if you're a journalist. It can mean so many things. I am just quixotic enough to understand it's greatness."

As he narrows his eyes, Trevor triumphantly spells roux using the X. "Okay, whatever you say."

"I don't know if it's such a great thing that you agree with me that I am weird and eccentric," I tease.

Trevor raises an eyebrow. "Hmm, Is that really what I agreed with or are there alternative meanings?"

My eyes widen. "You fib! You knew all along what quixotic means."

Trevor rolls his shoulder nonchalantly. "Well, I do find you charming and sensual — perhaps even quixotic."

I rearrange the tiles on the stand and triumphantly spell insane. "I love you, but you're a little crazy, Trevor Black."

He leans over and kisses me. "Yeah, If this is what crazy looks like, I never want to be normal again. I used to watch my grandparents play cards. Back then, I didn't understand how they could be content just being in each other's company. Now, I get it. I wish we could bottle this feeling and keep it with us when we go back to the real world."

I nod. "I hate the reason we had come here, but I wouldn't trade it for anything. I needed this and much as I hate to admit it, I'd be lost without you."

I study the runway as we take off — it's a good thing we took off when we did, because the clouds look like they're going to erupt in a snowstorm at any moment.

Trevor interlaces his fingers with mine. "Happy to be returning to civilization?"

I lean against his shoulder. "Actually, not really. I enjoyed our time away. We should plan to do it again when I don't have a bad guy chasing me. It could be a fun tradition."

"I agree, it would be fun to have some land and a couple of kids to run a little ranch like Tyler does. I really enjoy working with the horses."

I look at him with wide eyes. "Did you pluck that idea out of my head? It so happens I have some land with some Arabian horses my grandmother gave me. I guess we're halfway there."

"How do you feel about kids?" Trevor asks in a joking manner.

For some reason, I feel compelled to be completely honest. "Personally, I'd love to have some kids. I like kids a lot. I'm not sure they like me so much, but I love them."

"What makes you think kids don't like you?"

"Well, they always seem to shy a little bit away from me. You know, like Becca did?"

"Have you tried kneeling down on one knee because you're awfully tall. Kids might find it intimidating."

"You know, you're right. Heather always gets down

on Becca's level, and she thinks Heather is the bee's knees."

"Bee's knees?" he asks with a grin.

"Hey, don't judge me!" I protest. "It's just something Grandma Lydia used to say. It's somehow found its way into my lexicon. So sue me."

"Just when I think I have you pegged, you go and show me your southern genteel side. It's kind of throwing me for a loop."

"Multifaceted — yep, that's me," I jest.

Trevor nods. "It's true, you know. You are multifaceted. Every time I think I have you categorized as one thing, you show me something else. It's endlessly fascinating. I can't wait to spend the rest of our lives together so I can figure out all the sides of you."

The air flies out of my lungs and I grip Trevor's hand a little tighter. "Did you say what I think you said. You want to spend forever with me? Don't you think it's a little soon? We've been dating for only a few months, and I don't have a great of a track record with guys. You might want to change your mind, I don't know," I ramble on a little breathlessly.

"Not possible. I feel like I know you better than anyone else I've ever known in my whole life, and I've been married to someone before. My relationship with you is closer than it was with my wife. Melinda Jo and I tended to coexist. In retrospect, I don't even think we were truly friends. I think we were more in love with the idea of being in love. I don't feel that way with you. I feel like you're my best friend and will be my best friend for the rest of our lives. Yes, I admit I love you, and when I see us together, I see us together forever. Call me old-fashioned that way, but it's the way I was raised. I hope this marriage goes better than the last one."

I swallow hard. "Trevor, I don't even know what to say. This feels too soon for me. Besides, are we making this move for the right reasons, or are we feeling pressured because of the artificial situation caused by the stalker? If you had to live with me on a daily basis when nothing exciting was going on, would you still want to? In case you haven't guessed, I can be a little neurotic. I don't know if you want to be around me all the time. Playing Scrabble and cards could get old." Panic makes my accent even more prevalent. It just underscores the differences between us.

"Remember when you told me you need warnings about changes in your major life events in advance so you don't get freaked out? Consider this your advanced warning. I'm not going to ask you to marry me today, or probably tomorrow. It might be in a few, days, months, or a couple years. But make no mistake — even with all your personality quirks and tendency to be quixotic — I plan to marry you. I'm giving you a little time to get used to the idea so when the time comes, you don't reflexively say no because you weren't expecting the proposal."

I close my eyes for a second to gather my thoughts. I'm not sure whether to be touched or offended by the fact that he understands me so well. If he had sprung a full blown proposal at me, I probably would've said no because it's so scary for me. I've been engaged once before, and he turned out to be a jerk. I'm a little gun shy. Yet, even as I think those thoughts, I know Trevor has more integrity and character than anyone I've ever met.

If he tells me he'll marry me someday; it will happen. I don't think he would be boinking his secretary for kicks and giggles.

When I open my eyes, Trevor is studying me with the look of dread on his face. "What's wrong?" I ask.

"Well, I'm a little afraid I jumped the gun. You seem a little freaked out by the idea of marrying me. I thought we were there after spending all the time we did together in the cabin. I thought we had learned enough about each other that this wouldn't be so unexpected. Now I don't know if I completely misjudged the situation or not," he answers with a frown on his face.

"You didn't misjudge the situation," I concede. "I'm a little leery of my ability to keep you happy long-term. I don't exactly excel at relationships."

"If the last few months are anything to go by, I'm sure you'll do fine. I'm happier with you than I've ever been in my whole life. Why would that change?"

"I don't know. I guess I'm afraid of disappointing you like Melinda Jo did. I don't ever want to let you down like that. I love you too much to have you be disappointed with me," I respond as I stroke his shoulder.

He lifts my fingertips to his lips and kisses them. "I say this from the voice of experience, we won't have a marriage where we never disappoint each other. That's not the measuring stick. The measuring stick is how we cope with the stresses of marriage. Whether or not I go back into the military or pursue something else, we're both going to have active careers, and no one is ever perfect. Juggling our personalities and our careers together with any children we may have will make for an environment rich in stress. It's how we recover from our stress which matters."

"Speaking of the military, what have you decided?" I ask. "You don't talk about it much."

Trevor looks out the window as he explains, "Well, I'm sort of in a holding pattern right now. Tyler asked his commanding officer to review the findings of the panel and see if there's anything that can be done. Tyler is a huge supporter, and he doesn't want to see me kicked out of the military for no reason."

"But, they didn't really kick you out of the military did they?" I clarify.

Trevor looks directly at me. "If I were chained to a desk for the rest of my career, it would be worse than being kicked out. That's not where I belong."

"That's really hard." I run my hand down the side of his face in a show of affection. "It's difficult to know if there is a right answer, but I feel the same way about my journalism career. I don't know what I would be if I wasn't a journalist. I like doing good in the world by sharing information with everyone. If I couldn't do it anymore, I'd be lost."

"About all I can do right now is wait. It's all out of my hands at this point. I've done the physical tests, the mental tests, and all the emotional tests. It's up to them to decide how valuable I am to them as a soldier. If they don't value me as a soldier, then I guess I will have to find something else to do with my life. At this point I'm clueless as what I would do."

"I guess I am not the only person who has things to figure out. We'll untangle them together. We make a great team."

It's been a whirlwind since we landed back on planet Earth, as it were. Javier says there should be results back on the DNA very soon, but I don't have time to worry. Heather's wedding is keeping me insanely busy. Trevor and I haven't even had a chance to see each other except in passing. Who knew there were so many details which need to be taken care of last minute when you get married? I figured you got married and that was the end of it, but there are a thousand things to do.

All this is made more difficult because Heather's venue where they got married the first time unexpectedly closed down when their sprinkler system ran amok. Heather decided to move the wedding to the barn and corral. Heather's rather ambivalent about the move — I think she had her heart set on the grand ballroom. But, Tyler is pleased as all get out because his horses will be present at the wedding. Apparently, horses have played a huge role in bringing Ty and Heather together. Therefore, Tyler feels like it's only appropriate that the horses be at the wedding. In a way, they are both right. So, I'm like Switzerland in this debate. Because I can't win for losing if I choose a side. I just line up and do what I'm told when Heather bosses me around like the big sister she is.

On my list of things to do today is to collect Carlton and Whitney from the airport. I guess my brother volunteered to give Heather away. I never thought I'd see the day. When Carlton and Tyler first met, they were like oil and water. Carlton could not stand him. Yet they seem to have reached some sort of truce. I don't know what kind of magic Tyler used on Carlton. Once Carlton has a grudge against you, it usually lasts forever. I'd like to know Tyler's secret because I'm not so sure I'm not actually on Carlton's bad side. I sort of left him in the lurch with Dad's business. I don't know how that's going because Carlton never talks about it. It can't be a joy to work next to Mom and Dad with their hyper-criticalness.

I give him mad respect for coming out here to support Heather. It's hard to say what the ramifications of choosing Heather's side will be on his business. As I see his rich dark hair and blue eyes, it's clear he doesn't care what Mom and Dad think. He has an ear to ear grin when he sees me, as does Whitney. They greet me like it's been years since I've seen them instead of a few months. But, I guess they have a point. I feel more like a different person now than I've ever felt in the past. I wonder what they'll think of the changes in me.

Carlton is the first to speak. "Well, you look like you've grown up in the last few months. I'm so thrilled to see you happy for a change. Is there a reason for this dramatic change? Do I need to get the shotgun out?" he teases.

"No, it's highly unlikely you'll need one. Even if you had one, Trevor could probably disarm it in half a second and hold you at gunpoint. I wouldn't recommend the shotgun approach."

"Still, I have to do my big brother thing and ask a bunch of questions, like big brothers do. For example, where did you meet this guy? How serious is it? Is he good to you?"

"Well, I met him when I came here to stay a few

months ago to get away from a situation back home. He was helping Heather out while Tyler was still on active duty. He works as a farrier right now, but he has a background in forensic accounting."

"You're lucky. If he's an accountant, Carl may actually like him," Whitney remarks.

"I'd say it's pretty serious. It took me a while to understand Trevor likes me for me — even with my weirdness. I think I can accept his love now. Eventually, I think he'll marry me. He treats me better than anyone's ever treated me my whole life. Please don't mess this up between us," I plead desperately.

"Didn't Heather tell you? I've turned over a new leaf. I now try my best not to be like dear old Mom and Dad. They almost ruined our marriage with all their cutting remarks. So, Whitney and I have decided to focus on each other and screen Mom and Dad out of our lives. I think it has finally started to sink in with them that they're missing out. Whitney and I have stood firm despite their criticism and doomsday predictions about our marriage. I think things are starting to turn around."

"You don't actually think they'll show up, do you?" I ask with trepidation.

"No, I don't think so," Carlton replies.

Whitney nudges Carlton. "Wouldn't it be fun, though? I'd like to see your parents be brought down by a couple of tough military guys and see if they can handle a little of their own medicine."

Carlton laughs. "Actually, I think Ty is the reason they won't come. They've gone toe-to-toe with him before and lost their dignity. I don't think they'll have the guts to show up here. Besides, I think they're still pissed at Heather for winning the lawsuit."

"As far as I'm concerned, they can stay ticked off. They had no reason to bring a lawsuit to begin with. It was stupid. It put Heather through a lot of stress she didn't need to go through. Everyone who knew Heather and Grandma Lydia knew they were planning to start a bakery together, it was no big secret. I can't understand why Mom and Dad bothered to challenge the will. It was bizarre. I mean, I know they're power-hungry, but really? Did they really expect to win?" I angrily interject.

Whitney pats me on the shoulder from the back seat. "It's all right Madison, you're preaching to the choir. We already know what kind of people they are. That's why we shut them out of our lives. I'd like to hope it's not too late for them to change. But who knows?"

———•———

Two years to the day after Heather and Ty got married the first time, we are standing outside on a crisp winter day witnessing them repeat their vows. I'm not sure how they lucked out with this weather. It's been rainy all week, and we're expecting rain tomorrow. But for today, the sun is shining on my sister. Then again, why shouldn't it? She looks amazing, and she's got one of the kindest husbands I've ever met in my whole life. God has a lot to smile about today. I'm a little *verklempt* — which is bizarre for me. Usually I'm not so sentimental but, I missed Heather's first wedding, so I didn't get to see her go down the aisle. The fact that she's made me maid of honor is mind-boggling. I figured it would be Kiera or Tara, but Heather insisted it be me. At the moment, I'm trying to balance on my heels when they're sinking into the grass. It is not an easy feat. Trevor notices and he walks over to stand beside me and offer his elbow so it's easier for me to walk on the uneven ground. I look at him in his military greens and I'm in awe. I know now why stereotypically women tend to go for men in uniform. He looks phenomenal. He's not sure yet if he'll stay in the military. Since his appeal is still pending he's been allowed special dispensation to wear the dress uniform.

I can't help my goofy little grin when William Gardner, the judge who officiated their first wedding, needles my sister about whether they have everything all lined up to go this time without interruption. It must be an old joke because Mindy is giggling. Given the chilliness of the weather, the judge keeps the ceremony blissfully short. He joked with Heather and Tyler that he didn't have to give the whole spiel because they were already married.

Ever the romantic, Tyler insists the judge say all the vows as they were said during the first wedding. It was an effective strategy as Heather tears up and practically swoons at his feet. Although, I have to admit I'm feeling lightheaded, too. All this testosterone is enough to make a girl dizzy.

After the ceremony, we went into the barn for the reception. I visit this barn every day, but I hardly recognize it. It looks like Gwendolyn's flower shop has exploded in here. There must not be any flowers left in the store. It's sweet and romantic. Heather and Kiera have knocked themselves out cooking. There are so many kinds of appetizers, I've seriously lost count. Every time one of the catering staff comes by with a different type of food, I'm impressed all over again. The cake is an amazing steam punk creation with handmade gears, brooches and delicate fans interspersed with giant gum paste roses painted a delicate pink and mauve. Heather's cake rivals any I've seen in magazines or cookbooks. When I asked Heather about hosting her own cooking show or writing a cookbook, she just said she wasn't interested in show business. She insists cooking for her friends and family makes her the happiest, and she'll gladly leave the show business stuff to Aidan.

Aidan is set up in the corner of the barn with his band. I can totally understand why he's at the top of the charts.

As I'm organizing gifts on the gifts table, Trevor comes up behind me and kisses my neck. I guess there are advantages to wearing my hair in this weird up-do.

"Madison, will you please come dance with me?" he asks with a strangely intense look on his face.

"Sure, let me take these shoes off though—they're killing me. My sister has good taste and I love these dresses, but the shoes need to go."

"Well, I think you're a vision of loveliness, with or without shoes."

"Thank you, you clean up rather nicely yourself." I grin.

I take my shoes off and flex my arches. Trevor places his arm around me and escorts me to the middle of the dance floor. I see Trevor flash a sign in American Sign Language, but I don't know what he said, because he did it so quickly.

Trevor pulls me close and whispers in my ear, "You know I love you, right?"

I nod against his chin and reply, "Yes, you've made no secret of your feelings. I love you too."

"I just want you to remember I love you regardless of what happens."

"Are you expecting something to happen?" I ask in a confused tone.

Something flashes in Trevor's eyes. "You never know what could come up."

Just then, Aidan and the band transition to a new song. I turn my head to watch them for a moment as they play *Marry Me* by Bruno Mars. I wonder if Heather told them that this is one of my favorite songs. I get a little lost in thought as I watch them play. So I'm taken off guard when I hear rumblings in the crowd on the dance floor. I turned around to ask Trevor what's going on and I'm shocked to see him on one knee with a ring in his hand.

"Oh my gosh!" I exclaim. "I thought you were going to wait to ask me to marry you. You promised," I say with panic edging my voice.

"No, actually that's not what I said. I promised you I wouldn't ask you on the day we talked. But, I warned you I would eventually ask when the time was right. What better time to ask you than in the middle of this romantic fantasy land Heather and Tyler have created. So, Madison Paige LaBianca, will you please do me the honor of agreeing to be my wife?"

I take a deep breath and consciously make an effort

to set aside my nerves. Is this what I really want? I can only come up with one answer. So, I stick my hand out and will it not to shake as he places a ring of diamonds on my ring finger. They are glittering like the sun, but small and delicate at the same time. It is quite simply the most beautiful ring I've ever seen.

"I want to make sure I understand your answer correctly, is that a yes?" Trevor asks as he kisses my ring finger, after he finishes placing the ring on it.

A tear rolls down my face as I see Trevor kneeling on one knee and looking up at me expectantly. Finally, I find my words, "You are certifiably crazy. You know that, right? Despite this insane proposal, I will marry you because you've infiltrated every aspect of my life with hope and happiness. I can't ever imagine trying to get through life without you. It's like you've become the other half of my heart. I didn't realize love could be easy and fun. I want a lifetime of love naturally. Trevor Christian Black, I would be honored to be your wife," I commit as I help pull Trevor to his feet. Vaguely, I hear the crowd around us break out in applause, but I'm ensnared by the look on Trevor's face. It's a combination of joy, relief and desire. Trevor completely ignores the crowd as he pulls me close to him and plunders my mouth with a deep, sensual kiss as Aidan finishes the song.

Aidan grabs the microphone and says, "Congratulations my friends, may you be as happy as Tara and me. I'm a firm believer in love and the perks of being married — despite what you might read in the tabloids," he finishes with a grin.

Trevor gives Aidan a thumbs up sign as he quips,

"How early do we have to book your band for our wedding?"

Aidan winks at Trevor and replies, "All you have to do is say the word and I'll make the time."

Tyler hops up on stage and takes the mic from Aidan. "I can't tell you how happy I am an honorable man like Black here is going to marry my sister-in-law. Seriously, Madison, if I could have handpicked a man for you, it would've been Trevor Black."

Heather's voice floats up from the back of the room where she's serving cake. "I don't know, Cowboy, how are you so sure you didn't?"

"Didn't what, Gidget?" Tyler asks with a puzzled expression.

"How do you know you didn't pick Trevor for Madison? Remember when we were talking about the impact Jeff and Kiera's relationship has had on everybody's love-life? We talked then about how great it would be if our love story changed someone else's life. I think it just did. Without you and I, there would be no Madison and Trevor. We've created a legacy of love. How cool!"

"I think you're right, Darlin'. You made me a huge believer in love. I had to pass it on."

"Well, whoever's responsible for introducing us, I'm grateful beyond words. My life is so much better with this man in it," I have a huge cheesy grin as a I show off my sparkly ring.

Trevor looks at me and then glances up on stage to see Tyler, "I agree with Madison. Our introduction felt more like fate than an accident. If you had a role in that, I will be forever thankful. I'm honored I'm going to be part of your family now."

"That's the funny thing about it, it always felt as if you were," Tyler responds with a crooked grin.

CHAPTER FOURTEEN

TREVOR

Our sense of euphoria lasts about two weeks. But like everything in life, everything good must be balanced by pain. The pain starts with a phone call from Lyle Beckel while we are out riding the horses. Madison's phone rings and she fumbles around in her saddle pack to retrieve it. At first, everything seems normal enough as she greets her boss. Then I hear her shout, "That's not fair! I've done nothing wrong. How can you fire me? I don't care what anybody tells you, it's not my money. I didn't authorize it … I have the police force here looking into it since they wouldn't do anything when I was back home … No, I don't think there have been any definitive findings yet, but I swear to you I didn't do anything."

I watch as her body takes on a defensive posture and badges of red-hot heat are displayed on her face. One thing I've learned is Madison has a need for things in her life to go according to script, and this is completely off of her radar. She seems blindsided by this, and I don't blame her. It's a dirty thing to do.

"So, that's it? You don't even want to hear what Tyler and Trevor have to say? … Fine. I'll be there," she states with disgust. She hangs up. She looks like she's about ready to throw her phone down in the ravine.

When she rides up beside me, she looks like a raging thundercloud. She glowers at me. "You won't believe what's going on now. I don't know exactly when my life got this crazy, but allegedly a second source has come forward to say I'm doing something hinky with the charities. I have to go defend my job. It's insane. How can someone anonymously report me for something I absolutely did not do when I'm the one who's being threatened? Lyle wants to fire me for something I would never do. You would think he would know better. We've worked together for years. He knows what kind of work ethic I have, so it's bizarre he believes these quote-unquote anonymous people."

"I don't know. I can't explain it either. I'll push a bit on Javier to see if he can find any more clues in the materials they collected."

"Wouldn't he already be processing it?" Madison asks.

"I don't know, but you're probably right. Just to make myself feel better, I'll still call him to remind him this is a huge issue on our plates. I feel so helpless because I can't do much to help you. Do you want me to go back east with you so you've got support?"

"Yes, that would be helpful. Besides, I want to show you my Arabians."

Sometimes, my inspiration can come from some strange places. In this case, I was watching a bloopers show on television with Mindy. It was intended to be funny, but it got me thinking about whether there might be some additional blooper rolls with the elusive Mysti Winter.

I am methodically going through YouTube videos to see if I can spot her. I've got two more to open before I can finally crash for the night. Today has been a horrible day. One of the horses I shoe was struck by a car. Unfortunately, his injuries were severe, and he had to be put down. I know it's the cycle of life, but it's still hard when it could've been prevented.

Rubbing my eyes, I click on the next video. I don't have much hope since this video is titled, "Blonde Bimbos Read the News".

After a few minutes, I'm about to give up because this is stupid, but then something catches my eye. I rewind the video and watch again. *Oh hello!* I didn't imagine it.

"Madison!" I bellow down the hall, "Come here! You need to see this."

Madison must have been able to read the urgency in my voice because she came around the corner with her toothbrush hanging out of her mouth. Without taking the toothbrush out of her mouth she walks over, stands behind me and asks, "What?"

"Watch carefully and tell me what you see," I instruct.

She comes and sits on my lap as she closely

examines the computer screen. She rears her head back so hard I'm afraid she might have broken my nose. "Did you see that? That is Barbie Light, I'm almost sure of it. Look at the way she tilts her head, that's exactly what the creepy lady did at the Portland Saturday Market," she practically shouts after spits her toothpaste into my garbage can.

"Do you want to know the spooky part?" I ask.

"Of course I want to know the spooky part, I am a reporter after all," she replies with a small smile.

"I found this on a site which has B roll footage from reporters."

"Don't tell me … is that Mysti Winter?" Madison asks with trepidation.

"It would appear so," I say with a frown.

"What station is it from?" Madison inquires.

"I don't know yet, I found this on a YouTube video, it doesn't list full credits, but I'll do some more research."

"Trevor, do you know what this means?" Madison asks in a breathless whisper.

"That we're one step closer to finding your stalker?" I guess, unable to hide my excitement.

"No … well, yes, but this *also* means I have concrete proof my stalker exists. When I have to go meet the muckity-mucks at the paper, I'll have something to show them."

"I still have a hard time believing they think you made up the whole stalker thing. They've gotten letters and emails. I don't know why the paper hasn't done more to protect you."

"I think they think I came to Oregon just for a vacation. If I had done that, I wouldn't be taking months and months off. As much as I love Heather and Tyler, I don't like the feeling of being indebted to somebody. I want to get back to my own house and figure out if my cat even knows who I am. She might have adopted the little neighbor lady. I'm pretty sure Linda feeds her better than I ever could. I just want to go home."

Her words make my heart stutter. I guess it's a little too easy for me to forget Oregon isn't her home. I'm not sure I've adequately prepared for the eventuality that she might want to go back to the East Coast. Things are still up in the air with my military service, I'm not sure if I'll be able to transfer everything to wherever she wants to live. I wish these decisions were easier to make. It seems as soon as I settle one thing in my life, something else comes up. It's a little frustrating. I wish everything would line up in a neat row somewhere and that the path we need to take would be clear.

Madison is so distraught at the moment, I refuse to add more to her plate. We'll just have to figure everything out later.

I place my arms around her waist and kiss her earlobe. I know it's hard, but we're getting there. This will all be over soon and you'll be able to resume your life. We will not let this person ruin our happiness. You are too important to me for that to happen."

"On one level I know, but it's so scary to think this person has completely invaded my life and changed the way I do things. I never thought I would be that person. I thought I was stronger."

"Madison, you are so strong. If you were weak, you would have curled up in a ball, not tried to save your job, and not tried to figure out who was stalking you. To me, you are the epitome of strength and resilience."

"Really? Do you think so? Some days I don't feel strong at all. On those days I feel like this person has already won. That's disheartening — I hate it when the bad guys win."

"Then let's not let them win. It's as simple as that. I promise, we will figure this out. Together."

CHAPTER FIFTEEN

MADISON

I FORGOT HOW LONG it stays bitterly cold in Massachusetts. I've been spoiled by Oregon weather. I hope it doesn't take Moses too long to get here. Although he hates it, he's usually the person who brings me to and from the airport. Since he's late, he probably got stuck in traffic. I'm likely to hear all about it from him. Sometimes, he treats me like I'm a wayward teenager instead of a full-grown adult. I think it's because he has a fourteen-year-old daughter.

I can't get over how tired I am. I slept most of the way home. Of course, it could've had something to do with the fact that Trevor kept me up most of last night. He had to stay in Oregon because he has to work a horse show today. He was completely devastated, so he spent most of last night showing me all the creative ways he loves me. All I can say is the man clearly loves every inch of me. The thought of it makes me smile — and frankly blush.

I'm so wrapped up in my thoughts I don't hear

Moses approach until he's right beside me. "Do I even want to know what you're thinking about? That's some kind of grin you have on your face," Moses teases.

"I'm just thinking about my life and all the things I left behind in Oregon," I admit.

Moses gives me a sly grin, exposing the charming space between his teeth. His belly is shaking with silent mirth as he struggles to contain his laughter. "Oh Maddie-girl, I *know* that look. You're missing a *someone* not a *something*."

"All right, you're too smart for your own good. Or you know me far better than you should." With that, I take my hand out of my pocket so he can see my new engagement ring.

"That's pretty impressive bling. Who is the guy who's going to steal you away?"

"Well, I think you would like him. He's a soldier who is on medical leave. He's working for my sister and her husband as a farrier."

"Does this young man have a name?"

I giggle at my own oversight. "Yes, silly. Of course he has a name. His name is Trevor Black. He's about the most honorable man I've ever met in my life. He is nothing like the last guy you met."

"Oh Lawdy child, I hope not. That guy was bad news from the get-go."

"Moses, why didn't you say something back then?" I ask incredulously. "We've been friends long enough we can talk about anything. Heck Moses, you're one of the few people who know I have to stuff my bra to appear on camera. That kind of knowledge comes with privileges. So, if you get a weird feeling about anything, please talk to me. I've got some strange crap going on in my life right now. Even if I told you about all of it, I don't know if you would believe me. Trust me when I say I don't think I'll be able to look at roses the same way again."

"Are you sure you want to know it all, even if it has the potential to hurt your feelings?" Moses asks tentatively.

A feeling of dread makes my stomach muscles clench. It's enough to make me nauseous. "Moses, tell me what's going on. I can tell you want to spill the beans. We might as well get it over with."

"Okay, but I don't even know if this is important so, don't blow it all out of proportion, okay?"

"I'm listening," I answer, waiting to hear my job has been eliminated.

"Remember, you asked for this and I'm sorry if it upsets the applecart," he stalls.

"Moses —" I warn.

Moses sighs as he pats the wrought iron bench in the breezeway. "Okay, you know that I had to pick up freelance work when you were gone so I could feed my family," he starts out hesitantly.

"Yes, I'm so sorry. I appreciate your flexibility."

"Well, you might not once you hear what I'm going to tell you. I think there is a reporter gunning for your job," he reveals.

I shrug. "What else is new? People are gunning for

my job all the time. Everyone thinks what we do is easy and anyone can do it. What's different about this one?"

"Well, not everyone I've worked with knows every single statistic about you since you worked at the college newspaper. This woman even knows what size underwear and shoes you wear. It's creepy."

"I suppose she could be an overzealous fan," I suggest weakly.

"I don't think so. I think she's trying to be you. She even had it on her online-doohickey she works for The Towne Sentinel. I told her she was being unethical because I've known everybody who's worked at this paper for twenty years, and she never worked for us. I told her it was a lie and her momma and daddy raised her better'n that."

"Do you think she made an honest mistake?" I ask, holding on to dimming hope.

"No, Child!" Moses practically shouts. "Hear what I'm sayin'. The woman wants to be you. Although, I don't know how she can possibly think she's going to be a decent reporter, because every time I turn around she's going off on vacation somewhere. I can't keep track of her long enough to film a whole story."

I feel woozy as a frightening thought occurs to me. "Moses, describe this woman," I request in a shaky voice.

"Well, she looks like she is some sort of bar-fly. Now, don't get me wrong, she likes to dress all up and put on airs. But you know me, I see beneath all her crap. So, I have to ask myself what kind of con is she running here? She talks like she's all cultured and everything, but her behavior is definitely like a street rat."

I shudder as he says the word rat. My eyes tear up as fear runs through my body and makes my heart beat faster. Finally, I meet his gaze with mine and ask the one question I need to know. "Name ... Moses. I need a name."

"You know, she's got one of those Hollywood names. You know, one of the ones you can kinda tell aren't really real because of the way they're spelled?"

I narrow my gaze at him.

Moses takes in my expression. "All right, all right, I'm getting there. What happened to your journalistic appreciation for letting a story unfold dramatically?"

"Moses, I don't think you understand, this could be a matter of life and death for me. I need a name please." I plead.

Moses looks like he's in shock. "Really, Child?" he exclaims. "Why am I just now hearing about this? You ought to know better. How many times have I saved you from something dangerous? It's kinda my job as your cameraman to keep you out of trouble. But, I can't keep you out of trouble if I don't know about it. I don't know exactly what you're talking about, and I expect you to tell me the whole story sooner rather than later. But, the young lady I've been working with — her name is Mysti Winter. But, it's spelled all weird. She gets all bent out of shape when people misspell it. She thinks her name will make her as famous as Katie Couric someday, so she makes sure everybody and their dog knows how to spell her name," he says with disgust.

Under normal circumstances, I would find this amusing because there's nothing Moses hates worse than vain reporters who can't do their job. But these are not normal circumstances. I don't know if I'll ever have normal circumstances in my life again. As I think about how much fear I've lived in for the past year, I get angrier and angrier.

"Moses, we have a new assignment," I say decisively.

"Maddie-girl, what are you talking about? You're going to have to give me more background information about what's going on — because I can't follow where you're going with this."

"Moses, you know how I had to leave town suddenly? It wasn't all about my sister's wedding — although she did have a nice one. Some crazy person has been stalking me for over a year and she's been trying to get Lyle to fire me. I want to get answers from this so-called reporter. I'm tired of this nightmare and I want it to end."

"Okay, okay. I understand you're upset, but don't you think we should call the police?" Moses asks, concern tinging his voice.

"If the police were going to do anything about this, they should've done something a long time ago," I snap. "I went to them day after day and week after week when this first started, and they treated me like I was a moron. So you'll pardon me if I don't think they have my best interest in mind."

"What are you planning to do?" I hope this isn't another harebrained scheme by you. You tend to put yourself in some real pickles. I'm getting a little old for all this."

"Relax Moses, we're just going to go talk to her. Nothing clandestine requiring a big set up. This is just going to be two women talking."

"Why don't I believe you? Oh, maybe it's because nothing is ever simple with you. I've known you too long to think this is going to go smoothly."

"Moses, I swear. This is personal between her and I. There's no big story involved, we don't have to get editorial clearance or anything. I want to talk to her, and I want it on camera so I can show Trevor what we've come up with. You know my brother-in-law is a cop, so he might find it helpful too."

"Have you ever considered this might be dangerous? You know this Mysti knows everything about you. She probably remembers your brother-in-law is a police officer. She's not likely to tell you anything. Are you sure you want to risk it?"

"Yes, Moses I do want to risk it. I flew all the way back here so I could clear my name. I have a feeling this Mysti chick is a big part of that. I want to know what's going on with her and why she's doing this."

"Okay, but at least wear a pin camera so she doesn't know we're filming," Moses acquiesces.

"Consider it done. I've got this funky necklace my honorary niece made me, there's a little hole in it so you can stick the camera there."

***

As Moses drives me up to her condominium in the ritzy part of town, I start to lose my nerve. But, I take a deep breath and decide I have nothing to lose. As far as she knows, Moses is there to talk about assignments with her. She's not likely to be armed or anything.

"Just for the record, Maddie-girl, I want to say I think this is a bad idea. I know you won't listen to me, but I just want to put my opinion out there," Moses warns.

"I'm a tough girl, Moses. Don't forget I've got tons of martial arts training and a few MMA bouts under my belt. I'll be fine."

"I thought you said you were just going to talk —"

"Yes, that's the plan. But if it doesn't go to plan, I'm prepared anyway. I'll keep you safe so you can go home to your wife and children, I promise."

I walk up the driveway with purpose and knock on the door. Moses decided he'll talk first. I step out of the way and let him be the one standing in front of the door.

When Mysti answers the door, all of my worst fears are confirmed. Although with a cleansing mask on her face and foil in her hair, she doesn't look as intimidating as she did when we ran across her at the Portland Saturday Market.

"Moses? I thought we didn't have a shoot until later in the week?" Mysti asks when she sees him at the door.

"We don't. But, I came to talk to you about some other stuff."

"Don't you think it's a little dangerous for a family man like you to come to a woman's house late at night? Who knows what could be said about that?"

That's it. I've had enough. It's one thing for her to threaten me and Trevor, it's another thing for her to threaten Moses, who has done absolutely nothing wrong to her. I work hard to tamp down my anger as I step out of the shadows and say in my best enthusiastic cheerleader voice, "Oh hi, my name is Madison LaBianca. It's nice to meet you. I hear you've been taking good care of Moses while I was gone."

"Yeah, I guess so," she stammers. I can practically see the gears turning in her head as she tries to figure out my approach. "Aren't you supposed to be in Oregon?" she asks, stunned by my presence.

"Yes, but I have a meeting with Mr. Beckel tomorrow. We're going to go over a couple of critical stories I've been working on."

"B-B-But, I thought he already fired you," she says in a hoarse voice.

I glare at her. "Really? How would you know something about my private personnel issues? How did you know I was in Oregon? Even Moses wasn't sure exactly where I was going to be."

"Well, I think someone told me —" she hedges.

"See, that's the funny thing about having a stalker. People get really protective of you and they don't talk about your private life when they know you're in trouble. So, the only person who should've known where I was going was Lyle, and I'm certain he didn't tell you anything. You can't even get him to give you the weather forecast if he thinks it's confidential and private. You'll have to excuse me if I don't believe you," I challenge, while I wildly gesture with my hands.

Moses catches my eye and motions for me to put my hands down. This is a long-standing debate with us because he says my wild Italian gesturing interferes with the shot and I argue it gives emphasis to the story. In this case, because I'm wearing a pin camera, I suppose I should listen and put my hands down.

At that moment, a wave of nausea passes over me. "Crap, I knew the chicken salad smelled off. Remind me not to eat at the airport," I vaguely explain as I push my way past her and run down the hall in the direction I hope is the bathroom.

Fortunately, I find it on the first try because I don't have a moment to spare before I literally lose my lunch. This is hardly the dramatic showdown I had envisioned. After I noisily throw up in her toilet, I do what every good reporter does and look in her medicine cabinet. She's got several unmarked pill bottles on the very top row. I turn the water on to buy myself some time as I peek inside.

When I look inside, I feel faint again. My heart is beating a million miles a minute. Quickly, I dump a couple of pills in a Kleenex from my purse. I screw the lid back on and put the medicine back in the cupboard. For good measure, I take a picture of the pill bottles.

When I emerged from the bathroom, I look at Moses and say, "Well, thank you for introducing me to another reporter, but I'm really beat and would like to go check on my house. I bet my cat misses me."

Moses is understandably confused because I think he thought there was going to be some huge confrontation between Mysti and me. But, based on what I found in the bathroom, I need some more information before I go head-to-head with her in a knockdown drag out. As much as I would like this to be all over tonight, things have become incredibly dangerous.

Moses recovers nicely and bids Mysti goodbye and promises he'll be on time for their shoot.

We're about two blocks from the house before Moses demands, "Okay Maddie girl, are you going to tell me what the heck happened back there?"

I sigh. "Yeah, you probably need to know the whole story. But, I think it's going to require a good stiff drink for me to get through this."

"But you don't drink —" Moses counters, confused.

"I know, but I might start now. That's how freakin' serious this is," I admit.

"Oh Lawdy! I knew this was going to be a big mistake. There is a quiet place around the corner where I play cards at with my buddies. The guys there aren't too offensive. You should be fine."

"Thanks Moses. I am so grateful you always watch out for me."

"Child, you have no idea —" he murmurs under his breath.

"Oh, I think I probably do." I take a deep breath and try to calm my nerves.

After the waitress sits us down, the bartender walks over to our table and says, "Mr. Mo. What can I get you tonight?"

My stomach turns at the thought of food, so I decide to stick with 7-Up. After I order, Moses comments, "7-Up is isn't much of a stiff drink."

"I thought better of it. My stomach is pretty queasy and I don't want to baptize your new car."

"As much as I appreciate that, it doesn't explain why we're even here. I thought you were going to get answers from Mysti, what happened to the plan?"

"Well, that plan went out the window when I found Roofies in her medicine cupboard."

Moses groans. "Do I even want to know why you were digging around in her bathroom?"

"Don't you look at the stuff in other people's bathrooms? You can find out all sorts of dirty secrets."

Moses sighs. "No Maddie-girl, when I go to the bathroom, I take a pee. I was taught to mind my own business."

"I was taught to mind my own business too, but sometimes you've got do something for the greater good. Take tonight for example — I found Roofies and Special K in her bathroom. I have no idea why a woman would even go near that stuff, let alone keep it in her house." As I voice my opinion, I shake uncontrollably.

"Are you going to be sick again?" Moses asks with panic in his voice.

This is where it gets hard. Moses is like a father figure. Scratch that, he's a thousand times better than my own dad. Hearing what I have to say is probably going to destroy him, especially since his daughter, Pamela, is a freshman in high school and has many years of school ahead of her.

I take a quick gulp of my soda as I struggle to continue. I try to keep the emotion out of my voice and keep it as cut and dry as possible, but it takes an almost Herculean effort to do so. I don't want to make this any more difficult on Moses than I need to. "There's a reason I know what Roofies and Special K are," I disclose carefully, watching for Moses's reaction.

"Oh, Child no —" he exclaims sadly.

I nod as I continue my story, "A long time ago, when I was in college, I went to a party at a bar. I had no business being at because I was only sixteen. While I was there, somebody put drugs in my drink and raped me. Sadly, he was never caught."

"Well, for sure you should bring in the police now."

"Oh trust me, I will — but they won't be the police she expects. This police force takes my complaints seriously. So, they'll do an actual investigation instead of telling me it's all in my head."

"I hope you know what you're doing, Madison. It seems like you're playing with fire," Moses declares as he sighs deeply and pats me on the knee. "I can tell I'm going to have to say some extra prayers for you tonight. Because I'm not sure I have enough skills to keep you safe if this is what we're dealing with."

"Don't worry Moses, as soon as my family and my fiancé get wind of this, you'll have more backup than you could've ever imagined."

———•———

I knew the conversation with Trevor wouldn't be easy, but I am not prepared for the amount of disappointment I hear in his voice. He sounds almost resigned to the fact that I'm probably going to be hurt before he can get to me. Despite all of my reassurances I'm being extremely careful, Trevor sounds insulted I didn't wait for his assistance. I guess I should've known better than to try to handle everything on my own. Trevor seems pissed. Ticking him off was the last thing I wanted to do. Apparently, he feels like it's his duty to save and protect me, even from myself. I never wanted to disappoint Trevor — in fact, it's pretty much my biggest fear. After hearing Trevor's promise to bring the cavalry, I roll up into a ball on my bed and cry myself to sleep.

I wake up to the incessant beeping of my phone. I am so tired. I'll be glad when this whole stupid thing is over so I can finally get some sleep. I feel like I could sleep for a week. I roll over to check my phone. It's probably Moses — he and his wife were going to meet me for breakfast.

When I read the text message, I sit up bolt upright in bed. *Whoa! I need to move a little slower*, I think as I get a little dizzy. I guess the effects of food poisoning haven't run their course.

When my vision settles down, I look at my phone again and read the text message. I have to read it four times to even start to wrap my brain around what I see. Don't think I didn't see your ring, but your little soldier man was mine first. Give back the pills or I'll tell him you made the whole story up about the rape. Who's he going to believe? You've got the pills in your purse. I'm clean. Good luck with that. Who knows? You may want to have a little fun while he's away. Just like the good old days.

I drop my phone in horror as the words sink in. There is only one answer I can come up with which ties all those clues together. But if I'm right, my whole world will implode.

Chapter Sixteen

Trevor

One of my strongest memories as a child, before my dad had his stroke, is of going on unscheduled drives with him. Every time he and Mom had a tiff, we could take off in his old Jeep. My dad would crank up 80's heavy metal and we'd drive. Sometimes we would be gone for a few minutes, other times we would be gone for hours at a time. I don't recall where we went, but almost always my dad would go on epic tirades where he constantly muttered not quite under his breath while he drove.

He would mumble, "That woman is so stubborn, she's going to drive me to distraction." Of course, when I was young, I had no idea what he meant. I just knew I didn't want to go there.

Well, let's say, after my conversation with Madison, I have new sympathy for my dad. If my mom had a fraction of Madison's fire, he had justification for those drives.

If I didn't need to tend to Tyler's horse with colic, I'd be on one of those famous drives myself. I am so mad at her I could spit nails. I want to know what the heck she was thinking, but she took exception to the question when I posed it to her. Okay, I may have roared it, but can you blame me? What kind of fool goes into the house of their stalker and pays a social visit? This woman sent Madison mutilated animals. How much more indication does she need that this chick is off her rocker?

I about had a heart attack when she told me all of this. All I could think of is how grisly the headlines would be. I remember how awful the media was after Melinda Jo disappeared. Even though I could show I was serving overseas when she disappeared, they still speculated that maybe it was a murder for hire. I almost lost my commission then, too. So, I can sympathize with her need to clear her name, I really can. But, darn it! Does she always have to try to do it alone? All I could express was my disappointment she didn't wait for Tyler and me to get there. After all, we're trained to fight.

Part of me wonders if she thinks I'm incapable of defending her because of my amputation. Most of the time, she doesn't even seem to notice, but stunts like the one she pulled tonight make a man wonder.

My phone rings. I answer it immediately, hoping it's Madison. "Go for Black," I answer without thinking.

"Trevor?" Javier asks. "Are you okay?"

"No man. I don't know if I can be okay until this monster is off the streets and Madison is safe in my arms again."

"Well, hopefully this will make you feel a bit better.

I was able to weasel some results out of the lab tech. These are not complete, of course. There was so little left behind they'll have to run PCR to replicate it. But the prelims indicate we're dealing with a Caucasian female."

"Tell me something I don't know, Javier," I practically growl. "Madison was in her house today. How crazy is that? I admire her moxie and dedication to finding answers, but the woman needs a keeper."

"I thought *you* were her keeper."

"I thought so too. Apparently she didn't get the memo."

"I'm sorry. That's hard."

"I can't even get out of here because I have to work at the horse show and Tyler's horse has colic. I have to hope she cools her heels for a few days until I can get there."

"I've met Madison, Trevor. I hate to tell you this, but your woman only has one speed and that's hot. There is no way she'll sit on a lead. There will be no cooling of heels," he jokes.

I growl. "Again, tell me something I don't know, Javier."

"Okay, try this one on for size. My cousin is a vet tech and he worked as a farrier to help pay for school. I bet I could get him to cover the horse show for you, if you don't mind losing the business," Javier replies.

"Thank you! Now we're getting somewhere. At this point, I don't care about losing clients, I just want to get to Madison."

"If I were in your shoes and needed to get

somewhere fast, I'd call the Judge or Aidan," he suggests.

"Thanks Javier, you're a genius. I'll make some calls."

Javier chuckles lightly as he quips, "Well, I do try." He may have said more, but I've already sprinted out of the barn toward the main house. I hope Tyler is ready to go out in the field again because I'm dragging his butt out there anyway. I need the back-up since it appears I need to corral not only the bad guy, but my fiancée as well.

When I hit the kitchen, I notice Mindy is sitting at the breakfast bar with cookies and a large glass of milk. She is coloring a large, intricate picture. She looks up at me and comments, "Uncle Trevor, don't be mad at Aunt Madison. She was trying to protect you from the bad guys. She thought if she could solve the mystery, everyone's stress would go away and you could fall in love like regular people."

The corner of my mouth hitches up. "Regular people?"

Mindy shrugs. "You know, going to the movies and roller skating — stuff like that. Anyway, she's really scared and maybe she won't be brave enough to tell you, so don't be too hard on her for her stupid decision, okay?"

"Okay," I drawl repeat slowly stretching the syllables as I try to process what happened.

I just got off the phone with Javier. There is no possible way he could've contacted Mindy — not to mention he would've had no reason to gossip with her about my situation. "Mindy, I have to ask, how did you even know I am upset with your Aunt Madison? I was on my own private line, and there is no way you could've overheard the conversation."

I swear I feel Mindy's disappointment more than hear it as she gives a small sigh. "I thought you were one of the people who understood, Uncle Trevor. I don't know why, but I just know stuff. I think I was born this way. It's part of the reason my Nana thought I was possessed by the devil. Personally, I don't think I'm evil. I try to help people, so I don't see how helping can be bad. But, she never understood that I tried to use my power for good. Before I met Tara, I never knew another person who was like me. It was kinda scary."

Immediately, I feel humbled by the wisdom of this extraordinary young woman. My life has been tough, but I have not been through a fraction of what she has been through and I had a much smoother start in life.

"Mindy Mouse, I'm sorry. Sometimes I forget what an extraordinary gift you have. Other times, it's hard for me to wrap my brain around how much you understand about what's going on. It's odd to realize you often know more about the situation than the grown-ups involved, including me. I'm sorry if it sounded like I doubt your skills. It's not that exactly, it's more like I don't understand them."

"It's okay, Uncle Trevor. I don't understand it all either, but Aunt Tara is helping me with that. I read lots of books, too."

"I can tell you I appreciate the help, and I don't think you're evil or weird. I think you're totally awesome. I will do my best to remember not to be angry at your Aunt. I know she loves me very much, and I understand she was only trying to help. I wish she would be more careful."

"Uncle Trevor? You know Madison is very strong and smart, right?" Mindy assures me. "You guys will be just fine."

Something about her simple reassurance seems to calm my racing heart as I run to grab clean clothes from the dryer and stuff them in a duffle bag.

CHAPTER SEVENTEEN

MADISON

I HATE WAITING. I always have, even as a child. It's my own personal pet peeve. I'm as fidgety as a kid waiting for Santa Claus as I pace in front of Lyle's office. I've decided I need to tell him about all the things going on. I know he will probably go ballistic on me. I've violated every safety protocol in existence. In retrospect, after talking to Trevor, I've gained enough perspective to conclude I'm a total idiot. But what's done is done, and I can't go back.

Unfortunately, I can't ignore my growing suspicion. I have a very strong hunch Mysti Winter and Melinda Jo Whitmore are the same person. If I'm right, I have no idea how this will impact my relationship with Trevor. I've been a nervous wreck for days. I can't seem to stop throwing up. I must have an ulcer or something. I've always been stupid skinny with no boobs or butt, but this is ridiculous. My clothes feel like they're going to fall off. I hope we figure this out soon. I can't afford to lose any more weight. I already look like a prepubescent basketball player.

I haven't been sleeping worth a darn either. I've gotten so used to sleeping with Trevor, it's like my body doesn't know what to do if he's not around. I stifle a yawn as I take another lap around the circuit in front of Lyle's office. Even though Moses is used to my nervous, neurotic energy, he finally throws up the white flag. "Maddie-girl, you're going to wear a hole in the floor if you don't sit your butt down. I'm sure Lyle's meeting won't last much longer."

"Moses, what if he fires me on the spot? It was totally stupid of me to go to her house. I don't know what I was thinking. I touched the evidence. I know better. If Tyler knew everything I did, he would hate me. I probably messed up the whole investigation."

Moses grabs my hand and pulls me into the plastic chair beside him. He looks me directly in the eyes and says, "Maddie-girl, as my grandma used to say, 'There's no need to cry over spilt milk.' You're forgetting something important. I was there with you, remember?"

I bury my face in my hands as I wail, "Oh my Gosh, don't remind me. What if I get you fired, too? Your wife would never forgive me."

"Madison, you have to stop this. You're going to make yourself sick. Look, I had my big boy pants on when I went with you. You didn't have me held hostage at gunpoint or anything; I could've said no. If there's any music to be faced, we'll face it together."

After a few minutes, Lyle's door opens and some people I don't know in suits file out.

Lyle gestures for us to sit in his office. He takes one

look at me and says, "Don't take this the wrong way, but you look like crap. I thought a vacation was supposed to make you feel better."

I raise an eyebrow at him. "If I had actually gone on vacation, I might look a little more refreshed. If you'll remember, I was running from a crazy stalker. It tends to wear you down a little when you have dead animals delivered to your front porch."

Lyle pales as he leans back in his chair and rubs his temples. "Point taken. Tell me what you know, and please, for the love of God, put some good news in there. I'm sick of dealing with bad news."

"Trust me, you and me both. I'm not sure you'll find any of this to be good news."

"Somehow, I had a hunch you were going to say that," he replies as he shakes his head.

"This will take a little while, do you have something to write on? This is a twisted little drama. You might want to take notes."

"Normally, I would be all about a complicated story with lots of twist and turns, but I have a feeling this is more than just your average story."

"Lyle, you have no idea…"

Moses and I spend the next hour and forty-five minutes laying out all of our evidence. From the confrontation at the Portland Saturday Market to the bizarre text message I received from Mysti. I outline all the threats and how they contained confidential information only a person who knew Trevor intimately would know, as well as her obsession with me.

Lyle blanches as I recount the story of the black roses and mutilated rats.

"Do we have anything concrete to tie this Mysti Winters to the stalking? Or is this mere conjecture? I agree your theory sounds at least moderately plausible, but I still think were missing a piece. We don't know the why."

"Does there have to be a why?" I ask as the aggravation flows through me. Reliving all of this crap has not been fun. "The woman appears to be Looney Tunes. But, yes we have proof. When we were at the Portland Saturday Market, Trevor snapped a picture on his cell phone. We have the testimony of the guy from the photo booth. She destroyed one of those old-fashioned photographs we had taken at the fair."

"Don't forget the weird stuff with your computer," Moses adds.

"Yeah, that's true. I forgot to tell you. She accessed an encrypted file. The only way she could have done that would have been to get the password out of my office. Personally, I believe she did it at least twice, if not more. If she's a reporter worth her salt, she would've used the information in my file to scoop the paper. There were lots of confidential sources and a basic story outline in the file she stole. Mysti probably could've put together a decent story just based on the information I have in the file without even having to look any further."

"Did you say her last name is Winters?" Lyle asks as he digs through piles on the desk.

"Actually, it's Winter — Mysti Winter. But, I don't believe it's her real name. I suspect her real name is

Melinda Jo Whitmore."

After a few more seconds of digging, Lyle smiles as he victoriously holds up a piece of paper.

"Let's see how much reporting our mystery lady has done," he declares as he reads the paperwork.

"What is that?" I ask.

"This is her resume. She sends it practically every other month — even though I've repeatedly told her we are not hiring anyone. Nothing seems to dissuade her. Her resume shows up here almost like clockwork. I happen to have this lying around because I haven't had a chance to clean my desk recently. Otherwise, I usually toss them in the garbage."

"Where does it say she went to college?" I ask with trepidation, fearing I already know the answer.

"She seems to have tried to bury information about her schooling deep within her resume. She doesn't even mention it in her cover letter. It's an odd strategy. Most people who have gone to journalism school want to tell me exactly where they graduated from. It's like a badge of honor," he explains.

"*Where* did she go to school?" I repeat my question again this time with more emphasis.

"Well, it looks like she went to a community college in Oklahoma first. But then it looks like she transferred to the University of Oklahoma. It seems like she's been trying to hopscotch through several markets to receive bigger and better promotions."

My heart is in my throat. I did *not* want to be right. In fact, I would have given anything to be wrong. How exactly does one tell someone that their wife who they adored is not really dead? Not only is she alive, it appears she's gone completely around the bend. I have no idea how Trevor is going to react to this. I tremble when I consider the ramifications.

"So, what's this lady's beef with your boyfriend?"

"Actually, he's my fiancé now, which might be part of the problem. Mysti-slash-Melinda Jo was married to my fiancé, right after high school. Then, she disappeared. Her parents had her declared dead."

"You know boss, I think Madison's probably right," Moses says. "When she told me who her fiancé was, I about fell out of my chair because this Mysti chick has been yapping about him for weeks. Mostly, I try to ignore her and do my job like a professional, but her rage was a little hard to overlook."

"What? You didn't tell me that!" I declare as I look accusingly at Moses.

"I didn't want the boss-man to think we've been comparing stories, in case there's some sort of investigation. I learned that watching Cagney and Lacey."

"Well, I admit all of this is creepy as heck. But, we still have the other issue of your conflict of interest with the charities you been investigating. My bank guy says the money is coming out of your account."

"That's just it — it's not from my account. Well, the first couple did because I didn't know I was being scammed. Once I figured it out, I put a fraud alert on my account. Now they're not paying anything — not even my power bill. So, it's a little inconvenient to say the very least. I have nothing to hide. I will show you every bank statement for the last ten years if you want. I wouldn't ever do this kind of crap." I stand up and pace the room. I'm too antsy to stay in the chair. I walk over to Lyle's desk and stand directly in front of him as I insist, "I'm a professional. I worked too hard to develop my professional reputation to have it all go down the drain over some donations to causes I don't even support."

"Madison, I want to believe you. But the evidence is the evidence. It's pretty hard to argue with."

I'm not a violent person but, I swear I want to hit something right now. "This is insane. How do I prove a negative?" I ask, unable to keep the anger out of my voice. "Think about it for a minute, Lyle. How many charities have I brought down in the last four and a half years? At least two a month, right?"

Lyle glares at me, but nods as he leans forward in his big office chair.

"It stands to reason I've brought down at least a couple dozen charities which were up to no good. Because of the work I do, people are not spending money on charities which aren't very charitable. So, does it make any sense to you at all that I would look into charities I believe are fraudulent and then turn around and give them money?"

Lyle slumps down in his chair. "It didn't make any sense before. But when you put it that way, it *really* doesn't make any sense. Tell me, what is your theory about what's going on?"

"I don't know what Madison's theory is, but I can give you one —" Moses interjects.

Lyle turns his attention to Moses as he gestures for

him to continue.

"I think this whole stalking issue and the anonymous reports are related. Whoever this Mysti Winters is, it's clear she's on a mission to destroy Madison and everything she loves. I've worked with Madison since she was fresh out of college. I can tell you without question the most important thing in Madison's life is her job. She loves it here. She wouldn't do anything to jeopardize it," Moses asserts with more passion than I've seen him display for anything else other than his wife and kids.

"Okay, Mo. You've made your point. When I examine the story on the whole, there really is no motivation for Madison to give money to bogus charities."

"Thank you for finally believing in me," I respond, the hurt and anger is still present in my voice.

"I'm sorry, Madison. I couldn't give you any favoritism because we worked together for so long. I had to look at this as objectively as I possibly could. I've never personally doubted you, but what I had to do in my job as the news manager is completely different from how I feel about you when we go bowling on Tuesday nights."

I think about Lyle's assertion for a moment before I carefully answer, "I can appreciate your logic; but do you know how painful it was for me to think you didn't believe me after all the time we've spent working together? I had so many sleepless nights over that. If I've lost credibility as a journalist, I have nothing left. I couldn't bear to think you didn't have faith in me."

"It's just a tragedy we all had to go through this. I

didn't like this process any more than you. I'm sorry to tell you it's probably not over yet," Lyle answers as he pinches the bridge of his nose.

I sigh. "Sadly, you're probably correct. Still, I don't know what we can do to prevent the fallout. Heck, I don't even know if I'll still be engaged after I tell Trevor his wife is still alive. I feel like my life is spinning out of control."

"I know it might not seem like it, but I am in your corner. I'll do anything I can do to help. In fact, I might call a colleague from another newspaper and have them do some investigating on Ms. Winter. I think our editorial board would have a bit of difficulty if I authorized an investigation within our own paper. It might be considered a conflict of interest."

"That's a shame," Moses posits. "Madison is the best reporter in the biz. I'd hate to see all the secrets she could unearth."

———— • ————

For my safety, and to ensure any further contact between Mysti Winter and me is recorded, Lyle arranged for all of my calls and texts to go through an answering service and he gave me more safety gadgets than I'll ever use in a lifetime. I'm a little taken off guard when I receive a message on the answering service instructing me to have dinner at one of my favorite restaurants. The answering service said they were unable to retrieve the name of the caller, but they assured me it was someone on my approved list. Perhaps it's Carlton and Whitney planning to take me out to an early birthday dinner. I left everyone else I love in Oregon. There's something really discouraging about my thoughts. How am I supposed to re-build my life here when everything I love is there?

Suddenly, I'm starving. It seems like all I've done today is wait. Unfortunately, I can't get up and walk around in the busy restaurant. Much to my dismay, I have to sit … and wait.

There isn't anyone more surprised than me when the hostess produces Trevor instead of my brother. I thought there was no way he could be here. I look down at my shapeless yoga wear and wonder what in the world I was thinking? Oh that's right, I was thinking it would be a casual dinner with my brother. I didn't realize the love of my life would be sitting across from me. I know he doesn't care how I look — but I do. If I had known he was coming, I would've dressed up and at least attempted to look cute.

Trevor puts his hands on my shoulders and cups my jaw as he briefly kisses me. It's a little disconcerting, because Trevor usually is not big on company manners. For him to opt for the polite PDA is a little scary to me. Perhaps he is angrier with me than I thought. Why else would he be keeping his distance? Unless, of course, he got DNA results back and hasn't bothered to share it with the rest of us. I pull out of his embrace and sit down. "I'm so glad you're here, but I thought you couldn't come?"

"Initially I couldn't, but Javier has family who stepped in for me as a farrier so I could leave without guilt. I need to be here with you. I didn't realize it before today — I'm only truly happy when I have you right by my side. If someone's threatening you like that, they need to be taken out with extreme prejudice."

"Did you just quote me a cheesy line from a movie?" I ask, my mouth hitching up with humor.

"I did quote you a movie line. It happens to be the most appropriate one for the situation. I used it for illustrative purposes," he responds with a grin.

"Okay, I was just checking — because it's so corny."

"So, what have I missed? I'm trying to completely overlook all the crazy stuff you've done this week. But, please — whatever you do — don't do stuff like that again. If you do, I won't live past thirty-five. It's too stressful."

"I'm sorry I worried you so much. You're right, I was out of line. I took far too many risks, I'll try not to do it again," I acquiesce.

"Apology accepted. Tell me what's been going on," Trevor prods.

I've had this conversation over and over in my head. There just is no good way to approach it. Taking a steadying breath, I forge ahead. "There's been an unexpected break in the case —" I start to say hesitantly.

"Well, great. That's what you were waiting for. Mad … what did you find out?" he prompts eagerly.

"Well, it might not be what you expected," I hedge.

I can tell Trevor is getting really agitated as he declares, "Madison, I don't think there's anything worse than what we've been going through. Just tell me what's going on."

Something tells me the news I have for him is a little

more upsetting than we've been going through. Yet, I can't find a way to tell him that without going into the whole story. I hope he really is prepared to hear what I have to say.

"Umm, I'm not sure where to begin. But, I guess I can start at the beginning," I start to explain. I'm frustrated because I sound so disjointed. "Remember when Mysti Winter confronted us at the market and we were baffled about how she could know so much personal information?" I ask, rhetorically.

Trevor shrugs. "I figured she is some sort of social media guru, or maybe she's somebody's research assistant."

"I wish that were the case, it would be so much easier than what I have to tell you." Nervously, I twist my hair between my fingers.

Trevor sighs deeply and then commands, "Madison, it's gonna be fine. Tell me what you know. No sugar-coating it. I'm a soldier in the Army and I've had my leg cut off. I've been through some heavy stuff before, this can't even compare to that, I'm sure."

"Okay, but please don't hate the messenger. I believe the reason why Mysti Winter knows so much about your personal life is because … she is actually Melinda Jo Whitmore," I announce somberly, bracing myself for his reaction. This could be the very last time we see each other, for all I know.

Trevor looks like I've given him a roundhouse kick to the temple. He picks up his Coke and guzzles it. He takes the napkin and wipes his whole face as if he's broken out in a cold sweat. Eventually he takes a shuddering breath before he says, "I'm sorry. I must not have heard you correctly. Did you say you think Melinda Jo is actually alive? How do you know this? Do you have any proof?"

I expected to be pummeled with questions, but it's still difficult to answer them.

My eyes mist up as I try to keep myself composed during the scariest conversation I've ever had in my life. How do I tell him this without destroying him?

"Well, we don't have the DNA back yet, but there are so many other things which point to the fact that Mysti Winter is actually Melinda Jo. You yourself said it was extremely strange she knew about your reaction to blood and that you had your wisdom teeth out. She also knew medical information about your amputation and your departure from the guard. She damaged a romantic picture of us, and then she makes fun of your disability."

"Okay, you have some points there. However, you didn't even meet me until after she'd been stalking you for a few months. How do you explain that?"

"I don't have an explanation. I wish I did. I don't know why she's got something against me. I had only met her one time prior to the time she confronted us in Portland. It was so benign, I barely remember it. It was one of those journalism events where we all stand around and talk to each other like we've got something important to say. All I can remember about her is thinking that her hair would be a lot prettier if it was a natural color because the platinum blonde clashed with her eyes. I know that's a bizarre thing to think when you meet someone, but her hair was so out of place with the rest of her, it was odd."

Trevor smirks. "Trust a woman to notice that stuff."

"Anyway, I remember that she asked me a bunch of career-related questions, but everyone at those events does the same thing. It's like you have to wear your resume on your sleeve," I add.

"Okay, I have another question. Where has she been all these years? Does her family even know? She was really close to her brother. I think his name was Andrew or Alex. It was something like that. I know he's named after his grandfather and his dad. I only met him briefly once or twice because he was always gallivanting around the globe on his daddy's money. I always thought it was funny that he goes by the name Trey. He acted like it was some sort of badge of honor to be the third person in your family to have the same name."

Oh no, not again, I think to myself as the world spins. I sway in my chair and Trevor rushes over to help me as I crumble toward the floor.

I wave him off and take a big drink of the lemon water the waitress provided. In true Trevor form, he completely ignores my resistance to his efforts to be chivalrous. He slides his chair as close as he can get it to mine and moves the silverware across the table. He's so close he's practically sitting in my lap.

He examines me carefully. "Are you all right — are you getting sick again? Maybe we should go back to the doctor and get you some more antibiotics."

"No, I'm fine. I'm not getting sick again, at least not that kind of sick. I'm heartsick," I respond as I shake like a leaf.

Trevor reaches over and swipes the hair out of my face and tucks it behind my ear. "Sweetheart, you'll have to give me a little more than that. I'm completely lost."

"Unfortunately, I don't think I am," I retort as I try to keep bile from erupting in the back of my throat. "You just provided me the why."

"I did?" Trevor asks with surprise.

I nod sadly. "You gave me the last piece of the puzzle. I think I understand why Mysti Winter has been after me."

"I'm glad it's clear to you, because I'm still in the dark," he remarks.

"I have every reason to believe that your brother-in-law raped me when I was sixteen years old," I whisper in a broken voice. "Clearly, I'm not as 'over' all of this as I thought I was because my body can't decide whether it wants to pass out or throw up."

"What? How did you reach that conclusion? I thought this was all about Melinda Jo," he asks with befuddlement on his face.

"I thought so too — until you mentioned her brother. I didn't know him, but I knew of him. Around Oxford, everyone called him 'Trey Whitty' — I guess he thought of himself as a real comedian. Everyone knew who he was because he was a star on the rowing team. His flat was allegedly epic. Everyone wanted to get an invite to his parties because I guess he had access to the best alcohol and women. I once heard my teacher's assistant in political science wax poetically about a party at his house for more than a half an hour. He acted like he'd been visited by one of the Royals."

"Are you sure he's the same person? There could be other people with a similar name."

"Am I a hundred percent positive — as in would I print it in the newspaper? The answer to that is no. However, it's the piece of the puzzle the ties it all together. It's probably the reason that I've been stalked for so long and that the attacks are so personal. It even explains the presence of Rohypnol and Ketamine in Mysti's house."

"True it could, but what I don't get is why would they go after you when you were the victim?"

"Since when does anything these two do make any sense? They're both deranged. Trey Whitmore raped me before I had even grown up enough to start my period — let alone have sex, and his sister pretended to be dead for almost a decade. Exactly why would we expect either one of them to be normal?"

The look of stark despair on Trevor's face makes me regret being so blunt. After all, technically Melinda Jo still has rights to him, and I've likely lost all of mine.

"Oh, I'm sorry, Trevor. I know that Melinda Jo was your wife and at some point you loved her very much. I'm sorry for being so in-your-face about all of this. This is probably hard for you too."

Trevor blinks as if he's coming out of some sort of trance. "Well, the way I see it, if Melinda Jo wanted anything to do with me, she knew where to find me. Do you know I've kept the same PO box we had when we were married all these years, even after she was declared dead? I've even kept the same cell phone number in hopes she might actually call someday."

"You did?" I gasp in a stunned whisper, but Trevor continues on as if I said nothing.

"But you know what? She *never* did, I can't tell you how much it *pisses* me off that she was alive and well enough to terrorize you for an *entire year,* but couldn't so much as drop me a text message or a Christmas card. So, pardon my French, but screw her. She has no place in my life now. I'm a different person than I was in high school, and she can go back to being gone for all I care. I'm completely and totally in love with someone else now."

Relief surges through me when I hear his words. I sink a little in my chair when I consider what it means. But, my overwhelming thought is, *Thank goodness. I don't have to give Trevor back.*

The adrenaline crash overtakes me as I suddenly have to throw up. Consequently, I have to confess my extreme gratitude and undying love as I'm running toward the restroom as I try not to toss my cookies. This is so totally *not* the romantic scene I envisioned in my head.

CHAPTER EIGHTEEN

TREVOR

As I watch Madison run to the bathroom, I have to tamp down my panic and remind myself that if she wants my help, she'll ask for it. It's hard for me to sit around and watch her be in pain, but I can understand her reaction because I'm feeling queasy myself.

I don't even know how to process what I was told today. It seems too far-fetched and obscene to be true. Still, my gut tells me Madison is correct. I've spent months trying to come up with the reason Madison was stalked long before she ever met me. Yet, this theory seems to unify it all in some sick, twisted way. I always suspected there was something more going on than a fan who is attention seeking or upset with Madison. The stalker doesn't seem to just hate her — much of the vitriol seems to be focused on me.

To be honest, even after Melinda Jo's parents had her declared dead, I never quite believed it. I assumed I was the one who was a little nuts — because after all, who believes their spouse is still alive after so much time has

237

passed? I wonder if I'm still married to her or if the fact that she was declared dead makes my marriage null and void.

I try to set all the complications of my first marriage to the side because if Madison is right, there's a rapist loose on the streets. We have to deal with that first. It is so hard to think logically when all I want to do is tear the creep apart piece by piece.

I grab my cell phone and call Javier to see if he's gotten any more results back from the lab. I hope he has, because a lot will hinge on being able to prove Mysti Winter and Melinda Jo Whitmore are the same person. If we can tie Melinda Jo to the case, it shouldn't be too much of a stretch to go back and figure out when Alex or Andrew — or whatever his name is, went to school with Madison and establish a connection.

As the phone continues to ring, my frustration mounts. I wish we had all the answers yesterday. I leave Javier a brief message explaining I need to talk to him as soon as possible.

Movement from across the room catches my eye, and I notice Madison is coming out of the restroom. She looks pale and shaky. I rush to her side and offer her my elbow as an escort. For once, she accepts the help without protest.

I place the cinnamon tea I ordered for her in front of her with a flourish. "I put sugar in it just as you like. I think you may feel better if you have some."

"Thanks, it's been a rough morning," she admits as she gratefully sips the tea.

"Unfortunately, it's likely to get rougher before

things get easier."

"I suppose so, but it has to be a good thing that we've discovered who the stalker is."

"It's good *and* bad," I observe. "You have the chance to go back and rewrite some history. You told me one of your biggest regrets was not going after this guy. Now, you have a chance to make him pay."

"It's more complicated than that. First, after my experience with the stalker, I'm not even sure anyone would believe me. A good defense attorney would tear me to pieces. The side effects of Rohypnol make me an unreliable witness. This doesn't even account for the fact that the trial might have to be in England. I don't know what the rules are about that. It'll be complicated. I'm not sure it's worth it. It's been years."

"Madison, you are one of the smartest people I know. If you have reason to think it's him, I totally believe you. The sexual assault laws have changed over the years, so it might be easier to report a rape now than it used to be. I can't see you being okay with the idea that he's out there running free. Your sense of moral responsibility is too strong."

Madison's eyes light up with fire as she snaps back at me, "Trust me. I'm not fine with that scum ball even breathing — let alone running around, potentially assaulting other women. I'm petrified. What if he comes after me again? Clearly, he knows who I am."

"Madison, you're a different person than you were back then. You've prepared yourself physically and mentally to take on anyone. Besides, the scumbag would have to get through Tyler, me and all the rest of your friends before he can so much as touch you. You've got world-class backup."

For the first time today, I see a ghost of a smile. "I do, don't I?"

I have a huge issue with men who feel entitled to take whatever they want, regardless of consent. I saw enough of this when I was in Iraq and Afghanistan. "Personally, I hope he tries to step out of line, because I'd like to annihilate him. He should pick on someone his own size for a change," I practically growl.

This time, Madison does give me a huge grin. "I'd like to see you set him straight. Maybe you should charge admission."

"The heck with that," I offer, cracking my knuckles. "I'd do it just for the exercise."

Madison smiles slightly. "That actually sounds like it might be fun." She turns somber as she continues, "I'll talk to Jeff when we get home and see what he suggests. Maybe I'll talk to Tara, too. She finally faced her rapist in court, and from what Heather says, things are much better in her life. Maybe some of her courage will wear off on me."

"That sounds like a perfect idea. Perhaps you'll get valuable information from them. You're one of their posse now, so they'll do anything they can to help protect you."

"Funny you should say that because Kiera told me exactly the same thing a few months ago. I guess I'm so used to doing things myself I don't usually consider asking my friends to help much. Yet, the Girlfriend Posse seems to be made for situations like this. I guess I'll have to adjust my approach to life."

"Well, it couldn't hurt to ask for help. It's a talented group of folks."

Just then, my phone rings and I check the number. I look up at Madison. "Speaking of the group, this is Javier."

"Go for Black," I answer. "Just a second, Javier, let me put the headphones in so Madison can hear our conversation."

"Sure thing," Javier replies.

I dig out a set of earbuds from my jacket pocket and place one in Madison's ear and the other side in mine. We must make quite a picture sitting in the middle of the restaurant with our heads placed together ear to ear. It's not ideal, but it will work under the circumstances. Sometimes, I miss all the communication gear we had when I was in the National Guard. It would make things like this so much easier.

"Okay Javier, we're situated. What did you find out?" Madison asks anxiously.

"Oh, hi Ms. M. I hope you're doing well. I'm sorry it took me so long to call you back. I had to go take my daughter to dance lessons. All I can say is I'm glad it's not me doing hip-hop — that would've been a disaster. Anyway, the lab results were confusing ... to say the least."

"What do you mean?" asks Trevor.

"Frankly, I'm not exactly sure where to start. This was not a result I was expecting. First of all, there are two DNA profiles. Madison, the local police where you live found male DNA in your office they couldn't exclude. Apparently, they tested every person who has access to your office. This is the only profile which doesn't have a match."

"Really?" Madison responds, surprise evident in her question, "I wasn't aware the local police were doing anything for me. They didn't even believe I had a stalker."

"I can't speak to the politics of it, but perhaps the local LEO's were a little intimidated by the fact outside help was coming in. Maybe they figured they'd needed to protect themselves."

"Law enforcement officers are notorious for being territorial. What did you find so weird about the result?"

"Well, the prints on Madison's laptop belongs to a female with a familial match to the blood found in Madison's office. If that wasn't strange enough, when I ran the DNA off of the flower box with the dead rats, it came back to a person who's been declared dead. When I received the result from the lab, I had them run the test again. That's why I took a few more days to get the results. I wanted to double check."

It knocks the wind right out of me. I reach over and squeeze her hand before I collect myself enough to respond, "If I were to hazard a guess, I would bet the prints belong to Melinda Jo Whitmore, correct?"

There is a pause on the end of the line before Javier responds, "Yes, that's correct. How in the world did you guess?"

"Because she used to be my wife," I explain succinctly.

Even the word *wife* echoes through my body. Was I supposed to predict this or stop it? Supposedly, I knew her better than anyone.

"Seriously, dude? What is she doing leaving dead animals at Madison's place?" he asks incredulously.

"We wish we knew the definitive answer. Unfortunately we don't. All we have are theories. The leading theory is it has to do with Melinda's brother, but we don't really know because Melinda Jo Whitmore disappeared off the face of the planet and no one was able to find her."

"No kidding? This case keeps getting stranger and stranger. I didn't even know you were married."

"Well, I don't think I am now. Melinda Jo's parents had her declared dead, so my hope is the declaration somehow nullified my marriage. The woman is a serious psychopath. I don't know why I didn't see it when I was married to her. I mean, we had our problems, but it wasn't anything like this. We mostly fought about career stuff," I clarify.

"It must be strange to have her suddenly come back to life. Do you know where she's been all this time?"

"I don't have a single, solitary clue. The first time I saw her after I went away to serve in the sandbox, was when we ran into her at the Portland Saturday Market. But, she's changed so much I didn't even recognize her. Her hair is completely different. Usually, it's brown and very curly. When I saw her in Portland, she had bleached blonde hair and it was straight and long. It looks like she's also had some plastic surgery done. Her nose looks different to me, as does her... bust." I glance over at

Madison. "When we were together, she was always telling me she would have to undergo a radical makeover to be competitive in the news market. I guess she followed through. I'm not surprised because her parents are loaded. Money has never been an issue for her."

"Oh, that explains a lot. I was wondering why you didn't recognize her when we first ran into her," Madison remarks.

"Do you remember what color her eyes were?" I ask as a thought occurs to me.

"I do. They were green. I remember being a little jealous of her green eyes because mine have always been a very boring brown. Consequently, I always notice when people have interesting eye colors. Hers were a bright emerald green, why?"

"She must've been wearing contact lenses too. Melinda Jo's eyes are very pale blue. They are so pale they're quite noticeable. It doesn't shock me she was wearing contact lenses if she wanted to stay under the radar."

Madison shutters and blanches. "Don't talk about those creepy eyes. They are so light blue, they almost look clear. Those eyes haunt my nightmares."

"Yes, but how would you know that?" I ask, completely confused.

"Because, her brother has the same weird eyes. It's part of the reason I never tried to be like one of the popular girls and work my butt off to go to one of his parties. He just creeped me out in a weird way."

"How did you end up at a party with him?" I ask,

seeking details.

"One of the upperclassmen in our dorm was having a birthday party at a local bar and several of the other students started pressuring me to go saying I was a baby. Well, of course, I couldn't let that fly. Against my better judgment, I went to the party. Because I'm so tall, I've always looked older than my age. No one challenged me when I went to the bar. It seemed pretty normal at first. People were just standing around dancing, then this big group of guys came in. I remember everybody cheered and said, 'Finally, Trey Whitty is here. Now the party can really begin.' I don't remember much after that, a few flashes of faces, clothing and smells. I might as well have not existed during those few hours because they were a total blank. After the rape, I almost wish I hadn't lived those hours. I was ready to throw in the towel on life."

"So, you're telling me your ex-wife started stalking Madison months before she ever met you because of a sexual assault allegation from years ago?" Javier asks.

"Unfortunately, yes that's what we're saying," Trevor answers.

"Well, you won't like the rest of what I have to tell you," Javier responds with a sigh.

"Are you serious? There's more bad news?" Madison asks with a trembling voice.

"Yes, I'm afraid so. The DNA profile we lifted from Madison's desk drawer matches an unknown profile from several home invasions which include sexual assault. The perpetrator used chloroform to subdue the women."

Madison looks at me with shock as she gasps and

moans.

I know exactly what she's thinking. "Madison, Sweetheart, it's not your responsibility. You were sixteen years old and all on your own in a foreign country. I know adults who wouldn't be able to navigate that system. You've got to let the guilt go. It's not warranted and it won't do you any good. The only person responsible for the rape of those other women is Alex Whitmore III," I insist.

"Madison, are you sure this guy is the one who assaulted you?" Javier asks. Through the phone I can hear him typing on a keyboard.

"As sure as I can be — considering I was drugged," she answers bluntly. Madison turns to me and adds, "I forgot to tell you a few days after the attack, I overheard a couple of students in my English class pointing at me, snickering and joking about how Whitty had gotten some fresh meat and that he was really happy it was veal. I was completely mortified because all I wanted to do the whole time I was at Oxford was fit in. I wanted everyone to forget I was still only sixteen."

"What a freakin' sociopath!" I mutter under my breath.

"Your response was understandable, Madison," Javier answers. "This time you won't be the only person testifying. We have solid DNA evidence linking him to other attacks. Those victims will have their own stories to tell."

A tear rolls down Madison's face. "This time, I have to say something. I have to help them stand up for themselves and advocate for any other women he hurt.

Maybe, if there are enough of us, we'll be able to stop him this time. Like Trevor said, this time he doesn't have the upper hand."

I place my arm around Madison's shoulder and pull her to my side as I kiss her cheek and say, "That's my Madison. I'm so proud of you. Let's go stop these creeps and give them what they deserve."

"I admire your tenacity and bravery Ms. M.," Javier compliments. "Please know we're working on this as hard as we can. There's no way we're going to let him slip through our fingers again."

"I agree. Madison is the strongest person I've ever met. If anyone can handle this, it's her," I tell Javier.

"Trevor, what are you going to do about your other loose end?" Javier asks.

"What loose end?" I ask, distracted by Madison's tears.

"You know, the one you're *married* to? Assuming it's still in effect. It could mess up your relationship with Madison — if you don't take care of it."

I sigh. "I don't know where things stand with Melinda Jo. I don't consider her to be my wife anymore, and it's been several years since she was. If I have to, I'll get a divorce because the only woman I plan to spend the rest of my life with is Madison."

Madison starts to fan herself. "Trevor Black, you completely lied when you said all the romance has gone out of your soul. That was pretty much the most romantic thing I've ever heard in my life."

Chapter Nineteen

Madison

TREVOR TOOK THE NEWS about Melinda Jo far better than I ever expected him to. I can't tell you how much better Trevor makes me feel about our relationship. He didn't even consider going back to his wife for a single second. Yet, it isn't all good news. We met with Jeff and Tyler to have a status meeting of sorts. Jeff told us if we had only gotten married before we located Melinda Jo, our marriage would've stood uncontested. However, since she's now been found, Jeff recommends Trevor file for divorce. Fortunately for Trevor, Jeff has agreed to assist him with the process. I feel much better — Jeff is a consummate professional and will help Trevor navigate those choppy waters. I suspect if she's crazy enough to stalk me over something which happened while I was in college, she won't take the news of divorce well.

Trevor and I are having a mild disagreement over this. He thinks because she's left him alone for so many years means she's no longer interested in him. I know how jealous women work. They might not want something and may be ready to discard it — but if someone they perceive as competition decide it is valuable and the fight will be on. I don't think she'll give up easily.

It is refreshing to have an honest to goodness disagreement with Trevor and still feel like he values my opinion. This was not true with my ex-fiancé. He would always belittle me if I disagreed with him. We tended to disagree a lot. I've noticed Trevor doesn't like to fight simply for the purpose of fighting. We've had many philosophical disagreements, but when it comes down to it, Trevor always respects my opinions. It's fun to be allowed to be a smart girl again. I hated hiding my knowledge or opinions to make someone else happy.

The big unknown right now is Alex Whitmore. At the moment, we're not even sure where he's at. That fact all by itself is enough to give me nightmares. Trevor and Tyler decided it's probably safer for me to be back in Oregon, and fortunately for me, Lyle gave me unlimited leave to deal with the situation. After he determined none of this was my fault and there was a bigger story at play, he has become extremely supportive of what I need to do to deal with the mess of my life.

Aidan generously offered part of his security team to help watch my back. Therefore, I'm getting movie star treatment when I go to Dutch Brothers to get coffee. It has taken a bit of getting used to, but I'll take overprotective bodyguards any day over being stalked by a psychopath.

It turns out my hunch was correct, and if I elect to press charges, the rape trial would have to take place in

England. Fortunately, there isn't a time limit on when I can bring charges against Alex. But there are still issues about whether or not I can prove what actually happened to me since I wasn't really conscious. The fact that I found Rohypnol and Ketamine at Melinda Jo's house, and we have proof the two of them were working together helps bolster my story. But, it's still a huge risk. The other option is to testify in the home invasion cases here in the United States. At this point, I'm torn about what I should do. I need to make sure he can't harm anyone else, but I don't know what the best approach would be.

Emotionally, I'm not prepared to deal with all of this. For so many years, I put it completely out of my mind as a coping mechanism. To have to deal with it head on is its own kind of terror. I can't remember everything, but I do remember how I felt afterwards. Those feelings have come rushing back and have made me tearful and afraid. It's a good thing Trevor loves me so much, because I'm an absolute basket case. I can be functioning fine and then suddenly, a wave of fear and sadness will overtake me and I'll collapse in a heap of tears. This is so frustrating. It's not who I usually am.

Trevor has been incredibly supportive. He has tried his best to anticipate every single need I might have. This is a mixed blessing because in some ways all the protection feels stifling. As a journalist, I'm used to being able to pick up and go where I need to go without having to check in with a dozen people. I'm trying to put myself in Trevor's shoes and understand how frightening this is for him too.

Currently, I'm helping Mindy make cookies to take to school for St. Patrick's Day. Actually, more accurately,

I'm watching Mindy make cookies because she's had far more practice at it than me.

As she pipes frosting around a four-leaf clover, she looks up at me and asks, "Aunt Madison, why are Uncle Aidan's bodyguards just standing around? Shouldn't they be protecting him and Tara from the paparazzi people?"

I know with Mindy there's no sense in trying to sugarcoat the truth because she probably knows the whole outcome by now. She has lived through her own assault, so even though she's young, she's especially attuned to the dangers in the world.

I sit down at the breakfast bar and pat a seat next to me. This is an incredibly difficult conversation to have with a young girl, but I push ahead. "Mindy, do you remember your mom telling you about the disgusting packages arriving at the house?"

Mindy nods and responds, "Yeah, those were gross. I don't know why someone would want to do that to those poor mice. We have mice in a classroom at school and they're nice. They let you hold them and everything."

I shudder with disgust. "Well, to each his own, but I don't think you'd catch me holding any mice. I prefer dogs, cats and horses. Anyway, those were sent by a lady who doesn't like me very much and wanted to scare me."

"That's the Barbie lady I told you about who was pretending to be somebody else, right?"

"Yes, you were absolutely right about her. This lady's real name is Melinda Jo Whitmore, but she was going by the name Mysti Winter."

"Aunt Madison, she has my middle name and I

don't like it. You shouldn't be able to be evil and have the same name as a nice person. We need to give her a nickname because I don't want to share my name with somebody like that," Mindy insists with her arms crossed and a scowl on her face.

I can't say I disagree with her logic. I'm pretty sure I would feel the same way if I found out someone truly evil had my name. "I don't have a problem with that," I reply with a smile. "Don't tell anybody, but Trevor calls her Deranged Barbie. Before I knew who she was, I used to call her Barbie Light."

Mindy ponders this for a bit. "It would be fun to call her Deranged Barbie, but people might get mad at us because we're being mean. So, I think we should call her BL. That way, it's kinda like a secret code and nobody really knows who we're talking about."

"That sounds like the perfect plan," I agree.

"Why was BL after you?" Mindy asks with curiosity written all over her face. Mindy is an avid reader, and it seems she's figured out this tale is a tangled mystery.

"Well, when I was not much older than you, I had the chance to go to Oxford University early. I was trying to fit in with the older kids so I went to a party. While I was there, this man, Alex Whitmore, wanted me to kiss him and stuff. I didn't really want to because I didn't know him and he was older than me. So, he decided to give me some drugs to make me loopy, so I would forget what happened. Then, he kissed me and had sex with me while I was completely asleep. When somebody does that to you, it's called rape."

"Did you call the police? My Uncle Tyler works for

the Sheriff's Office, he could probably help you."

"If I had known your uncle then, things might've been different. I was too embarrassed to ask for help, and I was afraid I would get in trouble for being at the party. So, I didn't tell anybody," I answer honestly.

"That's not good. People who do bad things should get in trouble."

"I agree. I'm working on trying to tell the right people now and maybe he'll be brought to trial."

"But, what does that have to do with BL?"

"Well, this is where it gets complicated. BL turns out to be Alex's sister. In a weird way, I think she was trying to stick up for her brother by messing with me — but, the story gets even stranger. It turns out that Trevor is married to BL. They were high school sweethearts. A few years ago when Trevor was serving in the military with your Uncle Tyler, BL decided she didn't want to be married anymore and she pretended to die. Up until a few weeks ago, Trevor didn't even know she was still alive. When she was spying on me, she got jealous because Trevor is my boyfriend, so she decided to try to freak out Trevor, too."

"She's not very smart is she? Tyler and Uncle Trevor are really strong soldiers, they don't freak out easy."

"You're right, everybody got mad when she started picking on me. They started trying to figure out who she was and eventually we solved the mystery. Now we know who she is and who her brother is."

"Is she going to get in trouble for what she did to you?" Mindy probes.

"I hope so, Mindy Mouse. I really hope so. She made my life miserable for a long time. She was helping her brother do bad things to other women. She should face some consequences."

"I know she will," Mindy retorts. "By the way, make sure your cell phone is charged up."

Something in her tone makes the hair on the back of my neck stand up, so I ask, "Mindy, is there something I should know? You're pretty good at knowing what's going to happen."

"Ms. Tara says I can't tell you unless it's a matter of life and death. But, don't worry. I think you'll think this is good news," she assures me.

"Thanks for telling me, Mindy. It makes me feel better. Can I take a couple of cookies with me? I need to go work on some paperwork in the barn."

"Sure you can," Mindy smiles with a crooked grin. "I've been in this family long enough to know I need to make lots of extra cookies. My Uncle Tyler is a big cookie monster. I almost have to make a whole batch just for him."

"Thank you so much for listening Mindy, you make a great friend," I say as I head out the door with a plate of delicious cookies.

———◆———

I'm trying to concentrate on wading through the spreadsheets of contacts I'm working on. Although, I'm technically on leave from the Towne Sentinel, Lyle gave me permission to continue to investigate the story about the basketball players and recruitment violations. As I look at the receipts from the escort service, I have a startling realization perhaps I wasted far too much time getting a fancy college degree. Some of these women make as much in three months as I do all year.

When my cell phone rings, I practically jump out of my chair. Ethel looks at me like I'm a little nuts as I yelp in surprise.

"Hello?" I answer tentatively. Trevor is a few miles outside of town helping a farmer deliver a set of twin calves, so I'm not expecting to hear from him anytime soon.

"Hey Maddie, how are you today?" Tyler asks.

"I'm okay, a little stressed as usual. Mindy's keeping me well fed with cookies though."

"Oh man! It's my lucky day. I can't wait to get home. Are you ready for some good news? It might relieve your stress a bit."

"Sure, I can always use some positive news. I haven't had much of it recently."

"Well, law enforcement has arrested one Melinda Jo Whitmore on charges of drug possession and extortion."

"You're kidding! That's the best news I've heard in forever!" It's a good thing Tyler can't see me because I'm practically jumping up and down in my chair.

"I thought you might like the newest development in the case. The rumor is she's singing like a canary about her brother. She didn't have much choice when she heard they discovered her diary in the search warrant. Apparently, it's like a sick treasure map of all the women Alex Whitmore attacked. It seems he's been at this for a very long time. His sister apparently blames the women involved instead of her own brother. So, she set out to destroy everyone. You're not the first woman that she's stalked, but hopefully you'll be the last. Her connection to Trevor was a random coincidence."

"I find that hard to believe. I mean, what are the odds?"

"I don't know, you'll have to ask your fiancé. He's the math geek, not me. I draw pictures of buildings for fun, I don't do the whole statistics thing," Tyler teases.

"What happens now?"

"Since she had the Rohypnol and Ketamine in her possession and admitted it to you in the text messages and her diary, it is likely she'll be held without bail. Additional charges of being an accessory to breaking and entering and rape are likely to be added."

"Oh my Gosh, Tyler!" I exclaim. "She was in my house, and within feet of Trevor and I in Portland … and when we all went dancing. If that wasn't scary enough — I went to her house like an idiot. Can you imagine what she would've done if I hadn't left in such a hurry?" I ask, nearly hyperventilating.

"I know Madison, it could've gone sideways at any time during all of this, but luckily it didn't and you're safe. You should take comfort in that. Hopefully, you'll have a little more common sense the next time you go charging into a situation without any sort of backup," Tyler says dryly.

"I know I really screwed up. I don't ever plan to do anything like that again. In fact, it might be a while before I'm out in the field again. The world around me is just too bizarre."

"I agree, the world is a tough place, but you've had great stuff come out of this situation. In a weird twisted way, if hadn't been for Melinda Jo, you and Trevor might not have met. So, that's karma for you, right?"

"I suppose it is poetic justice in a way. She gave up a phenomenal guy. That speaks to her mental acuity." I take a deep breath and ask the really hard question, "What about Alex Whitmore?"

"Well, his sister's meticulous record-keeping will likely be the cause of his capture and incarceration. She documented every attack he's been involved in. Not only that, she kept newspaper clippings and private school records — we're still trying to determine how she got her hands on those — and banking records on all the victims. It's too bad she's using her powers for evil, she would've made an excellent private investigator. Her files are more complete than most police dossiers. She's made prosecuting Alex Whitmore III a piece of cake."

"Have they found him?" I ask with trepidation.

"No, unfortunately not yet. But I believe it's only a matter of time. Are Aidan's guys still in place?"

"Yes, my sidekicks are still around. Last I checked, they were having a rousing game of Texas Hold'em on the porch of the barn. I feel pretty safe because you parked your front loader to block the back entrance to the barn, so there's only one way in and out."

"Well, I didn't get my badge out of a Cracker Jack box. I do know what I'm doing."

"Tyler, I don't tell you this enough, but I really

appreciate all you and Javier have been doing for me. If it hadn't been for you guys, the police force in Boston wouldn't have taken my case seriously. I owe you guys so much," I gush. Unexpectedly, I'm close to tears.

Tyler must've heard the emotion in my voice because he says, "It's okay Madison. It's my job. But, even if it wasn't, I would protect you with my life because you are family."

Well, that's just about enough to put me completely over the edge, and I tearfully whisper, "Thanks Ty, I love you guys too. Thank you so much for calling."

———◆———

I'm sure Trevor did not expect to almost get a face full of pepper spray when he accidentally bumped the bed as he was taking off his boots, but things like that can happen when I have had months and months of very little sleep and several days of horrific nightmares.

"Madison, you can stand down. It's me. I'm sorry I'm so late, but it took a while to deliver the calves."

I sit up in bed and try to kiss him, but Trevor backs away. "Sweetheart, you don't want to touch me right now I'm covered with things you'd rather not be exposed to. Calving is a messy business. Let me take a shower first."

I giggle. "Go ahead. I'll be right here." I'm laughing because the conversation we just had is almost exactly the conversation we had on the first day we met. Who would've thought I would go from holding the guy at bay with pepper spray to being his fiancée? My life has certainly been a whirlwind.

I try my best, but there is no way I can stay awake.

I am exhausted to the bone. I didn't even wake up when Trevor came to bed.

I'm surprised when I wake up in the morning with my head on his chest and my arm flung over his waist. For the moment, I'll relish our casual comfort. This is the best feeling on the planet.

"Mornin' Madison," he rumbles in a sleep roughened voice.

I kiss the center of his chest. "Good morning. I am glad you're here. I missed you yesterday."

"How was your day yesterday?" he asks casually.

I sit up in bed so quickly I almost break his jaw with my head.

He looks around, alarmed. "Did I miss something?"

"No, it occurred to me you probably haven't heard the news. Tyler called yesterday and said they had arrested Melinda Jo for drug possession and extortion. Apparently, the case is strong against her, and she's not likely to get out of jail anytime soon."

"I take it she didn't throw out the pills like she said she was going to?"

"Apparently not, and it gets even more incriminating. It seems she kept a detailed diary of all of her activities, including the ones that weren't exactly legal."

"What about her brother?" He pins me with a lethal gaze.

"Unfortunately, I don't have any great news about him. He's still on the loose. I guess he slipped through their nets."

"I wonder if she'll turn in her brother in exchange for getting out of jail? Unless she's changed, Melinda Jo can't stand small spaces. She used to have an anxiety attack every time she went to the doctor and had to sit in a small room, and she wouldn't set foot on an elevator.".

"I guess she's already started. According to Tyler, he heard through his sources she's 'singing like a canary' about Alex."

Trevor makes a sound of displeasure as he shakes his head in disgust. "Yeah, that about sums up her ability to be loyal. It's great for our side, but sucks for her brother."

"Oh, that's not the only thing that sucks for Alex. Allegedly, she kept detailed files on all of his sexual assaults," I report happily. I can't keep the cheesy grin off of my face.

"Wait, there are even more victims?"

"Yes, I guess he's been doing it for years. You know what else? I'm not the first stalking victim. Apparently, she blames the women for 'ruining' her brother's life and set out to destroy us all — one by one. Tyler seems to think her involvement with you is just coincidental to the case."

"Wow!" Trevor exclaims. "Still, I have a hard time believing my relationship with you didn't escalate her attacks."

"I know, that's what I told Tyler. It's too much of a coincidence to be ignored," I agree.

"What have you decided about testifying? I know

you were on the fence there for a while."

"Well, it's safe to say I've completely jumped off the fence. I want to see Alex's butt in jail for as long as possible. It wouldn't hurt my feelings if Melinda Jo spent a few years there herself." I declare with conviction.

"This might surprise you since she was my wife for so long, but I want her to face jail time too. What she did was dangerous and wrong and enabling her brother is unforgivable in my book."

<hr>

Aidan and Tara flew us back to the East Coast so I can confront Melinda Jo at her bail hearing. As a reporter, this is not the first time I've witnessed a court proceeding, but it's the first time I've ever been involved.

I grip Tara's hand as the bailiff motions for us to stand. My stomach is in my throat. This is so nerve-racking. I feel like I'm about to throw up.

Just then, Melinda Jo turns around and sees I'm in court. Suddenly, she screeches, "You witch! You ruined my brother's life. He was supposed to be a doctor, but you had to go parade your hussy little self in front of him. It's your fault he has to do technical support for a medical supply company instead. So, tell me, Miss Priss, did you like it when I took your job away? You know what? Forget it. I should've killed your worthless behind when I had the chance."

My mouth is agape with shock as the judge pounds on the bench with a gavel and orders calmness to be restored. He orders Melinda Jo's attorney to control his client. The attorney walks up to the bench. "I apologize,

Your Honor, but in light of recent developments, the defense withdraws its petition for bail and will accept whatever the prosecution has suggested. However, I respectfully ask that my client undergo a psychological evaluation."

The judge looks over at the prosecution's table where the lawyer is busy scrambling through paperwork. She has a bewildered expression on her face. The judge addresses her, "Any objection?"

"No, Your Honor, we are requesting no bail; but clearly The State agrees a psychological examination might be appropriate."

The judge bangs his gavel. "It is so ordered."

He looks at the attorneys who are still reeling with shock. "Is there anything else we need to attend to today?"

The prosecutor stands up and says, "Your Honor, I know this is unusual, but the defendant's husband hasn't spoken to her in years and would like to say a few words before she's taken into custody."

The judge looks surprised but then shrugs. "Does he want to have this conversation in open court or in chambers?"

The prosecutor looks at Trevor. "Mr. Black, do you have a preference?"

Trevor stands and addresses the court, "No, Your Honor, what I have to say to my wife can be said in front of the whole world."

"Open court it is," the judge responds. "You may proceed whenever you are ready."

Trevor squeezes my hand and then walks to the prosecution table. When Melinda Jo sees him, her eyes darken with rage. I can hear her attorney advising her to stay quiet.

"Melinda Jo, I freely gave you all of my love and affection from the time I knew what it meant to fall in love. You let your quest for fame and acknowledgment destroy our love. I'll admit, I was not the perfect husband because I was too focused on being a soldier, but I did not deserve to look for you for years and believe you were dead when you are alive and well. As soon as the paperwork can be put into place, I am filing for divorce."

"Baby, you can't do that! I need you." Melinda Jo pleads.

Trevor sighs as he responds in an even voice, "No you don't Melinda Jo. If you needed me, you had multiple ways to reach me over the past several years. You didn't need me then, and you don't need me now. So, please leave me and the people I love alone. We are done." Trevor nods at the judge and returns to his seat.

The judge looks at the bailiff and says, "Melinda Jo Whitmore, you are now remanded to state custody until a trial date can be set and a verdict reached. I hope you find a way to gain some perspective."

"Court is dismissed," the judge says as he bangs his gavel one last time.

The judge looks over at Trevor. "Thank you for your service, young man."

Trevor looks up at the judge and replies, "Thank you sir. It's my honor to serve."

As we file out of the courtroom, Trevor pulls me closer to his side. "Thank you for allowing me to find peace. We did it. We won. That's one less bad guy on the street. I love you so much."

Chapter Twenty

Trevor

Jeff gives me a very understated high-five as I finish signing the divorce papers.

"I know it's not what you hoped for when you got married, but I think it's for the best. The woman in your life right now is phenomenal. She accepts you for all of who you are. Trust me, I know what a priceless gift that is" Jeff says as he pats me on the shoulder.

"I mourned the loss of Melinda Jo a long time ago. Frankly, I'm just relieved it will be over. Any feelings I may have had toward her disappeared the moment she threatened the woman I love. She had her chance with me and threw it back in my face. I have no regrets about signing these papers. Although, I must admit I'm shocked she agreed to the divorce settlement so quickly."

"She was pretty much out of bargaining chips. Did I tell you they have added more charges? It appears she actually drugged a young woman's drink in a Starbucks so she could deliver the victim to Alex. The store backs up all of their security footage off-site and they still had the footage from the day. It clearly shows Melinda Jo tampering with the drink. The prosecutor wouldn't have even known about it except she bragged about it in her diary."

"Jeff, that's so sick. How could I have ever loved someone like her? Why didn't she have signs of all of that when we were married?"

"Kiera is the expert in mental health issues. But if I were to guess, perhaps she has adult onset schizophrenia. It usually strikes in the early twenties."

"The only sign I saw that anything was amiss was her temper tantrums were getting more frequent and escalating in severity. I assumed she was getting bored with married life and was looking for a way out. I was gone on multiple deployments during our last few years. I didn't really have a front row seat to the demise of our relationship."

"Trevor, I don't know what to tell you. Kiera would tell you none of this is your fault. Whether it's a process of natural disease or her own personal choice, you didn't cause it to happen. So, you can take this whole mess off your shoulders, because it's not yours to carry."

"Tyler pretty much told me the same thing. But, it's still difficult to watch her decline even though I don't have any feelings for her. She was my best friend for many years. It makes me sad to see what she's turned into."

"I can understand that, I have a stepfather who's more than a little unbalanced. Yet, every once in a while we had good moments growing up. When I see what he's become — or maybe always was — its difficult. But I'm loyal to the people who really love me. I suggest you adopt a similar approach. You have a woman who believes you make the sun shine and the stars sparkle. Don't lose that because you're lost in the past."

I shake Jeff's hand. "Thanks man, that's solid advice."

"No problem, Trevor — just a few lessons I learned the hard way. Now, let's put all this business behind us and go have something to eat. Kiera and Heather have been working all day to make us a celebratory dinner."

Heather made an amazing roast with mashed potatoes and gravy. She even served corn on the side. How she knew it is my favorite meal, I'm not sure — but it's just what I need today. Our family dinner is ridiculously stereotypical, right down to Becca pulling on her grandpa's pant leg asking to go feed the ducks. Eventually, he caves and pushes his chair back from the table.

I'm chatting with Aidan about his most recent tour when our conversation is interrupted. "Mom, why aren't you eating? You usually like Aunt Heather's cooking," Mindy helps herself to a second helping of succulent roast and gravy.

"I have a bit of a stomach ache, that's all — but I'll be fine," Kiera answers.

"There must be something going around," Madison comments. "I haven't been feeling well either. I figured it was all the nerves."

Mindy's eyes widen and she gasps before she pipes up, "No it's not —"

Tara gives her a stern look as she interrupts Mindy and chastises, "Mindy Jo, remember what I said about privacy?"

Mindy practically swallows her words. I can tell that she'd like to talk, but she obviously doesn't want to upset Tara. "Sorry, Aunt Tara. I forgot."

Tara smiles gently. "It's okay Mouse, just be careful."

Mindy chews on her lip. "Is it always this hard?" Mindy flicks her hair out of her somber blue eyes and sighs heavily.

"It can be," Tara replies.

Jeff, Tyler, Denny and I look at each other in confusion as Denny sits back down at the table. I'm relieved I'm not the only one completely puzzled by the bizarre conversation between Tara and Mindy.

"It looks like they're having one of their psychic moments," Heather supplies.

Yes, that's exactly what it seems like. They can seemingly talk in their own shorthand and understand each other while the rest of us are all lost.

Kiera picks up her fork to take a bite then thinks better of it and sets it down. She shrugs as she looks at Mindy and Tara. "Okay, I feel compelled to put my daughter out of her misery, since I'm about to be busted anyway. The reason I'm not feeling particularly well is because I have morning sickness. Whoever calls it morning sickness doesn't know what in the Hershey's Bars they're talking about. It's all day sickness."

Jeff looks like he's been caught in a thunderstorm

and hit by lightning. "Pip, isn't it dangerous for you? I thought with your overheating issues, getting pregnant is potentially life-threatening."

"It could be. We'll just have to manage the autonomic dystrophy carefully because my body has different ideas and doesn't like to play by any rule book. Theoretically, I shouldn't have gotten pregnant in the first place since I'm on the pill, but I did, so we have to be vigilant. I guess it must have been a medication interaction. I was on antibiotics for my kidney infection, remember?"

"Well, I'm still worried. Autonomic dystrophy is nothing to mess with," Jeff replies in a somber tone.

Kiera grabs his hand. "Luckily for me you're a paramedic in your spare time, so I know you'll be especially careful with me."

Tyler slaps Jeff on the back. "Congratulations buddy. You'll be the father of three. What are you going do if it's another girl?"

"I suppose that I'll love her exactly the same as I love my other two girls. Still, it would be nice to have a little guy on my team."

"Don't worry, Dad. My brother will be just fine and so will Mom," Mindy states with confidence.

Heather laughs out loud. "Well Kiera, I guess you guys could save a bunch of money on ultrasounds. Mindy has spoken and she's rarely wrong."

Tara looks at Mindy and shakes her head. "Mouse, I thought we talked about this."

"We did, Aunt Tara. I followed the rules. You said

I couldn't tell anybody unless it was a matter of life and death. Daddy was afraid my mom might die, so I just told them that she's going to be okay. It's not fair for him to have to wait all those months when I already know the answer."

Donda chuckles and glances over at Tara. "I guess she's got you on a technicality."

Tara nods. "I think you're right. Mouse has always been way too smart for her own good."

I grin at the interaction between Tara and Mindy; it is clear they are very good friends. I look over to Madison to see what she thinks of the announcement. She doesn't seem to be paying any attention to what's happening. She still looks quite stunned. I notice her hands are trembling as she passes the gravy.

She looks intently at Kiera and asks in a shaky voice, "Is it all right if we have an emergency meeting of the Girlfriend Posse?"

Tara nods. "It's in the rules: all you have to do is ask. We're always here for you."

"Do you want me to come with you? I never know if I'm included in these things," Gwendolyn remarks.

All the women in the room simultaneously answer, "Yes!"

"Gwendolyn, we told you a long time ago you were a member of the Girlfriend Posse. So, let's adjourn to the den for a meeting," Kiera declares.

"Can I come too?" asks Mindy as she raises her hand.

"Of course you can," Madison answers. "You're a

junior member of the Girlfriend Posse, aren't you?"

Mindy pops out of her chair with a smug smile and shouts, "See ya —" as she runs towards the den.

After all the women leave the room, all the guys look at each other with complete befuddlement. "That was weird. I wonder what's going on." Tyler remarks, as he helps himself to more roast beef.

Aidan smiles mysteriously. "I have an idea, but I think I'll keep it to myself for now; I don't want to get in trouble with my wife."

Chapter Twenty-One

Madison

"Girl, that was a whole-lotta-drama. I hope it's worth it," teases Donda as she flops back on the couch.

"I don't know what to think, that's why I called the meeting," I reply.

"Madison, tell us what you're thinking." Heather pats me on the shoulder.

"That's just it — I haven't been able to have a coherent thought since Kiera announced her pregnancy."

"Sweetie, I'm sorry. I didn't mean to upset you. I wasn't even planning to announce it today. It just happened," she explains.

"Oh, I didn't mean that at all. I'm thrilled for you. That's not why I am freaking out. I'm freaking out because I think the same thing happened to me."

"I'm going to be an aunt!" Heather shrieks. How far along are you? I'm so excited. What does Trevor say?"

"Trevor has no idea. I just figured it out myself. When Kiera mentioned antibiotics have a negative impact on the effectiveness of birth control pills, I got to thinking about when I last had a visit from Aunt Flo. I think it's been a good four months. I didn't think much of it, because I thought it was the high level of stress effecting my cycle, but when Kiera shared her story, I realized it could have been from the time that I was on antibiotics from pneumonia. It didn't occur to me I might be pregnant because I take my pill like clockwork. It would explain a lot."

"Is anything else a little off?" Gwendolyn asks.

"Well, I've been sick for it seems like forever. I figured it was because I'm completely stressed out and I thought maybe I was developing an ulcer or something."

"I've learned the hard way the nausea can last all day when you're pregnant."

"Is there anything else that's a little off?" Heather asks.

"Yes," I exclaim, "things that I used to love like steak or barbecue sauce absolutely make my stomach turn. Also, I'm so tired I can barely stay awake. I haven't been sleeping because of the whole issue with Melinda Jo. I'm beginning to think it may be something else entirely."

"Well, Madison, I'm not a doctor, but I have had two amazing children and your symptoms sound quite familiar," Gwendolyn replies.

"Girl, you need to pee on a stick ASAP. You sound good and pregnant to me," Donda adds. "How do you feel about that? Have you and Trevor talked about kids?"

"The general topic has come up in conversation,

but I don't think he meant to have them right now. Our lives are a colossal mess. We don't even know where my rapist is. It's a lot to think about."

"That's the funny thing about life, it happens when you're making other plans," Tara advises philosophically.

"Well, I for one think it's awesome news," Mindy interjects. "It means I get to have more cousins. I like Gabriel a lot; he's like my favorite person ever, but he's my only cousin. Anyway, I'd like to see what it's like to have other cousins — even if they are only pretend."

"Honey, Gabriel really is your cousin, remember?" Donda corrects with an amused smirk on her face

"I know. I always forget because I met him before he was really my cousin," Mindy responds.

"I also think this is fabulous news. It means I won't have to go through this pregnancy alone. I'll have a pregnancy buddy. We can do classes and shopping and name picking altogether. I think it sounds like a blast. What do you think?"

Their unconditional acceptance of what is essentially a dicey situation makes me feel so much better. When Kiera asked me to be her pregnancy buddy, it's enough to bring me to tears. A wave of sadness overtakes me as I suddenly remember this isn't really my home. Funny thing is that it actually feels more like home than my home. I'll be sad to leave these friends who have become my family.

"Kiera, that sounds spectacular. Unfortunately, I don't know how long I'm going to be here. I'm starting to forget this isn't actually my home," I explain, feeling a little hopeless.

Heather sniffs and wipes her eyes with a Kleenex. "Oh, please don't remind me. I love having you here. I was looking forward to being a doting Aunt."

Mindy pats Heather on the knee. "Try not to be sad, I can always be your pretend niece, that way when Aunt Madison decides to move to Oregon, you'll already have lots of practice."

"You're right, it would be good practice, but I don't plan to move to Oregon," I confess.

"Like Tara said, life happens when you're making other plans," Donda proclaims.

"Is this meeting ever going to be over?" Mindy complains. "Uncle Tyler said I could help you guys brush the horses."

I chuckle. "Yes, I think this meeting is adjourned. Thank you for the help. I guess I need to do a little shopping before I have any real answers."

As everyone files out of the room, Tara pulls me aside and says, "Congratulations, Mama. I know you're scared, but it'll be all right."

Somehow just hearing that from Tara makes me feel much better.

As I help Mindy put on her coat so we can go outside and be with the horses, Trevor comes up behind me and gives me a hug. "Is everything all right, Madison?"

"Yes, I think things are much better than fine right now. I just needed some support from my friends."

"Okay. I wanted to make sure you are being taken care of," he offers.

"Around here, it seems being taken care of is kind of a mandatory state of being."

———◆———

Riding Velvet makes me nostalgic for my grandparents. I wonder what they would've thought of my situation. I consider whether they would be disappointed, but then I remember what a free spirit my grandma was. In truth, she would probably just celebrate the fact that the father of the baby is a handsome, loyal soldier.

As soon as I have that thought, I mentally stumble. I wonder if I should be more upset about my changing circumstances than I am. It is mind-boggling and not something I anticipated in a million years, but I can't honestly say I'm angry or distraught about it all. I'm scared because so much stuff is up in the air right now. I worry about the safety of my child because one of my attackers is still on the loose. Yet, having a baby with Trevor makes me inherently happy. I have visions of him teaching our little ones how to ride horses and catch trout. I can envision us as a family going camping in Trevor's magical spot in the woods. I hope he's as happy about this change of plans as I am.

His reaction may depend on how today goes. Trevor is meeting with his commanding officer. None of us know what the outcome of the meeting is going to be. This is one of the few times I've ever seen Trevor be uncertain or tentative about anything. It's a little odd to see him that way. The meeting today is to discuss what his commanding officer found out from the colonel above him.

Trevor considers it a make-or-break meeting. He's polished his shoes every day during the last couple of weeks. Hopefully, he'll come home with great news. It would make a wonderful birthday present. He's been so out of sorts ever sense the medical board issued its first finding stating he might have to be removed from the field. His life, which has basically been in total limbo may finally start making some sense. I hope it all works out because he shouldn't have to abandon his career because of a pressure sore that took a long time to heal.

Velvet lurches sideways for no apparent reason. I pull on the reins to correct her. I don't know what's with her today. She's extremely skittish. Usually, she's a mellow ride. Velvet is the horse Mindy rides all the time, and she is usually as predictable as they come. Finally, I get tired of being jerked around. I decide to get off and call Trevor to see if he will bring me an order of fajitas from our favorite restaurant.

As I prop my back up against the rough bark of the tree, I'm tempted to dose off in the warm sun. I'll be glad when the feeling of tiredness passes. It's a little overwhelming. I put my head back against the tree and close my eyes. Aidan had a huge outdoor concert in New York City, so I'm temporarily without my entourage. It feels a little decadent to be one with mother nature without interruption. I close my eyes and sigh as I try to remember all the reasons I need to go back to Boston. I never expected to fall in love with Oregon, but it seems I have.

I open my eyes and watch the water pass through a little creek on Tyler's property. The other day, Mindy jerry-rigged a fishing pole and line and actually caught something. It was pretty funny.

Velvet rears up on her back legs. Something about her odd behavior puts me on edge, so I roll up to the balls of my feet and sit on my haunches in a defensive crouch. Suddenly, I feel a knife pressed into the side of my neck as a voice growls, "It took you long enough to ride this way. I've been waiting out here for days and I'm getting hungry. You're going to pay for that."

Instantly, my mind goes back to the last time somebody said something like that to me. I don't even have to guess. I know this is Alex. I'm ashamed he got the drop on me. I know better. Adrenaline surges through my body as I spring to a standing position and whack him in the jaw with an elbow and follow with a roundhouse kick to his temple. He crumples to the ground like a melted candle.

On the other hand, I am breathing like I ran a marathon. My hands are shaking so bad I can barely push the rescue button on my smart watch. I feel like a safety rookie as I feel around my pockets for my pepper spray. Of course, I left it behind.

I can only pray Tyler or Trevor get here soon. I don't know what I am going to do when Alex wakes up. I look around my natural environment and find a sharp rock and palm it as I wait for someone to answer the phone. Finally, someone answers. "Maddie? Why are you calling Tyler's phone?" Heather asks. "He's out in the barn, but he left his phone in the kitchen. What do you need?"

"Heather, listen," I whisper urgently. "Send Tyler to the apple tree by the creek. Do it right now please."

"Okay done," Heather says after a second. "Stay on the line with me and tell me what's going on."

"I've got Alex Whitmore incapacitated at the moment, but I don't know how much longer I'll be able to hold him. I can't find a big enough rock to bash him in the head again. This time I won't have the element of surprise. Please, just make sure they get here like, yesterday," I beg, trying to catch my breath.

After what seems like forever, I see Tyler's Polaris flying across the field toward me. I breathe a sigh of relief. At least, now I won't be alone in dealing with this jerk. Tyler has his gun out and points it at Alex's head. I step back and collapse on the ground next to the tree. I can't believe my life has come to this.

Tyler unceremoniously scoops Alex up and rolls him over as he binds Alex's hands behind his back with zip ties he has attached to his waist. Fortunately, Tyler just got off work and still has his uniform on which has tons of equipment stashed in it. I watch as he tilts his shoulder up and murmurs, "One in custody, send backup," into the speaker which sits there.

This is the most bizarre game of freeze tag I've ever played. Neither one of us dare to move until Tyler has backup. I'm afraid to breathe for fear I might do something wrong and encourage Alex to wake up before backup gets here. Tyler has a knee pressed into Alex's back and his gun aimed at the base of his skull.

"Is it wrong for me to hope the sucker resists arrest? I'd like nothing more than to have an excuse to take him out," Tyler growls menacingly.

Waves of nausea overtake me and I have to duck

behind the tree to throw up. I'm still squatting on the ground and heaving my guts out when I hear Trevor roar, "What in the heck is going on, Colton?"

"Well, it's kind of self-explanatory. The stupid idiot thought he could come to my house and assault my sister-in-law. But, she showed him — his current state of consciousness is a testament to Madison's skills in self-defense."

Unfortunately, I can't stop throwing up long enough to answer for myself. Trevor runs over. "Are you sure you're not hurt? What's wrong?"

Finally, I stop throwing up long enough to catch my breath and answer, "Just feeling a little queasy. I think all the drama got to me."

"I think I should take you back to the doctor. You've been sick for a long time. This is the strangest flu bug I've ever seen in my life."

It's all I can do not to completely confess what's going on, but I refuse to share the happiest news of my whole life in front of the man who raped me. My news will have to wait. Heather is making a surprise birthday cake for Trevor's birthday, which will double as my pregnancy announcement. I just hope he thinks it's the precious gift I do.

"I think we should wait a few more days to see if this passes. I would hate to bother the doctor for nothing."

"Okay, but if you're not better by next Monday, I'm hauling your butt into the doctor," Trevor says as he helps me up on to the back of Jacques. He swings his long leg over the horse and snuggles up behind me. He addresses

Tyler. "I hope you don't mind, I'm going to take her away from all of this. She shouldn't have to look at him for a second longer than necessary. As far as I'm concerned, we can leave him hogtied in the middle of the field and let him die of starvation and thirst. I don't care, but I've got to get her home. She's not feeling well. She can answer any questions later," Trevor says with absolute authority.

I lean back into Trevor's chest so he can reach the reins.

"Actually, I was going to try to remove her from the scene with a department rig, but your method is far more romantic. Go take your woman home. However, I don't want her to bathe or change her clothes yet."

"Don't worry Tyler, I learned my lesson the first time. This time, I'll willingly let anybody test whatever part of me is necessary to nail this disgusting excuse for a man."

Trevor's posture goes stiff behind me and he yells in my ear as we're flying back toward the barn, "Madison I was so scared." After we reach the corral and he's tied Velvet up, he picks me up and gently places me in my favorite swing on the porch of the barn. He continues to speak, his voice heavy with emotion, "Madison, please tell me he wasn't able to hurt you again. If he was, I'll never forgive myself. I knew you were in danger, but I went to the meeting anyway. If anything happened to you, it would have been my fault."

"First, aside from the fact I think I broke my toe when I kicked him in the head, I'm not hurt. Secondly, it wouldn't be your fault. The fault would be on Alex — but you don't have to worry about that. He didn't get a chance to do anything but scare me with a knife before I was able to debilitate him. I guess there are uses for my MMA skills, even if I'm not an MMA competitor," I say with a lilt in my voice because things have become so serious.

Trevor rests his forehead against mine and he's breathing heavily. "Madison, this isn't a joking manner. I could've lost you today. That guy is seriously deranged — and so is his sister. There's no limit to what he would do to stay out of jail. You are so lucky you were able to get things under control. I know I'll have nightmares for months about what would've happened if you hadn't been able to fight back."

Even two hours later, I'm still in a state of shock. The rest of Tyler's team at the Sheriff's Office were there in almost no time flat. They showed up with an ambulance and carted Alex off to the hospital to be checked out. Trevor wants me to go to the hospital to have my broken toe examined, but I'm not capable of dealing with the drama of the hospital right now. I've broken my toes so many times when I was learning kickboxing so I know, although it hurts, it's not a matter of life and death.

My hands tremble as I put the peppermint tea up to my lips and take a sip. This is nasty stuff, but if it helps control my nausea, it might be worth it. I've been reading books on my Kindle about things to expect while I'm pregnant. Several of them suggest this concoction to help with morning sickness.

Tyler comes up behind me and I jump. "Oh, I'm

sorry, I didn't mean to scare you. Of course, right now you have all the reason in the world for your nerves to be frazzled. I came out to tell you it's unlikely Alex will leave jail anytime during the next four or five decades. It seems as if he was intending for today's events to include a 'suicide by cop.' He was profoundly disappointed when he woke up in the hospital chained to the bed. In preparation for the attack on you today, he posted a four hundred page manifesto on Google Docs outlining all of his crimes in sick detail. It turns out he even took Polaroid pictures of several women while they were incapacitated by date rape drugs."

"Oh no!" I breathe. "Does that mean he took pictures of me?" I can't help myself — I let out a silent sob as my shoulders shake uncontrollably.

Tyler shakes his head as he hands me a new Kleenex and responds, "As far as I can tell, there don't appear to be any souvenir pictures of you. Javier is keeping an eye out for them. Hopefully, we can keep the manifesto aspect out of the news so he doesn't get any more famous than he already is."

Drying his hands on a dishtowel, Trevor comes back into the room. "Darn straight he doesn't need to get famous for this. He needs for someone in prison to do to him what he's done to dozens of women. That would be true justice."

Tyler pats Trevor on the shoulder. "I don't think you'll find anyone who would disagree with that statement."

"Well, I'm not arguing — not in a million years. Thanks for having my back guys," I answer as I walk over to give Trevor a hug.

CHAPTER TWENTY-TWO

TREVOR

I SHOULD BE WORKING on my billing, I've done a lot of odd jobs the last couple of months and haven't been invoicing people like I should. But, as I try to concentrate on the accounting software, I can't really focus. I've got big decisions to make and not a lot of data to make them.

Tyler and the Colonel were able to come up with a compromise with the medical board. If I choose to rejoin my team, I'll be able to go out in the field, but if the mission will require long exposure to the elements, I'll be subjected to more mandatory medical tests to make sure my stump is in good condition and not breaking down with decubitus sores. I'm actually all right with the compromise. It makes sense logistically, and the last thing I want to do is slow down my team.

I can't get a bead on how Madison feels about all of this, she's been uncharacteristically quiet since she was attacked. I wonder if she was injured more than she's letting on. If she is, she clearly doesn't want me to know because she's been avoiding me the last couple of days.

I'm relieved to see she's talking to her sister. The two of them have had some intense conversations recently. Every time I go near Madison, she seems to freeze up and go running to Heather. I'm worried she's pulling away from me instead of toward me. Yet, I'm not sure what to do about it.

When I talked to Aidan, he advised me to go slowly and take my time. He said he and Tara have weathered many rough patches and they always come through stronger in the end. I'm hoping the same is true for us.

The decision about the military weighs on my mind. I know it's possible to have a great relationship with your spouse when you're a soldier because, I've seen Tyler and Heather as well as a couple of my other buddies pull it off successfully. Still, it's hard for me not to be haunted by what happened the first time. I still wonder if my pulling away while I was on deployments had something to do with Melinda Jo's mental state.

Madison has given me very few clues about which direction she would like me to go. She says she'll support whichever decision I make. She admits it will be difficult, but she insists she'll be able to handle it, regardless of what I decide. It would almost be easier if she had a strong opinion one way or the other because I'm honestly torn. There are so many more people to be potentially hurt now if I decide to leave and go back to the unit. It used to just be Melinda Jo and my parents who worried about me, but now I have a whole community of friends and family who care what happens to me. I know I can't make a decision based on their feelings, but it's a factor to weigh in my decision about whether to go back.

After a couple of hours of working on my business affairs, I finally throw in the towel and take a shower. Apparently, we're having a big family dinner tonight so Heather can try out a bunch of new recipes.

When I come out of the shower, I find Madison standing in front of the closet door. She's sorting through my dress shirts and holding them up against her body. When she sees me, she smiles widely and says, "Oh, hi. I was just raiding your stuff, I hope you don't mind if I borrow something to wear, I'm not happy with the choices in my closet."

"Of course, I don't mind, I think you look amazing in anything — it doesn't matter whether it's mine or yours," I respond.

She grabs one of my shirts and gives me a kiss on the cheek as she runs by. "Thank you, I'll see you downstairs."

"Okay, I'll see you in a few minutes," I respond. But, honestly I'm a little sad she didn't stop and talk for a while. I don't know what's changed, but she has suddenly become shy about changing her clothes in front of me. I kinda miss the Madison who would make love in the middle of the forest. I don't know if I should say anything because I don't know if it's related to her recent attack or if she is typically shy and our previous encounters were aberrant behavior. Yet, I'm amazed how much I miss our daily interactions. She's quickly become my favorite habit.

I'm surprised when I go downstairs and enter the kitchen. I expected the kitchen to be overrun with people as it usually is when Heather cooks. Yet, I only see

Madison standing in front of the dining table. I have to blink when I see her. She's wearing one of my favorite shirts, but I have never seen it look remotely sexy. She's wearing it with some type of black pants and a belt. Once again, I am struck by how beautiful she is. She could have a career in the fashion industry or something, she always looks impeccably dressed — even when there's no special occasion.

I'm confused about what's happening until Madison steps aside and I see the dining table has been covered in the crisp white tablecloth with long tapered candles on it. I suspect the agenda for tonight has changed significantly since I only see two plates on the table. My stomach pitches with dread as I ponder what this might mean. It looks like she's setting up to make a decree about our relationship. Things between us are okay overall, communication is just a little strained at the moment. I'm not sure what she's going to say, but I hope this isn't some big elaborate break-up scheme.

She smiles softly at me. "Do you want a regular green salad or do you want one with Caesar dressing and croutons?"

I look around suspiciously, but answer, "Caesar salad please, if it's not too much trouble."

"No, it's much easier now that Heather is teaching me how to cook and I'm old enough to want to listen," she explains.

I grin as I contemplate what kind of teenager she would have been. "What's going on? I thought we had a big family shindig to do tonight. Where is everybody?"

"Everybody had other plans today. Besides, I

thought you might want a romantic date for your birthday."

I relax a bit. "To be honest, with all the drama, I forgot it's my birthday."

"Well, you now have a bunch of people in your life who will remember when it's your birthday. You're not likely to forget again around this gang."

"I guess not."

After we sit down to eat, I reach for a bottle of spicy barbecue sauce. Madison turns a little green at the gills. "Please, Trevor don't use that tonight. The smell of it makes me nauseous."

"Still? I can't believe how long this flu bug is hanging around. I think you should go to the doctor and be checked out. This isn't normal."

Madison gets up from the table and goes into the kitchen. "What are you doing?" I ask, puzzled.

"Well, I was going to do this after dinner, however you brought it up so, I guess I'll have to change the scheduled events," she says as she brings a covered dish back to the table.

She uncovers it with a flourish as she declares, "Happy birthday, baby."

I smile from ear to ear as I look at my birthday cake. It's a cow print decorated with horseshoes and a red bandanna like the one that usually hangs out of the back pocket of my jeans. Along the top of the cake it says, 'It's Your Lucky Day'. As she lights the candle, I comment, "Madison you are so sweet. I can't remember the last time someone had a fuss over my birthday."

"Blow out your candle and make a wish," she directs as she takes a picture with her cell phone.

"I'm not terribly superstitious, so I'm going to tell you what I wished for," I state as I blow out the cowboy boot candles.

"Are you sure you should do that? I thought your wishes don't come true if you told someone," she replies.

"Well, that's the folklore. Since I already have the best gift on the planet, I don't really need much more. Although, I guess I could wish all the distractions in our life could go away so we can spend more time together. I'll be glad when this trial and everything surrounding it is over. I still don't understand why you had to rearrange dinner to bring me dessert."

Madison swallows hard and takes a deep breath. The look of trepidation on her face makes me nervous. She sinks down into the chair and grabs my hand. "It's a funny thing about life, it rarely goes according to plan."

I nod. "Yeah that's true. Nothing about my life over the last couple of years has been anything remotely close to what I had planned, but sometimes the new outcome can be even better — like you and me meeting."

Madison lets out a big breath of relief. "Boy, I'm glad to hear you say that because our lives are going to undergo a lot of changes in the next few months, I hope you think they are good changes."

"Madison, I don't understand. Are you sick or something?"

Madison shakes her head and flips her hair out of her face. "Gah! I'm doing a terrible job explaining this."

She takes a moment to give me a piece of cake. "No, I'm not sick, at least not really. The reason I've been throwing up so much is that I'm … pregnant. So, I should be well in a few months."

I look at her with my mouth agape. Finally, I find the ability to ask her, "What do you mean? I thought you were on the pill. How did this happen?"

"I don't know for sure yet because I haven't been to the doctor, but if I were to guess, I'd say we made a baby the night we made love in the woods. I recently discovered taking antibiotics can make birth-control pills less effective."

I think back to when she was on antibiotics, but the math confuses me even more. I must not be counting correctly. I shake my head to clear my thought process,. "Wait, I still don't understand. You took the antibiotics a long time ago."

"As nearly as I can tell, I'm probably about four months pregnant. I misinterpreted the symptoms because I've been spotting pretty regularly. I figured all the stress with the stalker was messing with my cycle and making me have a nervous stomach."

I lean back in my chair as I try to wrap my brain around the fact that I'm a dad. Part of me is still afraid to believe. Our lives have been so crazy recently, anything could happen. "Are you sure?" I can't stop myself from asking.

A look of desolation crosses Madison's face as soon as she hears my questions. She sighs heavily. "I guess I was delusional in thinking this would end like some perfect fairytale. I was really hoping this would be happy news for you." A tear slides down her face.

I reach out and wipe it away with my thumb as I respond. "Mad, I think you misinterpreted my question. I didn't ask it because I don't want you to be pregnant, I asked because I'm worried about you. I don't know much about being pregnant, but my buddies wives were getting chunky by the time they were halfway through their pregnancies. If anything, I think you've lost weight. I worry that being pregnant is too hard on you."

Madison smirks at my comment. "Well, it's a little late to debate whether getting pregnant was the healthiest decision for me, because I am."

"You have to give me a few minutes for it to sink in. After Melinda Jo disappeared, I wasn't sure if I would ever be able to love anyone again, and I thought that my chances of having a family were probably over. I thought I had hit the winning lottery when you said you'd marry me. The idea that I am lucky enough to be able to be a dad is almost too good to be true."

Madison lets out a little sob as she looks at me with tear filled eyes, "Really? This is something you want?"

"I'll admit I'm shocked and a whole crap load of scared, but I have to say I'm also over the moon. It means even more because it happened in a place which means the world to me. It's almost as if fate is determined to remind us something spectacular can happen in the middle of the darkest times."

"That was one of my first thoughts too. Our child will be a tangible reminder that we fell in love under the most chaotic circumstances yet created something absolutely beautiful."

I hop up from my chair and pull her into an embrace as I murmur, "Madison, you're going to make an amazing mom. I can't wait to go on this journey with you. I love you so much."

Madison kisses me with intense passion and emotion. When she breaks away, she says, "I love you too. Trevor, you'll be a phenomenal dad, too. Do you mind if we go upstairs and go to bed? I haven't slept well in what seems like weeks."

"Well, it's not a good thing for you to be sleep deprived, so I agree, we should go get some rest. I'll plate up the food and bring it upstairs with us. You know, I was a little afraid you were throwing me this elaborate dinner so you could tell me you were breaking up with me or something equally bad," I confess.

"What? Why would you think that?" Madison asks with the look of surprise on her face.

"Well, you've been so secretive and closed off the last few days, I wondered what was going on. I thought maybe the attack made you less certain about our relationship," I explain.

Madison chuckles. "I'll admit my behavior over the past few days has been a bit bizarre, but that's only because I was afraid if I was around you much longer you would guess what was going on with me and I wanted to surprise you for your birthday. I don't ever plan to leave, so you better get used to having me around."

I kiss her lightly and place my arm around her waist as we walk upstairs to our bedroom. "I'm perfectly fine with that, because I don't have any intention of going anywhere."

Madison climbs into the middle of the bed and looks at me with a frown, "Trevor, I don't know if you can promise me that. When you go back with your unit, Uncle Sam is in charge of your schedule. You could be gone for all I know," she says in a dejected voice.

"I've been wrestling with this decision for months, but what I need to do is now crystal clear. I'll accept the Army's offer of a medical discharge. I don't want to miss this time with you. We need to start our lives together like a normal family. There is no way I will leave you to do this on your own. I've paid a high enough price to serve, but I'm not willing to sacrifice my family life."

Madison looks very concerned. "Are you sure that's what you want to do? I don't want you to feel like you gave up who you are just to be with me. I have had to do that in a relationship before and I was miserable. I would hate myself if you were not happy with me because I changed who you were."

"Madison, honestly, I've been toying with this idea for a long time — long before we got engaged," I insist as I climb into bed and pull her back between my legs so her head is resting on my chest.

Madison looks up at me. "Then why did you fight so hard to get back in the military if you weren't sure you wanted to be there?"

I sigh as I admit my fears for the first time, "I don't really know the answer, other than to say I absolutely hate to lose. Giving up my military career because of my amputation felt like the terrorists were winning. I couldn't let that happen, but the military isn't my life like it is for some people. Aside from the whole service related injury, my time with the military has been pretty good. I made some great lifelong friends like Tyler and Matt. Now that I have you — and my child — in my life, the cost of staying in is just too great. I'm done paying the price for freedom. It's someone else's turn now. I'm leaving on my terms for *my* reasons; therefore, the insurgents who blew up my convoy aren't winning."

"From the moment you struggled to stay alive and helped Tyler put the tourniquet on your leg, you defeated the bad guys. You don't have anything left to prove. You will always be a hero whether you serve in the guard or not," Madison vehemently argues. Her faith in me is astounding and completely assures me I have made the right choice.

"Thank you, Sweetheart, your belief in me means everything."

"How could I not? You've supported me and this crazy search for my tormentors without question, I'm only returning the favor. For a few minutes, we're both lost in our own thoughts and I take a few moments to simply hold her in my arms. But, soon she asks quietly, "So, will you stay here and work for Heather and Tyler?"

"Well, I guess it depends on what decisions you make," I answer with a shrug. "Aidan has offered me a job sorting out his payroll. I guess one of his assistants decided he needed the money more than Aidan and helped himself to a large portion of Aidan's personnel budget. Aidan wants to figure out exactly how much he took and how to prevent it from happening again. He'd like me to come work for him. I can do that from anywhere. If you end up on the East Coast, I'll just follow you there."

"Is that where you want to live?" Madison asks.

"Well, my first priority is to be with you. I'll do whatever it takes to make that happen. If you're asking about my hopes and dreams for a place to live … I'd like to stay around here. This feels like home."

Madison is quiet for a few moments, and I'm afraid perhaps she doesn't approve of my answer. Yet, after a few beats of silence she replies, "You know, I never thought I would say this in a million years, but it feels like home to me too. I don't know what to do. I don't want to leave Lyle in a lurch."

"You're essentially telecommuting now, is there any reason you couldn't continue to do that? Being out here might make it easier for you to investigate a wider variety of charities and Beckel could brag he has a national reporter," I suggest.

Madison gives me a ghost of a smile. "You know, he might just buy that logic. It's worth a shot."

"Well, I guess I better look for a big piece of real estate, Arabian horses take a fair amount of space."

"How in the world are we going to get them from Massachusetts to Oregon?"

"A really long road trip and lots of patience," I respond.

"I would imagine," Madison replies with a smile. She takes a deep breath and stretches. "I don't know about you, but I'm feeling better about things. I think we made some solid plans. However, I'm ready to think about something else now."

"That can be arranged, Sweetheart," I respond as I scoot off the bed and pull her to the edge. I gather her hair and tie it in a loose knot on the top of her head. Slowly, I unbutton my shirt. I may never wear that shirt again because it looks so much better on her.

I give her a hot, sensual kiss. When I draw away, I study her body. "Now that I'm paying close attention, I do notice subtle changes and I think it makes you even more beautiful."

Madison's eyes mist up. "Trevor Black, I don't know how you do it, but you always know the perfect thing to say."

EPILOGUE

MADISON

"WILL YOU PLEASE FIND a chair and sit in it?" I snap at Trevor. "You're driving me crazy. Now I know why Moses was always complaining. Pacing is an annoying habit if you're not the one doing it. I never thought I would find someone who paces more than me. The technician got called in to do an emergency ultrasound on a person who has gallstones. Our appointment got pushed back. She should be done soon."

"I know, that's what the receptionist told me too. But, I'm so nervous. I just want to know everything is okay. You've lost so much weight because of all of your nausea. It scares me." Trevor finally sits down.

"Trevor, women long before me have had severe morning sickness and everything's been fine. I think it's a good sign. Besides, I am pretty sure I felt the baby move earlier today. It felt like I had a little butterfly inside."

Trevor gives me a beaming grin as he places his hand over the soft swell of my abdomen. "I want to feel little Lydia Paige kick," Trevor says as he moves his hand to a different spot.

"You're so silly, Trevor, little Vincent Trevor isn't big enough for you to feel yet" I say with a chuckle.

"Did I tell you my dad was tickled to death we decided to name the baby after him?"

"Yeah, I know. Your dad actually sent me a Facebook message to thank me."

"He did? I didn't even know my dad had a Facebook account."

"Well, he does. He got a new computer because he said he needs it if we stay in Oregon because he won't be able to see his grandchild in person. I think he wants us to move to Oklahoma."

"What did you tell him?" Trevor asks, still holding his hand against my abdomen.

I smile smugly and shrug. "I told him the truth: I have a friend who is going to loan us his private plane and we can visit anytime. Funny thing though, I don't think he believed me."

"Did Aidan really offer? His generosity blows me away," Trevor replies, shaking his head in disbelief.

I give Trevor a crooked smile. "Yes, I think his exact words were he would be thrilled to run a grandparent shuttle so they can watch Vincent grow up."

"You know, we have some pretty great friends. Maybe Aidan and Tara should be the godparents."

"I'm sure they wouldn't mind. I believe Heather and Tara are both godparents to Mindy and Becca, what's one more?"

A nurse comes into the waiting room and calls us back to a room with all sorts of scary looking equipment. Trevor helps me up on the table and pulls down my yoga pants a little.

"Are you ready to meet our little one?" he murmurs in my ear as he kisses the side of my neck.

Emotions overtake me as I nod. Despite the assurances I've given to Trevor, I am incredibly worried. I should've been getting prenatal care a long time ago, and I continued to take the birth control pills because I didn't know I was pregnant. Perhaps all the throwing up actually has done me a favor. I'm not sure how many of those pills I was able to keep down.

Maybe I have some maternal instincts after all. I'm still amazed I'm the first one to get pregnant between Heather and me. Heather has wanted to have kids for as long as I can remember. She used to volunteer to babysit the kids in the neighborhood so she could be around them. I don't dislike kids. In fact, I think Mindy and Becca are two of the coolest kids I've ever met in my life. If my son or daughter turns out like them, I would be thrilled. I just wondered if this moment would ever come for me, given my crazy past.

Trevor is looking at me expectantly. Nervously, I nod my head again. "I was ready for this from the moment I figured out I was pregnant."

"Well then, I won't make you wait any longer," the ultrasound technician says as she snaps on some gloves and grabs some cold, sticky gel and squirts it on my stomach. I grip Trevor's hand tightly as a grainy image of a baby pops up on the screen.

As I glance over at Trevor, I whisper, "Look at him, he's perfect."

I can see tears on Trevor's eyelashes. "She sure is."

After several more clicks of the ultrasound machine, the ultrasound technician has apparently finished all the measurements she needs. She hands me a towel so I can wipe my belly and looks at us. "Do you want to know who's right?"

Trevor and I nod simultaneously as we study the screen.

The ultrasound technician circles a shadowy area and says, "I'm not supposed to say this, but I'm about ninety eight percent sure Dad is right on this one. You have a very healthy, robust looking, twenty-two week old baby here, and she appears to be a happy little princess. If I don't see you again during your pregnancy, I want to say, 'Congratulations', you guys seem like amazing parents."

"Sweetheart, did you hear that? I'm going to have a Daddy's little girl. How perfect is she?"

We floated around on a happy cloud for over a month. Trevor made good on his promise to take early retirement from the military. Thanks to the stud fees I've been getting from the Arabian horses, we were able to put together a good down payment on a nice little ranch. We ended up outside of a little town called Sisters, but I fell in love with the quaint old farmhouse and traditional barns. It reminded me so much of Grandma Lydia's house that I felt like it was only appropriate for her namesake to be raised there.

Trevor was so sweet, when he saw how sad I was to leave Ethel behind, he adopted the cutest little black lab puppy from the Humane Society and named it Lucy. He already found a pony he wanted to adopt for Lydia, but I told him we needed to wait a couple years before we added another horse to the herd. My horses still need to get acclimated to life in Oregon. At least Sisters will get a little more snow than down in the Valley. Hopefully, their transition won't be too rough. Aidan decided it was too risky for me to be involved with the moving of the horses, so he hired a whole team of former rodeo clowns to assist with the move. I thought it was hysterical. Did he have them listed in his contacts list under 'Rodeo Clowns'? I don't know how he and Tara always come through with everything we could possibly need. They seem to know everybody in every industry.

I am busy painting the nursery with Donda — actually, she is painting and I am watching while I wear a respirator mask when a cloud arrived to dampen our happiness.

I'm shaking as I hang up the phone with the prosecutor in the case against Alex Whitmore, III.

Donda looks at me curiously. "Do I dare ask what that was all about?"

I can barely pull myself together long enough to hoarsely whisper, "Tyler, Trevor and I have all been told to come to a meeting. If we don't come, the prosecutor is afraid his lawyers will try to pull some fancy maneuver to throw out evidence."

Once again, I'm taking a flight across country to face a nightmare. When Heather and Tara heard about the meeting from Donda, they all decided to come along so I would have a built-in support system. Yet, this flight is so much different from when I ran away. I am in such a better place emotionally, I hardly recognize myself. Under Trevor's tender, attentive care, my self-esteem has come back and I feel ready to take on the world. I have a wonderful circle of friends who have my back. But, most importantly, I have a man better than I could've possibly dreamed sitting beside me. My life is so good that regardless of what happens in court, I've won.

When Trevor reaches across me to get a book from Tyler, his arm touches my belly at the same time Lydia kicks. His eyes widen in surprise. "Was that what I think it was?"

I grin at him. "Yep, your daughter was just giving you a high five."

"You guys are like my own personal miracle every day. As odd as it sounds, I say a little prayer of thanks every day because only God could be in charge of having my ex-wife help me find my future wife and the mother of my beautiful, perfect child."

I snicker at him. "Well, that's one way to look at the scariest time in my life, but I can't say you're wrong."

I smile to myself as Trevor busies himself proudly showing the prosecutor our ultrasound pictures. I suppose this is a better strategy than pacing. The prosecutor doesn't look all that interested.

Finally, Alex's attorneys come into the conference room. Geez, does he really need four lawyers? I shoot the prosecutor a panicked glance. She gives me a discreet thumbs-up. I try to take a deep breath. It's a little harder these days since Lydia has decided directly under my rib cage is her favorite spot to hang out.

The female attorney in the severe navy blue suit gives me the once over, but then she sticks out her hand for me to shake, "Miss LaBianca, had I known about your condition, we could have probably done this via video conference call." She looks at the prosecutor and says, "Kate, you should've said something. I've flown to San Francisco when I was pregnant, and I know the flight is a pain."

The prosecutor puts up her hands in a gesture of innocence and says, "Don't look at me. I'm as surprised as you are. I had a Skype call with her a couple of weeks ago, and she didn't look pregnant at all. When I was pregnant, I looked like a blowfish which had been over-inflated. I would've never guessed you're six months pregnant."

"I think it's because I'm so tall," I demure. I get that comment a lot, and I never know how to answer it, so I have learned to cite my height as a reason Lydia doesn't stick very far out. Of course, I can tell because my clothes are tighter, but it seems like most everyone just think I have a potbelly from eating too many fries. My impatience gets the best of me so I ask, "Why are we here?"

The female attorney looks at the three of us sitting at the conference table and says, "I'm sorry for any inconvenience, but it seems prison life has been harder than he expected — if you know what I mean — and my client wants me to relay a message."

I brace myself, gripping Trevor's hand so tight that I hear his knuckles crack.

One of the other attorneys starts to speak, "We didn't mean to alarm you, Miss LaBianca. We're here today because Mr. Whitmore wants to change his plea to guilty. Of course, we had to counsel him against making such a decision, but he would not be dissuaded. Accordingly, I've drafted paperwork to change his plea. I expect since his psychological exam came back within normal limits, the judge won't have a problem accepting the change of plea."

"You're offering this in exchange for what?" Trevor asks skeptically.

"Nothing. We are not requiring you to sign a waiver blocking you from further legal action or anything else for that matter. In fact, the defendant's parents would like to offer you a sizable amount to compensate you for the actions of their children," another attorney clarifies.

Something about the way he said that pushes all of my buttons so I sit up straight and glare at him as I spit, "He better not *require* anything of us, we will *not* make concessions to him in any form. I'll testify on the stand for a solid month if I have to, to make sure he spends the rest of his life behind bars."

The female attorney looks at me with alarm. "Calm down, it's not good for the baby —"

"Wait," I interrupt. "I wasn't even almost done. The Whitmore's can keep their filthy, dirty money. There isn't enough money on the planet to make what Alex and Melinda Jo did to me right. This isn't about money — it never was. It was about standing up for the right things. It's about being a good person and helping other people. With all due respect, you can tell the Whitmore's they can put their money exactly where their son violated me with a beer bottle when I was barely sixteen. Is that clear enough?" I ask, enunciating every word.

The attorney blanches a bit before she turns to Tyler. "Mr. Colton, since the attack happened on your property, the Whittmores' are prepared to compensate you as well."

"Even if my job did not preclude me from taking money for what I do in my role as a police officer, I would find your offer as offensive as my sister-in-law does. I guess you could say my answer is the same."

"Are you sure? You might want to reconsider. I understand soldiers and police officers don't make a whole lot of money," she says.

At this point, Trevor's eyes ice over as he jumps to his feet and challenges the attorney. "Ma'am, it is true that soldiers, police officers teachers, firefighters, and other public servants don't make very much money. However, the things we do have in spades are honor and integrity. I lost my leg to fight for those values, and I won't compromise them so your client and his family can feel better about themselves." He turns to the prosecutor and asks in a lethal tone that should've made their hair stand on end, "Are we done here? They said we didn't have to sign anything for the deranged creep to change his plea. My fiancé is too exhausted to hang around for this drama."

"No, I suppose you're free to go. Again, I apologize for the inconvenience."

Trevor gallantly pulls out my chair and helps me stand. "It's all right. I hope you'll understand if I say I hope I never meet any of you again."

A young attorney from their side who looks like he's barely out of high school, tries again, "But what about the money?"

Trevor practically snarls at him. "You know those soldiers, police officers, firefighters and teachers? Find charities which help them and give them the money." Trevor turns to me and says, "Madison, Sweetheart, are you ready to go home and live our dreams?"

I take a deep breath and answer with a wink, "Naturally, love."

The end (for now)

You can read more about Trevor and Madison's love story in *Love Seasoned* (Hidden Beauty #5).

Note from the Author

Dear Reader:

Thank you so much for taking the time to read *Love Naturally*. I hope you enjoyed it. The series continues with the unlikely love story which brings two families together in *Love Seasoned*.

You only get one great love in a lifetime.

That's what Denny Ashley believed when he married the love of his life.

Denny knew Gwendolyn was something special from the first time he saw her standing up to her louse of a husband.

Gwendolyn's marriage is over. She's never been so happy.

She is finally single and free — for now.

Denny Ashley is a force of nature. She treasures his friendship. Gwendolyn is unaware he is on a mission to court her and when her heart.

She never expected to find love again at her age.

She certainly never figured she would fall for her son's father-in-law.

Can Gwendolyn bet on happily ever after?

Is love better the first time around or seasoned by time?

Get *Love Seasoned* in paperback, e-book, or read for free with Kindle Unlimited now.

~Mary

Because love matters, differences don't.

RESOURCES

If you need help immediately, call 911.

National Sexual Assault Hotline:

1-800-656-HOPE (4673)

National Domestic Violence Hotline:

800-799-SAFE (7233) or 800-787-3224 (TDD)

RAINN (Rape, Abuse, Incest National Network) — The nation's largest anti-sexual assault organization. RAINN operates the National Sexual Assault Hotline at 1.800.656.HOPE and the National Sexual Assault Online Hotline at rainn.org, and publicizes the hotline's free, confidential services; educates the public about sexual assault; and leads national efforts to prevent sexual assault, improve services to victims and ensure that rapists are brought to justice.

Domestic Shelters.org— A tool that enables you to find a domestic violence shelter in your area by ZIP Code or address. You can search by the specific service you need. There are also informative articles about how to help someone who may be a victim of domestic violence or sexual abuse.

Take Back The Night—Media links, literature and other information about surviving and preventing date rape. Many of these resources are beneficial for helping survivors as well as their family and friends through the healing process.

When Georgia Smiled—A Foundation created by Robin McGraw to create and advance programs that help victims of domestic violence and sexual assault live healthy, safe and joy-filled lives. Initiatives include a phone app that helps create a safety plan for use in domestic violence date rape situations, education initiatives for use in high school and college settings and support programs for women.

Loveisrespect.org— Our mission is to engage, educate and empower young people to prevent and end abusive relationships. Highly-trained peer advocates offer support, information and advocacy to young people who have questions or concerns about their dating relationships. We also provide information and support to concerned friends and family members, teachers, counselors, service providers and members of law enforcement. Free and confidential phone, live chat and texting services are available 24/7/365.

Limbs for Life—The Limbs for Life Foundation is a global nonprofit organization dedicated to providing fully-functional prosthetic care for individuals who cannot otherwise afford it and raising awareness of the challenges facing amputees.

Wounded Warrior Project—The WWP mission is to honor and empower Wounded Warriors who incurred a physical or mental injury, illnesses, or wound, co-incident to your military service on or after September 11, 2001. You may also be eligible for the program if you are the family member or caregiver of a Wounded Warrior.

ACKNOWLEDGEMENTS

This book started writing itself in my head many, many months ago while I was writing Until the Stars Fall From the Sky as I developing Heather's character and envisioning what Heather's family would look like. It's an interesting thing when an author like me writes a romance novel. On the surface, I'm just writing about two people who fall in love. Yet, in reality it's about so much more. I'm telling a story about family, friends and community and I'm making a statement about the world around them.

As an author, I want to think you for giving me a platform to speak out about issues that I think are important like date rape on college campuses, the availability of date rape drugs, advances in prosthetic limbs, or the long-term effects of post traumatic stress. Most importantly, I enjoy the opportunity to present people who have been through real-life problems and still find love. Thank you for supporting my work.

I'd like to give special recognition to Sam Moon for her contributions as a sounding board for this project. She took my ideas and made them edgier and sharper. Madison is spunkier and smarter because of Sam's input. I look forward to reading what Ms. Moon publishes one day.

Huge kudos to my dream team of beta readers and proofreaders. You are the most underpaid but most appreciated group of people on the planet. I can't thank you enough Ruth, Heather, Laurie, Christine, Annie and Michelle. Linda Lloyd, you are a life saver. Thanks for saving me from my own bad habits.

Because love matters, differences don't.

~ Mary

ABOUT THE AUTHOR

I have been lucky enough to live my own version of a romance novel. I married the guy who kissed me at summer camp. He told me on the night we met that he was going to marry me and be the father of my children.

Eventually, I stopped giggling when he said it, and we've been married for more than thirty years. We have two children. The oldest is a Doctor of Osteopathy. He is across the United States completing his residency, but when he's done, he is going to come back to Oregon and practice Family Medicine. Our youngest son is now tackling high school, where he is an honor student. He is interested in becoming an EMT.

I write full time now. I have published more than thirty books and have several more underway. I volunteer my time to a variety of causes. I have worked as a Civil Rights Attorney and diversity advocate. I spent several years working for various social service agencies before becoming an attorney.

In my spare time, I love to cook, decorate cakes and, of course, I obsessively, compulsively read.

I would be honored if you would take a few moments out of your busy day to check out my website,

MaryCrawfordAuthor.com. While you're there, you can sign up for my newsletter and get a free book. I will be announcing my upcoming books and giving sneak peeks as well as sponsoring giveaways and giving you information about other interesting events.

If you have questions or comments, please E-mail me at Mary@MaryCrawfordAuthor.com or find me on the following social networks:

Facebook: www.facebook.com/authormarycrawford

Website: MaryCrawfordAuthor.com

Twitter: www.twitter.com/MaryCrawfordAut